The Reluctant P.I. and The Redhead

By Don Weston

Copyright

ISBN: 978-0-9968647-3-2

DEDICATION

Thanks God. Without a motivating force to guide me, I would never have written and finished this book.

If you enjoy a good mystery, check out other books or ebooks by Don Weston on Amazon, iTunes, Google Play, and Barnes and Noble/Nook.

Death Fits Like a Glove: A Billie Bly Short Story

Bleeding Blue: A Billie Bly Mystery

The Facebook Killer: A Billie Bly Thriller

Chapter 1

I didn't plan to become a private investigator. It was an accident, I swear.

I blame it on redheads. I have an incurable weakness for redheads. For most men, it's blondes I guess, but when I see a red-haired woman walking by, I notice her. It doesn't matter what color of red. It doesn't matter what age or what she looks like. It's the color red that makes my head turn.

So when I met the most beautiful redhead with the cutest freckles in just the right places. . . I got a little week in the knees.

It happened on a blustery March day. I was looking for work—again. Two years ago I was fired from my college-educated job for the smallest of infractions. I slugged, my boss, an editor on a large daily newspaper which shall remain nameless to protect the guilty. That would be me.

The result being, I had been mostly unemployed since then. It was unlikely I would ever find another reporting job on a Portland newspaper, or any newspaper for that matter, in the foreseeable future. Word gets around and the newspaper game is a small and gossipy community. Never mind, I had a legitimate reason for slugging my boss. No one would begrudge me that. Most would cheer. Who hasn't wanted to slug their boss? For editors it goes double.

They pick and pick and pick at your story and always come back at you with some screwy idea about how to make it better or suggest some new angle they think you should pursue after you've written five-hundred words of the sweetest prose this side of Harper Lee.

That's not why I slugged him . . . but I'm getting ahead of myself.

The day I became a detective I was between jobs and late for an appointment with a temp employment agency. I didn't know what I was qualified to do, other than writing, so I figured maybe they could plug me into a couple of jobs and I would see if anything clicked.

It was ten past eleven on a brisk windy day as I pulled my vintage '67 Mustang convertible alongside the curb in front of one of Portland few remaining historic brick buildings.

I was already late for my appointment and a cruel east wind, known for its ability to cut through Portlanders with a sharp blade of ice during the winter months, had raised its temperature to merely annoying. Still, it blew through my Mustang's rag-top frisking it for leaks and a strong gust played ping-pong with me as I jumped from my car and made a dash for the lobby of the Morgan Building.

I played tug-of-war against the wind with one of the building's formidable entry doors and lost. A gust held the door shut and released its grip just as I played Hercules.

Two women stepped over me, opened the door, smirked, and walked into the lobby. Neither of them was a redhead, by the way. Redheads may smirk, but not at someone who had the misfortune to be knocked off his feet.

I got up, slapped the dirt from my pants, tried to straighten my sports coat and tie, and followed the smirkers to the elevators. They were still smirking. A door across from the elevators led to a stairwell and climbing stairs seemed a logical alternative to watching instant replays in their heads.

On the fourth floor, wheezing and weaving in a now rumpled and stained suit, I opened the stairwell door and staggered down the embellished oak-trimmed hallway in search of suite four-thirty-four.

The rooms to my right had even numbers and odd numbers hung over the doors on the left side of the hall. "Let's see," I recited. "Four twenty-eight, four-thirty, four thirty-two, the next door should be the temp agency."

I looked at my watch. Damn! I was really late.

The thick oak door to the office seemed to stick, so I applied some subtle pressure with my shoulder and stumbled into my new profession.

The office was small. The décor featured rich walnut paneling, a cherry-wood desk in front of the window, and one of those S-shaped antique loveseats with worn and faded upholstery and scuffed walnut trim molding.

The desk was clean, except for one of those desk calendars, a phone, a computer monitor, and a picture of some guy shaking the mayor's hand.

Whoever worked here was an organized person. I hate organized people. My ex-wife organized everything, including her affair. I looked at the picture and surmised it must belong to the guy with the desk. He was thick with a big nose, brown hair and a cock-sure smile. He seemed proud to have his picture taken with Hizzoner.

"Hello?" I cried. The empty room beckoned to me. "You're late," it said. "They couldn't wait around for you forever."

I looked around for another door which might admit me to an employment counselor, and I realized this was the only office. Maybe I'd wandered into the wrong place.

I was in mid-turn toward the door, when it swung open again and the most beautiful redhead I'd ever seen appeared before me. She was tall, thin, yet shapely, with shoulder-length hair and the cutest freckles in just the right places. She wore a midnight blue business outfit with a dress that revealed long legs and her fresh strawberry scent grappled with sensuous ruby-red lips for my attention.

I was going to ask her if she was a job counselor when I realized I still hadn't recovered from the stairs. Or maybe she knocked the wind out of me. I paused to nonchalantly gasp for a breath while she spoke.

"Are you Mr. Steadman, the private investigator?"

Jeez, I hoped I was. I looked toward the desk again and saw a brass nameplate, which said: John Steadman, Private Investigator.

It seems I was.

"Just one minute." I flashed my most charming smile and

strolled toward my new desk to look at a calendar on the desk blotter and my luck held. Steadman was across town meeting a Mr. Weathersby for lunch, and he had another appointment afterwards. I grinned at my new client.

But in the end, I couldn't lie to this angel. It's one of my rules: Be credible, be on time, and don't lie to pretty young women. My confidence was healthy at this juncture though. Attractive red-headed women bring that out in me for some reason.

"Mr. Steadman is across town on a case. My name is Max Starr. I've been with this office for, ah, quite a while." (A while is relative, right?) "Can I be of assistance?" I motioned for her to sit in one of two solid padded chairs in front of the desk as I sat behind the stately piece of antiquity.

"My name Max, too." she said. "Well, my given name is Maxine. Maxine Andrews, but most of my close friends call me Max now. As a teenager, I was kind of a tomboy. I wore my hair in a ponytail and never put on a dress or makeup. I guess my friends thought Max fit me better than Maxine."

There was no way she looked like a tomboy now. She looked sexy and elegant and I thought Maxine suited her just fine. I conjured an image of her as a tomboy with the ponytail and a dozen boys chasing after her.

"We'll have to be careful when we're together in public. We'll both be answering to our names at the same time."

Did I say that? What an idiot. At least I didn't say we'll have to be careful when we're married because that's what I was thinking.

She managed a slight smile. "I'm rather desperate, Mr. Starr, and I need some help. Are you any good at making drops?"

"I'm an expert." I was recalling the fall outside the building steps a few minutes earlier. "What kind of drop are we talking about?"

"Well, there's this man, and he has something that would compromise me. He's offered to give it back, but he says he wants something for his trouble."

"Could you be a little more specific? I'll need to know as much as possible before I can decide if I'll take the case." As if there would be any doubt.

"It's a little embarrassing." She tugged demurely at a piece of her crimson hair, wrapping it around a finger. "I'm engaged to be married next month, and this man is an old boyfriend. Well, my engagement announcement was in the newspaper last week, and he saw it."

Strike one. How could I take this case? She had a fiancée.

"The man I'm marrying has money."

Strike two.

"He also has a family that is rather old-fashioned. They wouldn't think much of the pictures Scott took of me."

"So it's that kind of shakedown is it? The pictures are of a compromising nature?" There was hope for this case yet.

"They aren't pornographic. I was his model for some artistic pictures he took when we dated. He was a struggling professional photographer. Some of the photos were a bit risqué, but not explicit. But he's threatened to publish them on the Internet if I don't come up with $20,000."

My eyebrows sank in sympathy. "It's a tough spot to be in for sure. But why do you need me? Why not go to the police? Even if he gives the pictures back, he probably has copies."

She frowned. "I can't go to the police. Think of the scandal. Anyway, I don't think he'd really do anything nasty like that. He's a little down on his luck, and I believe him when he says he won't keep any photos."

"Then why don't you meet him and pay him off?"

"I'd prefer not to see him again. He might view it as an opportunity to get back together. I figure he'd be less likely to pull something against a man, especially against someone of your size."

"What do you mean try something?" My internal warning alarm hit high decibels. I can be brave to a point, but I'm not stupid.

"I'm just afraid he might try to get fresh. Will you take the case?"

I was trying to figure out what P.I.s charged. On an old television series, James Rockford charged two hundred dollars a day, plus expenses. But that was back in the seventies. At the rate of inflation over the years, P.I.s would be charging between one and two grand a day. We couldn't be charging that much. Still, this had the potential to be dangerous work.

Okay, confession time. I have watched a lot of old mystery

and P.I. shows on television. Think *Perry Mason*, any Agatha Christie mystery movie, and *The Thin Man*.

I also spent my teen years devouring books about hard-boiled P.I stories. Think Dashiell Hammett, Raymond Chandler, John MacDonald, Arthur Conan Doyle, and the aforementioned Agatha Christie. So anything I know about being a P.I., I got from books and TV. Probably none of my knowledge is accurate.

So I took a guess on my P.I. rates. "I get five hundred a day, plus expenses."

She gave me a long, hard look. I squirmed a little and tried not to show it.

"That's more than I thought." She reached into a black designer purse and withdrew a matching wallet. From the wallet she retrieved a wad of crisp new one-hundred-dollar bills, counted out five of them and placed the cash in my sweaty hand.

I stared stupidly at my good fortune. Good work if you can get it. I shoved the twist into my shirt pocket and re-buttoned my sports jacket. As I gazed into her lush green eyes, I wondered why I was fooling this charming lady. It's one of my faults. I tend to be impulsive. Still, this new job paid well.

She sized up my rumpled jacket, stained pants and spotted tie, apparently speculating whether I was legit. I probably looked like one of those above-mentioned hard-boiled P.I.s from the old detective movie noir.

"Here's the address where I'm supposed to meet him at the Buddhist temple," she said. "His name is Scott Hess. Here's a picture of him. The meeting is set for 11 o'clock tonight. My friend, Jon, is the monk at the temple, and he'll be there to let you in."

I looked at the picture. The guy appeared to be in his early thirties. He had oily black hair, a thin frame and a crooked smile. The girl in the picture with him was the doll standing in front of me.

She laughed awkwardly. "This photo was taken a few years ago. He looks about the same, but thinner if you can believe it." She pulled a sealed manila envelope from her purse and tucked it into my outstretched hand.

"This is the money for the payoff. There's also a note inside the envelope. Please don't open it. He'll give you another envelope with pictures and negatives." She gave me a desperate look. "I'm counting on you; don't let me down."

"I hope you don't expect me to be physical with him. To scare him off, I mean."

"Oh, he's really not a bad guy. He's in trouble financially and his morals sink a little bit every now and then. I don't think he'll be any trouble."

She clutched my empty hand in both of hers, squeezed it gently and warmly and drew herself to me, gazing into my unintelligent blue eyes. We floated together briefly on a cloud of air until the shrill ringing of a telephone interrupted the spell.

"Aren't you going to get it?" She looked at me like a lost little girl.

I debated. Finally, on the fifth ring I picked up the phone. "John Steadman Detective Agency."

"Is Steadman there?" a voice asked over the phone.

"No, he's not in right now. This is Max Starr, his, ah, associate."

"I need to talk to him right away. Can you tell him to call Richard Sealy?"

"Well, I'm on my way out the door." I was peeking at Steadman's calendar. "He'll be back at about two o'clock. I'd rather you call him back."

"I can't. I'm going into a meeting. Tell him to text me and I'll ditch the meeting and call him."

"Okay, Mr. Sealy." I scrawled a message on a Post-it note, signed it "Max" for Maxine's benefit, and hung up.

We arranged for me to call Maxine after my get-together with Hess. She gave me the number at a motel where she was staying, and I gave her my cell phone number, explaining investigators are hardly ever in the office.

I watched as she walked out the door. Her shapely long legs waved goodbye and I waved back.

After she left, I went to Steadman's computer and googled private investigators. Google came up with a web page for several local agencies. I picked one and dialed a phone number.

"Chris Johnson Investigations," a voice answered.

"Yeah, hey, I'm writing a story on speculation for a detective magazine. Can you tell me how much P.I.s charge a day?"

The gruff voice gave me a lot of trouble, as if he didn't want the word to get out about his rates. But in the end he broke down.

"Between seventy-five and a hundred dollars an hour," he said. Most P.I.'s ask for a minimum of three hundred dollars per day."

At this, I realized the rate I quoted Maxine might be a little on the high side. "How much for a drop?"

"A what?" he asked.

"A drop. My hero has to meet a blackmailer, pay off him off for a client, and retrieve some dirty pictures." It sounded dumb saying it out loud, even to me.

"Look pal . . ." The voice took on a fatherly tone now. "In a story, that's one thing. But in real life I wouldn't get near a scenario like that wearing Kevlar Body Armor. You'd be better off to have your hero refer a client like this to the police. In real-life, that kind of stuff can get you hurt. Even in a story it's kind of corny, don't you think?"

I did think. I thanked Mr. Johnson for his advice and hung up. What had I gotten myself into? Still, the vision had paid me nicely.

I put Steadman's computer back to sleep and looked around the office trying to leave no evidence of my visit. I did leave the phone message from Mr. Sealy. Steadman was an investigator. Let him figure it out.

On the way out I looked above Steadman's door. The numbers four-thirty-five were stenciled over it. I guess my first summation as a private investigator was a flop. The even numbers on one side and odd numbers on the other side theory was a bust.

On the door across the hall, suite four-thirty-four stared me in the face and I walked through the door. A mousy girl peered over her gold-rimmed glasses and patted at her brown hair to make sure her bun was intact. She rose from her desk with a clipboard in her hands.

"Are you Mr. Starr? You're thirty-five minutes late. Mr. Olsen won't be able to see you now. He has an eleven-forty-five."

"Tell Mr. Olsen to take me off his books. I found employment."

"Oh, good. Was it through one of our job referrals?"

"No, I found it on my own."

"Oh?" She looked worried, probably about their commission.

"What job did you find?" Now she was looking at the resume I had faxed her the day before.

"I'm a private investigator."

She took off her glasses, revealing tight brown eyes. "I don't recall seeing that job title on your resume."

"It's not there," I said.

"But you don't have any experience in that field."

She was right. I've had a lot of jobs before I went back to college and got my degree in Journalism at the University of Oregon. My only recent experience, other than as an investigative reporter, was punching out my boss and losing my wife.

But I figured I had some life experience and that ought to account for something. Yes, a lot of it turned out badly, but my luck had to change sometime. At least it's what I was telling myself at the moment. I had something to prove to the world and to myself and if I didn't take a chance once in a while . . .

As I left the puzzled secretary, my thoughts went to other matters. In the hallway I withdrew the envelope from my inside jacket pocket and rapped it absently across my knuckles.

I hadn't entirely believed her "get back the photos back" story. It would be too easy to scan the pictures and save them to a computer or post them on an online server, and I didn't think this Hess guy was much of a white knight. But when she held my hand, my mind clouded. As I stepped outside into the wind and gazed dreamily at the ugly-green Hawthorne Bridge spanning the Willamette River, I realized Maxine could have sold it to me on the spot.

She had been emphatic about me not opening the envelope. I wrestled with my conscience for a while--three or four seconds at least. Then, I inserted a car key into the corner of the flap, created a jagged opening, reached inside with deft fingers, and withdrew the contents. What I found was the kind of stuff of which cheap detective novels are made.

The envelope revealed a single page of folded stationary wrapped around a stack of scrap paper cut up from a Chinese newspaper in dollar bill sized increments. Tucked inside the stack of funny money was a computer flash drive.

Now here was a mystery. Was she setting me up? It was either something too dangerous for her or she was using me as bait for some kind of trap. Maybe she wanted to rid herself of this ex-boyfriend. Was she using me as a pretense to get close enough to shoot him? If so, why would she want a potential witness along for the ride? Perhaps I was the target. Or more likely, maybe someone was setting up Steadman. He must have made a lot of enemies in his line of work.

Thirty minutes into the new job and my head was spinning. What had I gotten myself into? I let a pretty girl and my ego talk me into believing I could be a private investigator. There must be licensing and training I would need to do this kind of work, and I wasn't off to a very good start ethically.

Also, I found myself thinking and talking in clichés, gleaned from years of reading pulp crime novels. I was an educated former journalist thinking in terms of dames and dolls and other tough talk to express myself in my new career. I figured I'd best be careful or this pulp dialogue would expose me as a hackneyed wannabe detective.

But you know, in the coming days, no one seemed to tumble.

I considered quitting the private eye business. Still, opening the envelope against my client's wishes proved I had good instincts for the job. The memory of the lovely redhead holding my hand in Steadman's office clouded my judgment again. Perhaps I could pull it off after all.

I walked briskly toward my car, the wind still laughing at me. Another one of my faults: I'm overly optimistic.

Chapter Two

I decided to grab lunch at my palatial two-bedroom abode in Northeast Portland, a 1940's white, two-story colonial house converted into a duplex.

As I climbed the wooden porch steps I felt an urgency to begin my new job. Once inside, the first thing I did was fire up my computer and slide Maxine's flash drive into a computer port.

The monitor displayed several folders with Chinese titles. A few titles were in English and one was in French. They might as well have been all in Greek, because even the contents in English were made up of indecipherable math formulas and medical jargon. One folder simply had a series of eleven eight-digit numbers, all neatly aligned to the left margin.

The flash drive would have to remain a mystery a little longer. I copied the hieroglyphics onto one of my spare flash drives. I don't know why. It just seemed like a good idea.

I made myself a turkey sandwich, returned to the computer and spent a couple of hours on the Internet searching to see if Oregon had any requirements for private investigators. Finally, I found a phone number for the state board of licensing on an Oregon Government directory, and I called to find out what I would have to do to become legal.

After talking with a sweet bureaucratic clerk named Betty, I realized I was in trouble. A few decades ago, the state of Oregon took over licensing of private investigators. I would have to pass an FBI background check, take a test on state privacy laws, pay $650 in fees and prove 1500 hours of investigative experience.

Betty said I could intern for a private investigative firm and knock off 500 hours experience by taking online classes. She also said I could wind up doing jail time if I represented myself as a private investigator without a license.

"There are people who try to do it, but eventually we catch up to them," she said. "It's a criminal offense, so make sure you have your I's dotted and T's crossed before you go into business."

I wondered if my part-time job with an insurance company might satisfy some of the requirements. I handled claims and did some investigative work while I was attending the University of Oregon in Eugene. Maybe I could parlay that with my investigative reporting experience.

It would take me a month to prepare to take the test and finish the rest of the paperwork. I reached into my shirt pocket and pulled out the $500 Maxine had given me.

The retainer would take care of part of the licensing fee, but I was a bit uneasy over the task ahead. Still, the requirements might not be enough to stop me from eventually hanging a shingle.

I'd left my cell phone in my bedroom charging, so I was more than annoyed that I missed a text from Maxine. I wasn't upset that the 11 p.m. meeting was moved up. It had felt like a trap anyway. But I certainly was troubled by her message saying she decided to meet this Hess character after all, and she wanted me to be there with her at 6 p.m.

I looked at my watch. It was a nearly six and the location was 20 minutes away. I ran upstairs to my bedroom and pulled clothes, videotapes, and my camera case from my closet. I was looking for a velvet brown box with a '38-caliber police special.

I had worked for six months as a salesman in a gun store in Southeast Portland after I was fired. I wasn't much of a salesman, but the owner, Ted Hughes, was. He sold me the '38, a 12-gauge over-and-under, and a hunting rifle that's never been out of its case. I had to quit the job. I couldn't afford to work there.

I found the revolver, inserted six rounds from a cardboard ammo box, and tucked the gun into the inside pocket of my sport coat. Cartridges splattered onto the floor as I fumbled to close the box, running from the room.

A sudden thought struck me at the front door. I had Maxine's packet of funny money with the flash drive and the backup drive I'd made was in my pocket.

Okay, this is where the stupid side of my brain took over. I asked myself what Marlow would do to hide the backup drive. I didn't want someone snooping around my apartment to find it. I didn't know what was going on or to what length they would go to get her prize.

Also, the adrenaline was coursing through me pretty strong in my delirium. I went to my desk and found an envelope, addressed, stamped it, and inserted the backup flash drive. This wasn't an original idea. I stole it from Raymond Chandler. His Phillip Marlow P.I. mailed things to himself in the movie, *Little Sister*.

It seemed like a good idea at the time. I never considered no one was about to come looking for it because no one knew I was in play. I decided to send it to my best friend, Joel, just in case someone came snooping. Big Mistake.

I jumped into the Mustang, backed out of the driveway and punched the throttle as I shifted gears up the otherwise quiet street. The car screeched to a stop at a corner near a blue postal box. My fingers were already chilly because of the dropping temperature, and I leaned across the seat of the convertible and fumbled the envelope into Uncle Sam's cold hands. I gunned the engine again and raced off to find Maxine.

Ten minutes later, as I eased my red Mustang into the driveway of the Kwan Yin Temple, I realized subtlety was not one of the many virtues of the Chinese Buddhism culture.

The sun set against a mammoth cement statue of a contemplative Buddha, which eerily welcomed me to the temple with the essence of tranquility. Inexplicably, the serene concrete Buddha was perched upon an animated beaver painted brown with a fierce snarl and curved fangs. It looked like the Oregon State University Beaver mascot logo. Exactly like it.

I stashed my car in an upper parking lot near Buddha and walked to the entrance of the modest brown building with its sweeping high-pitched roof. The parking lot was empty. Maxine's car could be in another parking lot on the back side of the building, and she might have parked there, I guessed.

An icy breeze blasted through me and seemed to switch on the streetlights. I shivered as dark menacing clouds merged with an evening sky to create an inky blackness. A sliding glass door to the temple was ajar so I scooted in out of the wind.

The foyer was filthy with ceremonial trappings. On my left, a large bronze Buddha held a golden spear with a lobster claw-like point. Several cherry wood tables with golden leaf ornamental designs were scattered about. On them rested candles, fruit, flowers, and oriental figurines. The sweet incense from ubiquitous urns stung my nostrils.

A pair of lady's sandals lay on the floor outside the main worship area. I slid out of my shoes out of respect and tiptoed inside. A whimpering, like that of a small child, broke the calm and I cocked my head toward the noise. Someone was crying or chanting inside.

I couldn't see anybody inside the worship area and there didn't seem to be too many places to hide. It became eerily quiet so I squinted into the darkness for the source of the chants. Along each side of the rectangular room, hundreds of arched-shaped mailbox-like cutouts lined the walls in symmetrical rows. Inside each cutout was a miniature bronzed Buddha. I lifted one out and felt its weight. There must have been a thousand statues.

The whimpering sound came again from somewhere between the altar and a stage. The only thing I could see were a pair of golden serpent-like dragons draped around two posts at each end of the stage. They seemed to be hissing at me. Across the top of the structure, two larger, fanged dragons guarded a crown and a trio of larger-than-life golden Buddha statues below.

The air turned frosty as I climbed upon the stage with the three Buddha. There was sort of a ghostly tranquility about the place that reminded me of a graveyard. A prickly heat swarmed up the back of my neck like death on an old man. I touched one of the Buddha figurines. It was smooth except for grooves cut into the bottom of the belly and its gilded skin was warm from the glow of the nearby candles and spotlights.

I knocked on the Buddha's oversized stomach and a moan seemed to emanate from within. I balled my fists and pounded on other two solid bronze figures and tried to push one aside, but it wouldn't budge.

A familiar pungent odor of cordite hung in the air, reminiscent of gunfire smells I encountered during my repeated trips to the gun range. Someone had been conducting target practice in the temple. I walked around the three idols and noticed a gap between them and the wall. Strewn carelessly on the floor was a velvet maroon drape, similar to another hanging on the other side of the stage. A familiar slender arm dangled at one end of the material.

I reached toward the drapery and tugged at it, revealing the still body of the woman responsible for bringing me into this mess. Her hair was a swarm of sticky redness. I bent over to touch the goo and she moved.

"You're alive," I cried.

She jerked away from my touch. "Please don't shoot me again. I told you, I don't have it."

"I'm not here to hurt you. It's me, Max, remember? You hired me to help you."

Her stiffened body relaxed a little and she groaned. I touched her hair, moving it away from the wound.

"Ouch. You're hurting me."

"It's not as bad as it looks. I think the bullet just grazed your skull. But there's a lot of blood. Whoever did this probably thought they finished you."

She struggled to get up from the narrow crevice her assailants had chosen to dump her body.

"Don't move. I'll call an ambulance."

"No ambulance. I'm okay. If they find out I'm alive, they'll come back."

"Who are *they*?" I asked.

"John wasn't here, so I let myself in. I should have waited. It was a trap."

Aside from her beauty, I admired her toughness. I looked around the room, but except for the watching eyes of a several hundred enlightened statues, there was nobody to help us.

I reached under her arms and tugged, dragging her slowly from her would-be grave. I leaned her against the front of one of the Buddha and waited for her to catch her breath. The only injuries I could see were some scrapes on her legs and the wound to her head. I applied my handkerchief to the side of her head and it came back only a little wet, the lesion already clotting.

"Tell me what happened."

"Let's get out of here, please," she said. "We can talk later. I picked this place because I believed Lu Fong wouldn't desecrate a religious temple of his faith. Apparently, I was wrong."

"Look sister, you may be beautiful, but you're not worth me

getting myself killed." Okay, maybe she was. "I need some straight answers. You told me this was about blackmail, but I looked in the envelope and found your Monopoly money."

She cried out into the bronze forest: "Where's the drive? You didn't lose it, did you?"

"I still have it." My voice had an edge to it. "I come here and I find you gunned down and lucky to be alive, and all you're worried about is some dumb computer flash drive. What's going on, Maxine?"

"I'm sorry. I was afraid if I told you too much, you wouldn't help me. I . . .'"

She struggled to get up, staggered and fell back into my arms. The unmistakable sound of car tires crunching against gravel came from the parking lot outside the temple and headlights flashed into the foyer. Maxine froze, and my heart pounded so loud I was afraid she would hear it and realize I was a fraud.

"Come on," I said, scooping her off the floor. "We're not waiting to see who that is." She was surprisingly light in my arms.

"My purse, it's over there."

I carried her toward a side exit door, bending to let grab her purse. Outside, Maxine seemed much heavier as I treaded gingerly in my stocking feet on the parking lot's prickly gravel surface.

I hoped we could make it to my car on the other side of the lot before whoever might be looking for Maxine realized she was no longer in the building. We could already hear angry shouts from inside.

Slowly, painfully, I hobbled up to the Mustang. I slid Maxine into the passenger side and tugged at the top to make sure it was secure in the wind. We would need the cover. There was only one way out of the parking lot and it was within sight of a green sedan now parked in front of the temple.

"Scrunch down so they won't see you," I said. I hoped nobody would pay attention to me if they were looking for a single woman.

As we spun out of the driveway to a side street, I saw three furtive dark shadows in front of the temple making animated gestures in our direction. One of them pulled something from inside his suit jacket and pointed it toward us.

I stomped maniacally on the gas pedal and we lurched toward the intersection. Then, like every bad dream, the probable happened. The Mustang's engine sputtered and stalled. I heard yelling and car doors slamming. An engine roared to life and there was the unmistakable sound of tires spitting gravel as the sedan peeled toward us.

I tried to restart my flooded engine. That's the problem with older cars. They have carburetors that tend to flood when they get overly excited, as when you stomp on the gas too hard. I cranked the engine: once, twice, three times.

"Come on, come on," Maxine and I cried in unison. The stubborn Mustang sputtered to life just as the green sedan screeched through the church driveway toward us.

I glanced left and instinctively punched the gas pedal as oncoming headlights from the main street screamed down on us. The Mustang's tires squealed into the intersection and immediately the lights from the oncoming car lit up the inside of my car like a solar flare. I gunned the engine waiting for the inevitable crashing sound I knew was about to happen.

Tires screeched and the odor of burnt rubber filled the air, followed by a thunderous metallic blast screaming in our ears. I switched lanes expecting to spin out any minute. We should have been hit, but I didn't feel anything. I looked in the mirror for a clue, but the plastic convertible rear window distorted the images.

Maxine climbed halfway out her side window. "A white van just demolished the green sedan. We made it. They didn't."

She pulled herself erect and managed a smile. For the record, I was a little tense. We both sat in silence for a few minutes, coasting down the street, unsure what to say.

"What was that all about?"

Maxine let out a long deep sigh that seemed to go on forever. "I'm sorry. I lied to you. You weren't meeting a blackmailer. You were to deliver information to an FBI operative."

"What?"

"I worked for a man in Hong Kong named Lu Fong. He dealt in human lives and maybe drugs. When I first went to work for him he seemed like a frail, charming old man, despite some rumors I'd heard about him.

"But over time I became more suspicious. I learned he could be ruthless, and he had some kind of secret dealings with the Chinese government. I began documenting some of his business ventures, making copies of stuff that I suspected were illegal. He had operations in several countries including the United States. At first I thought it was drugs . . ."

She was quiet for a minute. I guessed she was trying to decide how much to tell me.

"Anyway, he must have been spying on me too, because all of a sudden I was an outcast in the office. Nobody would talk to me and it always felt like someone was watching. It got so bad I packed up my stuff overnight and left Hong Kong."

I scrutinized my rear-view mirror as we talked. There was a car a few blocks behind us I'd been watching for a while. "I don't get it? What's this got to do with me?"

"Max, the packet I gave you, with the cutup newspaper, was for your benefit. It was supposed to have the money I was paying Scott Hess. The flash drive is what's valuable. It has names of anti-Chinese activists in Tibet and China and information about Lu Fong's illegal enterprises.

"Lu Fong knows I stole information about his activities, and he's tracked me here. Apparently, he'll stop at nothing to get it back." She touched her fingers to her wound as if to prove it to herself.

"So who is Scott Hess?"

"He's an old friend. He's works with the FBI in Portland. I called him when I got in Portland, and he offered to help me. He was coming back to town tonight from a case he's been working on, and he was going to meet me later at the Buddhist temple. But I got a text message from him saying he was back early and wanted to meet me at six. When I got there I was attacked by some of Lu Fong's thugs and they wanted the flash drive."

"Is that what you meant by it was a trap?"

"Yes. Lu Fong had my phone number. He must have spoofed me, texting me with a fake caller ID, pretending to be Scott. He moved the time up and they were waiting for me."

"How did they know about Scott?"

"I don't know. Scott thought Lu Fong or some of his agents might be looking for me. He suggested I lay low and hire a go-between to deliver the information to him."

"You mean me."

"Yes. I'm sorry, Max, I lied to you."

I frowned. "I don't understand why you didn't just go to FBI headquarters downtown."

"When I talked to Scott, he said there had been some trouble on a case he had been working on, and he was afraid there was a security leak inside the FBI. Since Lu Fong was involved in his investigation too, I assumed he didn't want to take the chance of us being seen together."

"It's quite a coincidence Hess is involved with Lu Fong, too."

"I know," she said. "Apparently Lu Fong had some business in the Portland area, and Scott stumbled onto one of his illegal operations. I don't know much more."

"So, why did they shoot you?" I checked for the headlights again. They were gone now and the anxious feeling inside me began to subside.

"They wanted what I stole. I told them I had given everything to the FBI but, of course, they didn't believe me. They slapped me around a little and searched me. When they grabbed my purse, I made a run for the door. I heard a popping sound and that's the last I remember."

"Does anyone know where you're staying?" It occurred to me that maybe Hess had set her up and was working with Lu Fong.

"I told Scott and you, that's all. Why?"

"Well, somehow Lu Fong's men must have learned where you were and they had your phone number. They knew about the meeting and flushed you into the open before your FBI buddy was in town, giving him an alibi."

"Scott wouldn't do that to me."

"All the same, you'd better be careful to whom you speak with at the FBI."

She sat quietly for a while, thinking. Then she stunned me by reaching up and brushing her lips against mine.

"I feel safer with you."

"Why?" I was scared to death.

"For the past week I've been on the run--afraid to stay with friends because I didn't want to pull them into this. I've been sleeping in different motels every night, eating fast food, and looking over my shoulder every minute of the day. Now I'm not alone. I've got you."

An oncoming headlight shone onto her face and I could see

her smiling at me. "I don't know what I would have done without you. Please say you'll help me." She took my hand in hers and leaned her head against my shoulder.

"What about your fiancée?"

"Oh." She yawned and snuggled into me. "That was just a story I created to get your help."

Was she using me again? Playing up to me to get my help? I didn't care at the moment. A little smile joined my face in the darkness.

"We'd better go to my place tonight in case someone's watching your motel."

It was quiet for a few minutes. Just long enough for guilt to creep into my conscious.

"Maxine, there's something you should know before we go on. I'm not who you think I am."

I looked down at her and she was asleep, her head tilted against my shoulder, a smile on her face.

So much for honesty.

Chapter Three

I woke Maxine when we got back to my apartment, and we tiptoed across the damp grass in our stocking feet. Our breath turned frosty in the cold night air as we padded up the steps.

"Seems like we left something behind," she teased, wiping the bottom of her nylon stocking with her hand.

I rolled my eyes. "My best pair of shoes."

I unlocked the front door and entered first, praying the place wasn't too messy.

"This is it?" she said. "Boy, your wife must be one lousy housekeeper."

Strewn over my brown leather sofa were my sweater, overcoat, some socks, newspapers, and a cereal bowl rested on a coffee table. The room was otherwise furnished with Berber carpet, a tired looking brown leather recliner, and a few small end tables.

"I'm not married. It just so happens I'm not compulsive about cleanliness."

She eyed me coyly. "You must be in your mid-thirties. How come you're not married?"

"I was once upon a time, but it was long ago and not very memorable. Have you ever been married?"

"Not even close. I think it's because I set my standards too high. Or maybe I'm afraid my father wouldn't approve."

"Your dad objects to your beaus?" I chuckled. "Kind of old fashioned isn't it?"

"Beaus? You sound kind of old-fashioned yourself. Daddy likes to look out for me and sometimes he can be difficult."

"Where is he now? Does he know you're in trouble?"

25

"He's a busy man. He's the head of Climatic Film Studios in Los Angeles. Anyway, I like to think I can take care of myself."

I gave her that. Not many people could take a bullet to the skull and bounce back with frisky repartee. She held herself with an air of confidence. Her red hair was more crimson where the bullet had grazed her, but she was sharp and sassy.

"I'm going to call a friend of mine since you won't let me take you to a doctor."

"Why? I feel fine."

"I want to make sure. I can't have my clients going around dying on me. Joel is okay. He's a physician's assistant at the local hospital and my best friend."

"Is there some place where I can clean up," Maxine said. I pointed to the bathroom and took the opportunity to phone Joel. I got a recording saying he was probably with a patient. I left a message asking him if he could come over and look at Maxine, then I texted him the same message.

Then I went into the kitchen to search for signs of food. Maxine reappeared a few minutes later and startled me as I closed the refrigerator door. Her red hair was freshly combed, except for a small sticky matted spot of blood. Her green eyes shone with excitement and her smile lightened my spirit. I think my heart skipped a beat or two.

"Are you hungry?" I asked. "I have some frozen dinners in the freezer. They won't take a minute to heat up."

"I'm starved. I haven't eaten since breakfast."

I slipped two teriyaki rice dinners from cardboard cartons and heated them in the microwave. I clumsily tugged at a bag of salad mix and it exploded onto the counter. I scooped up the salad in my fingers and tossed it into two bowls. I scattered salad dressing over the lettuce and tossed on some grape tomatoes. I found a bottle of Columbia Valley Johannesburg Riesling and two wineglasses.

"You said there were two men who were after you at the temple."

"That's right, one is called Jacky; the other is Shu Won."

"I saw three people getting into the green sedan as we were leaving. Any idea who the third person might be?"

She paused. "Was he tall and slender with a cane?"

"He may have been. It was dark."

"It must have been Lu Fong. Oh my God, he's here? I didn't expect him this soon." Her eyes widened and she licked her dry lips.

"I wonder how he could have known about your meeting with the FBI," I said. "Is there any way you can contact Hess tonight?"

"I only have his work number."

"How well do you know him?" I asked.

"I went to high school with him in Pasadena. We dated our senior year. There were some sparks and we saw each other off and on in college, but he left me for his training at the FBI Academy in Quantico, Virginia. I always played second to the FBI. He didn't even ask if I would go with him. Later, he was assigned to the San Francisco Bureau, but I was out of the state then.

"We emailed each other sporadically until he transferred to Portland a couple of months ago. That was when I emailed him my suspicions of Lu Fong, and he seemed very interested. He said the FBI had been investigating Lu Fong's activities in Portland recently and he wanted me to document anything that might seem noteworthy."

"So you took it upon yourself to play spy for someone who had dumped you."

She narrowed her eyes. "I was the one who started the ball rolling in the first place. But strange things began happening soon after my communication with Scott. Lu Fong had a series of meetings with his employees from which I was conspicuously excluded. I noticed no one was speaking to me other than about day-to-day business. Sometimes I would catch someone staring when they thought I wasn't looking. One night I was followed home from work. It gave me the creeps.

"I decided to leave Hong Kong. I was all packed and had even sent some things to Daddy when I received an urgent email from Scott. He said he was concerned for my safety, and that I should get out of Hong Kong immediately. I didn't understand why he was so concerned all of a sudden. Max, do you think that somehow Scott is involved with Lu Fong?"

"I'm not sure, but it sounds like he knows more than he's let on. It would be interesting to see if he keeps his date with me later tonight. It would prove he had nothing to do with the text sent to lure you there."

Maxine looked at me, perplexed. "What if he doesn't show up?"

This precipitated the first of many anxiety attacks to come on my part. "In that case we'd better be very careful."

"I'm going with you."

"You're going to stay here until Joel can look you over and then get a good night's rest. You can sleep in my room. I'll sleep on the sofa."

"If you think you're going to leave me behind, you're the one with the hole in the head, mister."

"Maxine, look at yourself. You've got blood all over your blouse and skirt, not to mention your hair, and you have no shoes."

"I can take a shower here, and we can drive by my motel and get my clothes and another pair of shoes. I've gone this far, and I'm not quitting now."

I don't think I've ever won an argument with a woman. Tricked a few? Yes. But our relationship was too new for that.

There was a sharp rap at my front door about thirty minutes after we'd finished dinner. I looked to the bathroom, where steam roiled from a crack in the door as Maxine showered and decided caution was a good mandate for a rookie P.I. trying to stay out of trouble. I squinted through the front door's peephole, breathed a sigh of relief, and opened the door to Joel's infectious grin.

Joel Powell was about my age, 33, taller than me, with long blond hair, deep brown eyes and a self-assured smile. He wore dark slacks, a colored long-sleeve dress shirt and a loosened blue tie.

"Hi, Max. I got your text message and decided to just head over. What's this about you being a private eye?"

I thought I heard the bathroom door open in the hallway. "I'll tell you later. Just play along, okay?"

"Sure, Max, sure. You've done some pretty nutty things over the years, so I don't know why this should surprise me. Where is the alleged victim?"

"I'm right here." Maxine stepped from the hallway draped in nothing but a white body towel, revealing shapely legs and a wee bit more. She dabbed her head gently with a smaller towel. "Mmmm, he's quite a looker, Max. I'll bet you guys probably go out and break hearts together."

It's the first time I've ever seen Joel blush. Maxine seems to have that effect on men.

"Max doesn't need my help," Joel sputtered. "It's those deep blue eyes of his. At least that's what the girls tell me."

"He does have nice eyes. But aren't you here to check me out? My eyes are green, see."

Joel's face reddened again. "Well, don't you want to get dressed first?"

"Why? You're a doctor. Besides, I haven't a thing to wear. Isn't that right, Max?"

Now, my face flushed. "Why don't you begin your examination? I'll try to find something for her to wear. And, Maxine, behave."

"I always do," she cooed. "I'm sorry, Joel. I guess I'm feeling better after my shower. Carry on."

I went through two closets before I found something suitable for Maxine and returned to see Joel shining a small flashlight into her eyes.

"How is she?"

"It looks like has been shot. I thought this was some kind of put-on. I'm going to have to report this to the authorities, you know."

"Ah, Joel. Couldn't you just overlook this incident? That's why I called you. We don't want any problems with the police."

"I can't, Max. I have an obligation . . ."

"Well then, I'll just have to tell everyone about your little fling with Misty Mary."

Joel's eyes widened and his face flushed. "Jeez, Max, you can't do that. You swore you'd never tell anyone."

"Who's Misty Mary?" Maxine asked.

"He's right. I promised. Let's just say Joel doesn't have the best luck with women. He's too trusting. Maybe you should hear this story. It has an important lesson to be learned."

"Okay, you win," Joel said. "I won't report anything to the authorities. Just shut up."

"But I want to know," Maxine said.

I shrugged. "A promise is a promise."

Maxine grimaced as Joel touched the side of her head. "It doesn't look like much but it hurts like hell, doctor."

"I'm not a doctor, Maxine. I'm a physician's assistant. No stitches needed up here, but I can give you some medication for the pain. Have you been experiencing any headaches?"

"One big headache right now," she said. But it's not throbbing as much."

"Any dizziness?"

"No."

"Have you been nauseous?

"We ate dinner less than an hour ago."

Joel allowed Maxine to comb her hair away from the wound, smeared on an antibacterial cream and wrapped it with gauze. I gave her a pair of my old blue jeans and a plaid sport shirt.

"You'll just have to make do," I said.

She disappeared into the bathroom for several minutes. Joel made some phone calls, and I paced the floor nervously, knowing another trip to the Kwan Yin Temple was in order.

Maxine returned wearing the outfit I'd given her. She had rolled up the pant cuffs and tied the tails of my shirt around her midriff.

Joel put the phone on its receiver. "You look great."

She pouted. "Except for the bandage around my head. How long do I have to wear it?"

"You can take it off in a few hours if you want. It's just in case there's further bleeding," He glanced at me. "I imagine it probably bled a lot initially. Did you keep pressure on it?"

"It had clotted pretty much by the time I found her," I said. "I used a clean towel from my gym bag in the back of the car."

"There are quite a few blood vessels very close to the skin. That explains the amount of blood you described in your text message. It's a minor wound so it shouldn't bleed much with the bandage on it. If it starts again, apply pressure and call me.

"If the bullet had struck at a slightly different angle, she might not be with us. She has some other minor abrasions on her legs, but otherwise she looks okay. Maxine, I would strongly advise you to get an MRI tonight just to be safe. I can arrange it easily enough."

She shook her head vehemently and put her hands to her ears in agony.

"I feel fine," she said. "I refuse to spend the rest of the night in some bland emergency room, with people coughing all over me and the stench of disinfectant, just to be told I'll live. Besides, we're sort of hiding out."

Joel frowned. "Make sure you stay awake for a few hours in case you have any side effects. Someone should wake you up every two hours tonight to make sure your condition doesn't worsen. Any dizziness, nausea or increase in your headache, you go straight to the Emergency Room. I didn't see anything in your eyes, but you could have a minor concussion."

She held up her hand as if being sworn as a witness at a jury trial. "I promise."

Joel looked at me sideways as we stepped onto the porch. "Good luck with this one. I have a feeling you're going to need it. And I would like an explanation later. While you were looking for her clothes, she insisted you were a private detective."

"What did you tell her?"

"I just played along. What have you gotten yourself into this time?"

"It's my new job, Joel. I'll call and fill you in later." I closed the door and turned to see Maxine's radiant smile.

"Looks like you're going to have to take me with you tonight so you can observe my medical condition."

I sighed. "It looks that way."

"But Max, first we have got to go to my motel room. I wouldn't be seen dead in this *Dukes of Hazzard* getup."

Chapter Four

I switched on the defroster to clear the fog from the Mustang's window and waited while the evaporating condensation revealed millions of white sparkling pinpoints of light in the black evening sky.

We drove to Maxine's motel, and I waited patiently as she changed in the bathroom. She came out wearing black slacks, a dark wool pullover, and a pair of black flats. She patted the gauze bandage on her head and winced.

"I'd better pack a few extras just in case," she said.

It was half past ten when we pulled into the upper parking lot of the Kwan Yin Temple. I parked closer to the entrance in case we needed to make another hasty retreat. Then I checked my gun to make sure it was still loaded. I was nervous, okay?

"Why did you want to get here so early?" Maxine asked.

"I like to see trouble coming rather than fall into it." I looked down toward the empty building. "The lights are all out. How are we going to get in if it's locked up?"

"When I got the text to meet earlier, I went to Jon and got a key."

We got out of the car and strolled up to the sliding door. I tugged at the door, but it was locked.

"Jon must have come by and secured the building after we all left." She rummaged through her purse for the key. "I can't find anything in my purse; everything is jumbled. Lu Fong's goons must have been looking for the . .. here it is." She held a brass key in her hand, inserted it into the slider and slid it open.

I hesitated before stepping inside. "How did you come to know Jon?"

"I practiced Buddhism with him in Hong Kong before he was transferred here. His temple in Hong Kong and the Kwan Yin Temple, here, both support the Dalai Lama's struggle to free Tibet from the Chinese communist government."

I worried the mixed religions might complicate our pending marriage, but as we stumbled around in the dark, I suddenly realized I hadn't been to church in years.

The candlelight emanating from the altar gave form to shapes as our adjusting eyes struggled to see. I heard a scratching noise, followed by a flickering flame and a strong odor of sulfur, as Maxine's lit some candles in the foyer with a match. Her eyes swept across the sanctuary to the altar and back to me. "This would be a wonderful place to get married," she said.

"It would?" I asked.

Her face changed and I thought I saw her blush, but figured it was my imagination. How can you see a blush in the dark? Suddenly, I felt my face warming and I turned away lest she see it.

"What's the matter?" Maxine said.

"Uh, I was wondering what happened to our shoes. Do you see them anywhere?"

She followed my gaze around the dimly lit foyer. "Maybe Jon took them. Still, we must take our shoes off before going inside."

"Fine. But this time we're going out the front door. I don't have any other shoes to wear."

We entered the temple in our stocking feet again, and I told her I wanted to look around to make sure there would be no surprises when we met Hess. I did a detailed search of the temple, exaggerating my task for her benefit.

"You can hide here." I pointed to a red curtain near the exit door.

"Why do I have to hide? I want to be in on the action."

"You will. After I'm sure we don't have any surprise guests, and that Hess is legit. Besides, he won't expect you to be here if he's on the up and up. No matter what happens, promise me you'll stay hidden until I call you."

"Legit?" She laughed. "You sound just like a private eye. Okay Marlow, you beat the truth from him and I'll lie low."

"It's private investigator." The guy from A and C Investigations had emphasized this over the phone. It seemed to be a sore point with him.

"Are you excited?" she asked. "All of a sudden I have an adrenaline rush."

"All in a day's work." I tried to sound confident, but it wouldn't have taken much for me to turn and run.

"You're kind of cute when you're lying," she said."

"I was hoping you'd notice." Fear, my only ally, had vacated the premises; stupidity had taken over.

She offered a coy look. "When this is all over, maybe we should go out sometime."

"How about we skip the preliminaries and just get married."

"Hmm. I don't know if you're that cute."

I leaned into her, for what I was sure was an invitation to kiss, when we heard a car door slam. "Get behind the drapes," I whispered.

I went to the wall of the hundred little Buddha's and pulled one from its arched shaped resting-place. I surreptitiously shoved the envelope with the flash drive into the alcove and replaced the statuette while Maxine walked toward the curtain to hide herself.

A cautious young man with black hair and a crooked smile entered the temple. "Who are you?" he asked.

"Max Starr. I'm the private investigator Maxine hired to meet with you."

"Oh yeah?" he said.

"Are you Scott Hess?"

"Yeah, that's me. You got my money?"

"You can drop the act. Maxine told me how you suggested she get a go-between to meet you here."

He looked at me doubtfully, his eyes narrowing. "Look, I came here to collect some money. She was to deliver it." He walked up the aisle toward me and stopped.

"I'm taking her place," I said. "You're supposed to have an envelope for me."

We were still playing a game, and it seemed to suggest his innocence in Maxine's earlier troubles. But it was time to get all the cards on the table.

"Maxine told me about how you and she went to high school together in Pasadena, and how you're now with the FBI. Did you know she got a text to meet you here earlier this evening?"

"What?" Hess said. "Where is she? Is she all right?"

"She's fine. But she says she got a text from you changing the time."

"I never..."

"Never what?"

"I never contacted her. We agreed I'd meet you here at eleven."

I stared him in the eye. "Then who texted her?"

"I don't know. Anyone can call or text from another number. You can get an App for that. It's called spoofing." He had abandoned all pretenses now.

"It had to be you or someone you told. She didn't tell anyone, and I certainly didn't."

"Christ, I didn't say anything to anybody." The fed rubbed his fingers against his forehead. "How could anyone know? Are you sure?"

I nodded. "It was either you or someone inside the FBI."

"Shit, I'll have to look into this. I don't know how it could have happened."

"Does anyone at the bureau know about Lu Fong and Maxine?"

"No. I didn't tell anyone. I thought it would be safer to wait until after I'd seen what Maxine had found. Which reminds me, you're supposed to have a package for me. I'd like it."

"I'm sure you would."

"So?" He stretched out his palm.

"I think I'd better hang onto it until we get some things sorted out. I wouldn't want it to get into the wrong hands."

Hess threw his shoulders back and glared. "I'm the goddamned FBI."

I could feel beads of sweat welling up on my forehead. Still, I managed a bluff.

"Yes, and I can see you're used to getting your way. I'd prefer a meeting at your office. This time we'll include your boss."

"Listen, asshole, you can give it to me right now, and I won't kick your butt."

There was a gasp from behind the stage curtain. Hess didn't hear it. He was busy reaching inside his blue suit-jacket. I didn't have time to go for my gun. He would have beaten me to the draw anyway.

Hess scowled, and I heard a snapping sound as he unlatched a holster button inside his coat. I closed the distance between us, grabbed his gun arm, kicked his leg from under him and threw him over my hip. He went down on his back with a thud.

The suddenness stunned him, and he gasped for air. I relieved him of his Glock 17 and stashed it inside my waistband.

"What happened?" Hess said.

"Judo. Four years training as a teenager, until I had to quit because I was too tall to throw the shorter kids over my hip. Just a reflex, I guess."

"You broke my leg."

"I doubt it. But you'll probably have quite a bruise. I used to go home covered with black and blue marks after my classes." I reached down and grabbed him by the lapels—the first major mistake in my very short tenure as a private investigator.

"Now, why the tough guy act?" I said. The next thing I knew, I was laying on my back watching solar flares on the back of my retinas.

I awoke some time later to see an angel, and figured I must be dead because I was in heaven. The angel was trying to tell me something, but when she opened her sweet lips no words came out. I smiled, watching her mouth move. Soon I began hearing her words, but they didn't make sense. The syllables were jumbled. I tried to rearrange the consonants to make sense of it.

"Are you with Mike?"

No. That wasn't it.

"Are shoes half price?"

Why would an angel want to buy shoes?

Slowly her aura diminished and she took human form.

"Max, are you all right?"

It was Maxine. "What happened? My head feels like it's been slammed by a cannonball."

"Karate," said a sarcastic male voice next to me on the floor. "I don't know what hit me the second time though."

"Tai Chi," Maxine said. Hess and I looked at each other across the floor in disbelief.

"You hit me?" Hess said.

"I did."

"Why?"

"You weren't acting very nice, and I didn't like the rough way you were going through Max's pockets."

Hess groaned. "I was afraid he was pulling a double-cross. I thought he might have hurt you and was planning to deal himself into the game. But he didn't have the envelope."

"What game are you talking about?" I tried to focus on his voice. It was hard work.

"The information Maxine has could be worth a lot of money. Lu Fong would pay to get it back. His enemies would also pay for it. Or, you might decide to use his bank codes to access his Cayman Island accounts."

"What is he talking about?" I vaguely recalled a sequence of eight and eleven-digit numbers I saw stashed on the flash drive.

"I told him about some bank codes I had found," Maxine said. "He was going to run it through the FBI computers. We think they had something to do with hidden bank accounts."

I attempted to get up, but Maxine put her foot on my chest and pushed me back. "Not until I see the envelope," she said. "Where is it?"

I can't say when I first decided to lie to my future bride. Oh yeah, it was back in Steadman's office. She didn't deserve my kind of chicanery, but I didn't want to turn the flash drive over to the FBI, and I certainly didn't want to give it to Hess. I didn't like him.

"I'm sorry Maxine, I lost it. I must have dropped it on our first visit to the temple. It could have fallen out of my pocket when I was helping you. I didn't want you to worry, so I didn't say anything. When we got to my place, I went through all my pockets and even checked the car while you were showering, but I couldn't find it."

"That's why you insisted on getting here early and looking around," Maxine said. "You wanted to look for the envelope, didn't you? Lu Fong must have found it."

I displayed a sheepish smile. She sat on the floor, crossed her legs and hugged her knees. It was then that I noticed Hess's Glock laying on the floor next to my revolver. They were there for the asking. Hess and I both asked, but I was faster. I turned to him with the Glock in hand.

"Stop right there," I said.

"What are you doing?" Maxine said.

"I'm getting us out of here in one piece. Mr. Hess, I'd like to see your badge. Take it out slowly." I was kind of anxious after his karate lesson. He pulled a badge from his pocket. It looked authentic, but I'll bet you can order them over the Internet.

I picked up my revolver and stuck it in my waistband. "I want you to set up a public meeting at FBI headquarters with your boss. What's his name?"

"Ken Thomas."

"Okay, we'll call you tomorrow at your office and you can arrange a meeting. Until then, we don't want any surprises. Understand?"

"Sure, sure."

I grabbed Maxine by the arm, pointing the gun at Hess every step of the way as we retreated. I dropped his gun inside one of his shoes in the lobby, after removing the clip and ejecting the bullet in the chamber. I tossed the clip across the foyer, and we slipped into our shoes and made a dash for the car.

"I'm sorry I was upset with you, Max. I know you did your best."

I pulled the gun from my pants and opened the door of the Mustang for her. Something about the way she forgave me thawed my heart. I slid into the seat beside her and took a deep breath, wondering if I had the courage to confess.

"I lied to you, beautiful." I blurted it out like I had just discovered how to talk.

"What do you mean?"

"I didn't lose the envelope. I didn't want Hess to have it just yet. Something about him just doesn't ring true."

"Oh Max." She leaned over the console separating us, snuggled up to me, draping her arms around my neck, and planted her delicious lips on mine.

We didn't have time for this, but I didn't argue. "You aren't angry?"

"Nope."

"You know, this means we're engaged."

She grinned. "I figured."

She fingered my earlobe playfully. "You know, Scott sounded mean and vindictive. He's not like the man I went to school with.

Maybe we shouldn't give him the envelope. Where is it?"

"I'll tell you later." I peered through the windshield, expecting Hess to be pointing his gun at us. "It might be better if everyone thinks it's lost. I think Hess might put the word out to others that it's missing."

"Please tell me, Max. I need to know it's safe."

"Do you trust me?"

"Yes."

"Then be patient. I have my reasons. The envelope will be safe."

"All right," she said, and she snuggled up to me in the chilled air. I put the car in gear out of the parking lot, pausing to look over my shoulder toward the temple.

Maxine shuddered. "What? Is he coming after us?"

"No, I was just wondering what happened to my best pair of shoes."

Chapter Five

The next morning Maxine called Hess and confirmed we had an appointment with Ken Thomas at 11 a.m. While she was on the phone, I hunted in my closet for a suit that might make me look more professional.

Maxine had slept in my room, and I had bivouacked on the couch. When I entered my bedroom something seemed different. My bed was made up and I could see carpet on the floor. A woman's touch, I thought.

I selected a suit and went to the bathroom to shower and dress. When I returned to the dining room, Maxine sat at the table with the morning paper and a piece of half-eaten toast in her hand.

"I made you some," she said. "Coffee's on, too."

"Thanks," I said.

"Did you see this?" Maxine drawled. "Some computer whiz in L.A. was kidnapped yesterday. I think my dad knows this guy."

"Mmm," I said, my mouth full of toast.

"Well, I guess there's always someone worse off," she said.

"How's your head this morning?" I asked.

She instinctively put a hand to the wound to see if it was still there.

"It's much better. There's a nifty scab that's forming, but I combed my hair over it. "I'm not going to wear that awful looking bandage anymore."

"Are you sure that's wise?"

"I'll bring some gauze and tape in case it starts bleeding again."

She gave me a look of finality so I dropped the subject. It was a beautiful spring morning and we were met by the sun and the chill was gone. The deciduous trees sported new leaves and crocus bloomed along the driveway.

Maxine looked stylish in a tan cotton jacket with lapels, matching trousers, an aqua green blouse and high-heel sandals with straps that wrapped around her ankles. I slid into the driver's seat in my best lightweight gray suit with a jazzy tie.

"Maybe we were wrong about Scott," Maxine said. "He set up the appointment without a hitch."

"It doesn't hurt to play it safe until we have a better idea of what's going on."

I tried to turn the key in the ignition when a curious thing happened. My door opened, and an iron appendage reached in and wrestled the keys from my hand.

"Max!" cried Maxine. I was trying to make sense of this extra arm, so I looked up to see to whom it belonged. A thick Asian face grinned at me and the fist attached to the arm retreated from the ignition and played a symphony on my chin. The first blow turned my head around in time to see another Asian figure struggling to place a gunny sack over Maxine's head as he pulled her through the open door. I felt a numb sensation followed by paralysis. I wanted to help Maxine, but my synapses stalled and blackness settled in like an uninvited guest.

I awoke with my face buried in a foul smelling rug, which seemed airborne. I was Aladdin hovering over a desert city on a magic carpet. My wrists were on fire and my head felt like it had run into a pyramid.

"Max, are you all right? Wake up."

I tried to get off the flying carpet, but found my wrists were bound together. I put my hands under my stomach and pushed, managing to lift up enough to see Maxine's worried eyes. A trickle of blood dried on the side of her face from the wound on her head.

The carpet fluttered erratically now, and I struggled for balance. A quick scrutiny revealed my flying carpet was made of blue pile and we were inside an older van with tinted windows. The two thugs who kidnapped us were laughing up front somewhere.

Maxine's hands and ankles were tied, like mine, with thin nylon rope. She sat upright and tried to give me an encouraging smile.

"What happened?" I fumbled to rub my sore jaw with my bound hands.

"We've been kidnapped by Lu Fong's men, I think. They must be taking us to him."

"How long have I been out?"

"About five minutes."

The loud chatter in the front of the van stopped, and I lowered my voice to a whisper: "Any idea where we are?"

"I can't see much from down here." Maxine snuggled closer, brushing my nose with her soft red hair. I detected an aroma of fresh strawberries.

"Is it Lu Fong's men? Did you see them?" I asked.

"No, they put a bag over my head. I managed to get it off, but by then they were in the front seat."

"The thug who nailed me was definitely Chinese. I saw his ugly face just before he turned my head."

"Oh," she said, solemnly.

I noticed a crimson streak on her cheek. "You're bleeding again."

"Oh, I didn't even notice. I've been so preoccupied about being kidnapped and worried about you and . . ."

"Worried about me?"

"Well, I got you into all of this. I feel responsible."

"Oh, I thought maybe . . . well, never mind. See if you scoot over here and untie me."

I managed to bring myself into a sitting position and turned my back toward Maxine. She inched toward me and picked at the knots. The laughter up front had died down as our captors apparently had settled into their official kidnapper duties.

"The knots are too tight," Maxine said. "All I've managed to do is break a fingernail."

I tried untying her hands with even less success because my hands were numb from the cord cutting into my wrists. I tried for few more minutes and gave up.

"What now?" Maxine said.

A horn blared outside and it gave me an idea. I remembered an old black and white movie where the hero and heroine retraced their way back to a Nazi hideout by having the woman close her eyes and try to identify sounds that might sound familiar. It led them to an old mill and the bad guys.

I don't know what I expected to happen to us, but I grasping at straws. What do you do in a kidnapping situation? I wanted to appear I knew what I was doing so . . .

"I think we should listen for any sounds that might give us a clue to where we are heading."

Her head bobbed back and she squinted at me. "Why?" she said.

"In case we can get to a phone and call for help. We'd have to know where we were."

"Oh," she said. "Well, obviously we're on a freeway. We're going pretty fast and it's been a while since we stopped for a traffic light."

I looked up at the blue sky through the tinted window above us and felt the rhythmic humming of the tires on the pavement. Maxine was right.

A disgusting, if not embarrassing odor, assaulted us. Maxine screwed up her face, and I smiled, knowing immediately what the emanation was.

"We must be going over the Glenn Jackson Bridge," I whispered. "That smell is a combination of the Columbia River Slough and Camas Paper mill. Camas is about 10 miles east of Portland on the Washington side, and the odor drifts through the Columbia Gorge like a funnel."

"Then we're leaving Oregon?"

"It appears so."

She scooted to me and I suggested we lean against each other--back to back-- for support. We agreed to try to observe clues to our route, to tell police later. If there were to be a later.

My senses became more acute. The foul odor was replaced by the sweet strawberry smell again and there was another fragrance. It was refined and flowery, a blend of fresh rose and ginger, like a field of roses on a warm spring day. Her body was warm and tender, and I had to keep reminding myself that this was a bad situation.

I tried to focus: We turned right, then left at the end of the bridge, ten more minutes of freeway driving, more foul odor, several gusts of wind, a steep grade, what felt like a wooden bridge, an occasional waft of strawberries and roses from Maxine's direction--must concentrate--a windy road, mud puddles, and we pulled into a driveway of some kind.

The van finally deferred to a lazy pace on a winding gravel road, and birds warbled outside.

"Well?" I said, softly.

"We made a right turn after the stinky smell," she whispered. "Then a sharp left on some kind of exit ramp. We drove ten minutes on another freeway. I smelled a spicy lavender and amber fragrance, felt some wind gusts shake the van, noticed we went up a steep hill, and then we went across a wooden ramp or bridge. I heard frogs croaking, and a few minutes later we splashed through some mud puddles. We've been on this gravel road the past few minutes, and I heard a house finch chirping above us."

I couldn't help grinning. She was better at this stuff than me and the spicy lavender and amber fragrance, she described, was my cologne.

The van rolled to a stop and the rough stuff started again. A gruff accented voice gave instructions over the headrest. "You will close eyes. We will put hoods over faces so you cannot see. Any resistance and we will have to carry you inside. Okay?"

We told them we understood. I saw glimpses of a yellow and green grass field leading up to a decaying cedar barn in the short span of time between the opening of the sliding van door and a gunnysack being jammed over my head.

The blindfolds gave me hope. They wouldn't take these precautions if they planned to kill us. Acids stirred in my stomach. It had been twenty-four hours since I entered my new profession. I had been lied to, beaten up by an FBI agent, kissed a beautiful girl, knocked out cold a second time, and kidnapped.

A pretty good job, so far, if you factor in the kiss.

We were deposited in a heap inside the entry of a 1940s style two-story house as our no-nonsense captors wrestled the gunnysacks off our heads. The vestibule was a room in itself with a living room off to one side and a formal dining room on the opposite. The furniture in the dining room was dark, ornate wood. Tapestries hung on the walls around us and the furniture in the living room was old enough to be considered antiques.

I looked up an impressive oak stairway in time to see an even more impressive woman descending in a long, silk, lime-green

Asian style dress with a slit up one leg. The woman displayed a crooked smile and perfect Asian features as she gracefully navigated each step. Her self-confidence and beauty intimidated me.

"Kay Lu!" Maxine shouted. "What is the meaning of this?"

"I'm sorry I had to bring you here like this, Max," the petite woman said.

"Do I know you?" I asked. Oops, forgot there were two Max's in the room.

"This is Lu Kay," Maxine said. "She prefers be called Kay Lu. She's the daughter of my former employer, Lu Fong."

"Hello, Miss Lu Kay," I said, my bravado betrayed by a shaky voice.

"I prefer to be called by my Americanized name, Kay Lu. I don't want to take my father's name. He is old fashioned in his thinking. It is I who convinced him to embark in new directions. If it weren't for me . . ."

Kay Lu stopped in mid-sentence, her confidence replaced by venom flowing freely on the subject of her father. The waves of anger gradually ebbed, and she offered a bitter smile, turning to Maxine.

"Who is he?" she demanded.

"His name is Max Starr," Maxine said. "He's a private eye."

"That's private investigator," I said.

"I hired Max to protect me from your father," Maxine said.

"Yes, father." Kay Lu's tone was sarcastic. "And has Mr. Starr been of assistance?"

"Up to now, he's done a very good job."

"Interesting. Max and Max. I suppose I will have to call you Maxine now."

Maxine glared at her. "Only my friends are entitled to call me Max anyway."

"Then let us get to the business at hand. When you left Hong Kong so suddenly, you took something belonging to Father. He is very angry. He wants it back."

"I don't know what you're talking about."

"You know very well. You stole information from his computer and corrupted the hard drive. He is no longer able to retrieve information from it. He has called in specialists, but they have not been successful."

Maxine smiled. "Computer viruses can be murder."

Kay Lu offered a conciliatory smirk. "Father hopes that you have a copy of the lost information. He seems to think you stole a list of his bank account codes, among other things. There is also a record of scientists he worked with and a list, I think, of Chinese activists and Tibetan loyalists, who would be considered less than loyal by the Chinese. China would be willing to pay a tidy amount of money for that roster of traitors."

"A lot of people will die or be put in prison if those names ever make it into the hands of the Chinese government," Maxine said.

Kay Lu wasn't in an altruistic mood. "Search them."

Two Sumo wrestler types in suits played ping-pong with me as they went through my pockets. "Easy boys, we don't know each other well enough, yet."

On the other side of the room, a third, slightly larger man with a pencil thin mustache, held Maxine's arms as Kay Lu patted her down. "Did you bring her purse?" Kay Lu said. It was more of a demand than a question. Pencil Mustache released his grip on Maxine and handed Kay Lu a saddlebag style brown purse he had brought from the van.

Kay Lu emptied its contents on the floor—one by one—and began tearing the pockets away from the seams. She methodically ripped and touched every inch of the purse, inside and out, and tossed the empty bag on the floor. "I couldn't be so lucky. Does he have it on him?"

"No." one of the Sumo brothers said.

"I hope you will forgive my rude behavior, Maxine. I had to find out if you had it with you."

Maxine bent over and picked up her personal belongings, carefully inserting them into the tattered remains of her handbag. "I would think your father has backup copies of everything on his computer, so why is he after me?"

"You know perfectly well his computer has been destroyed, as well as the backup flash drives that were in his safe. You did a commendable job, Maxine."

"So he doesn't have any other records?" Maxine's grin grew the size of a Cheshire cat's.

"No, you were too efficient and, as I said, he is very angry. That is why his men shot you last night. They thought if you didn't have the information, father meant for you to be killed. They were fools. When father learned they shot you without getting his lost data, he erupted. He risked his own security to return to the temple to find it."

"He must have been disappointed when he learned I wasn't dead."

"He does not know, Maxine. All he knows is somebody else was at the temple and escaped before he could learn anything. He supposes whoever was there removed your body."

"You didn't seem surprised to see her alive," I said. "You even sent a welcoming committee to bring her to you."

"How did you know I was alive, let alone where I was?" Maxine said.

Kay Lu flicked her open palm as if to swat away an annoying insect. "It is not important."

"There are only two ways she could have known," I said. "Either she had the temple staked out and followed us home after her father met with a traffic accident, or she has a well-placed friend in the FBI. Except for your friend Scott Hess, nobody else knew you were with me."

Maxine looked at me thoughtfully. "There was Joel. And besides, Scott wouldn't know where you live."

"Joel wouldn't tell anyone, even if he had someone to tell. Since Kay Lu doesn't want to come clean, I'm guessing it's Hess. Don't underestimate the technical skills of the FBI. They could have tracked you down through your phone's GPS signal."

Kay Lu scowled. "I really don't like you two talking as if I'm not in the room."

I turned and gave her a slight nod. "Why do I have the feeling you aren't working with your father on this. You seem to know things he doesn't. Perhaps you're striking out on your own."

"This guy is pretty bright, Maxine. That's right, mister private eye. Father and I have a difference of opinion. He wants his money back so he can keep me dancing to his tune. By holding money over my head, he assures I will be loyal to him. I am twenty-eight years old and would like a life of my own. Of course, I want all of his money too."

"And if I did have a flash drive, and it had a list of political activists?" Maxine said.

Kay Lu rolled her eyes. "I am not interested in all of that. Father's money and a few other items are enough for me. I will make you a deal. Bring me the flash drive, and I will let you live. I'm not all caught up in revenge like Father."

"I have a feeling the fruit doesn't fall too far from the Loquat tree," I said. "I'm sorry but I don't think we can trust you."

She smiled sardonically. "You are making a Chinese analogous joke regarding the chestnut not falling far from the mighty oak tree, yes?"

I shuffled my feet. "My father was a horticulturist," I said, almost apologetically. "Someone had to listen to his ramblings."

Kay Lu huffed. "Keep in mind, the leaves of the Loquat tree can be a bit poisonous."

"We'll have to take our chances," I said.

"That is too bad because it will be at Maxine's expense. Wong!"

The thick-armed thug, who attacked me earlier, ascended from the shadows of the doorway and put a hand on Maxine's shoulder.

"Make her talk," Kay Lu said.

Wong draped his huge arm around her petite waist and brought a long-bladed knife to her neck. His quickness surprised her. She made a move to elude him, but stopped when she felt the knife at her throat.

He moved the blade artfully across her neck, revealing a thin trickle of blood. It was more than I could stand.

"Wait." I said. "She doesn't know where the flash drive is. I have it."

Wong stepped toward me and pinched my shoulder in his Herculean grip. "Not on me," I yelped. "It's hidden away somewhere safe."

Kay Lu waved Wong back. "Ah, things begin to take shape. I assume, Mr. Starr, you would like to avoid watching the torture of your client."

"Yes. Let us go and you'll have it within a few hours."

"As you just said, I'm afraid trust is an issue. I will let one of you go and get the information. You will have three hours to return it to me. If you fail, the other will die."

I looked at Maxine. "Let her go."

"But you said she does not know where it is. You will tell her, I suppose?"

"Yes."

"Why not save time and tell me now. I will send someone to collect it and you will be set free when it is returned."

"No dice."

"This is becoming difficult. You will go and get the memory drive, Mr. Starr. Wong will accompany you. It is eleven-thirty, now. If you do not return by two o'clock, I will be forced to kill my former friend."

"That's cutting it pretty close. It's not hidden in a place that is easily accessible. There could be complications, and if I don't think I can make your deadline, we will not bring back the flash drive. I can guarantee you that."

Maxine pleaded with me. "Max, don't do it. My life is not worth all the lives at stake if she or her father gets the list of the Chinese activists and Tibetan loyalists. Kay Lu will turn their names over to the Chinese government, and they'll be executed."

"I'm sorry, Maxine. Right now it's you I'm worried about. We'll have to take our chances Kay Lu will keep her word."

Kay Lu stroked both hips with her hands and cooed. "Of course, I will keep my word. You may have until three o'clock as an act of my good faith."

"Max, you can't do this," Maxine said. "I've worked too hard to keep this information out of their hands. I won't have the loss of innocent lives on my conscience."

But it was what Maxine said as I walked out the door with Wong that stopped me in my tracks.

"I can't believe that I ever cared for you."

Chapter Six

Wong let me sit up front with him in the van on the way back to Portland. Of course I had a gunnysack tied over my head, but on the positive side I could breathe.

"Why all the cloak and dagger stuff, Wong?" My muffled voice didn't get a response.

I pulled at the bag with tied hands, and he nearly garroted me with his arm. I responded by gurgling through my nose while trying to breathe inside the restrictive sack.

"I thought you left," I said, upon regaining my voice.

Nothing.

"See what I mean. You're the strong silent type. You might say I'm a bit chatty. If you don't talk to me, I get lonely, and this sack doesn't make it any easier."

"When we get closer to our destination, you will be allowed to remove the bag," Wong said. "You must now tell me where we are going."

"I will when you remove the sack."

It was quiet for the next 20 minutes as a will of minds battled silently, each of us waiting for the other to flinch. Wong flinched.

"We are approaching Portland; you may take off the bag."

Not much of a flinch, I thought. My hands were still tied but Wong was busy driving, so I attacked the drawstring and wrested it off. I wiped my face with the course burlap sack and struggled to get the window open. The cool breeze felt good against my sweat-drenched face.

"You tell me where we go now," Wong said.

I gave him directions to the Kwan Yin Temple. He looked at me sternly, as if I was wasting his time, but nodded. We parked under the giant cement Buddha statue, and Wong reached over and untied my hands.

"You do nothing funny or I break you in half. Understand?"

"What's not to understand?"

We met the Buddhist monk Maxine called Jon in the foyer, and Wong talked with him briefly in their language. Jon finally bowed and went into his office. I navigated Wong past the ornate tables and around worship mats on the floor.

We approached the wall of Buddhas, and I hesitated. "It's behind one of those statues down here." I made a bold movement toward the lower row.

Wong caught my arm and pulled me back. "I will get it," he said, probably figuring it would be a good place to stick a gun. As he bent over and began removing the statuettes from their perches, I grabbed a much larger bronze Buddha from a nearby table.

I didn't want to kill him, so I brought it down squarely between his shoulder blades. I heard somewhere that such a blow would knock a man out. Wong fell to one knee. I waited to see if he was going to topple.

Another beginner's mistake. He turned with the agility of an elf and glared at me, arms spread apart. I swung the Buddha sideways, striking the giant in the stomach. This had the desired effect. He doubled over, gasping for air, but he wasn't finished.

When I hit him the first time my adrenaline pumped so hard I should have been flying six inches off the ground. The second blow, curiously, had sapped me of my strength, and I was about to give up when I thought of Maxine. I lifted the bronze figure over my head and sunk it into Wong's shoulder blades once more with renewed energy.

He collapsed in front of me in a heap. I looked around the empty room for witnesses to my brave deed. I was improvising on the fly now, and I knew I had to put Wong out of commission for a while.

I walked to the lobby and down a hallway until I found Jon reading at a tiny desk. He wore an olive colored gown that reminded me of an old army blanket. "Do you know Maxine Andrews?" I asked.

He nodded politely. "You are a friend of hers?"

His English was thick and accented, and I had to strain to

understand his words. I wanted to ask him about my shoes, but decided this wasn't the right time.

"Yes. She asked me to help her in a matter here last night. She said you were a friend from Hong Kong."

"We have mutual friends in Hong Kong."

"Lu Fong?"

"No, Lu Fong is not a friend to anyone but himself. Our friends are more centered with the Dalai Lama."

"You know the Dalai Lama?"

"I have been privileged to meet with him a few times, yes."

"Does Maxine know him?"

"She has met with him and practices his doctrine."

"Man, I'm way out my league with her. Look, the man I came with--King Kong--he is not a friend of Maxine's. He wishes her harm."

"What can we do to help her?"

"My friend, Wong, needs a place to stay for a few hours--a place where he won't be able to disturb anyone."

"Where is he now?"

"He's taking a little nap in the temple."

The monk looked surprised, but he seemed to grasp what I was saying.

"If you will help me carry him to a cot in the kitchen, I will fix him an herbal remedy that will aid in his meditation and give him time to reflect on the path he has chosen," Jon said.

"Is that another way of saying you'll give him a Mickey?"

"I'm not sure what Mic Kee means, but I believe he will sleep for several hours."

"You'd better triple your dose of herbs, because this guy's metabolism is something else."

Jon helped me drag Wong from the sanctuary into a small kitchen area, where he began brewing a strong tea-like substance. "It is better if we do not breathe the air in here too long once the kettle boils. The steam will relax our misguided friend."

I fished the keys to the van from Wong's pocket, thanked Jon and left without the flash drive. It was safer in the temple. I had devised a plan of sorts, but I was going to need help. I drove home and called Scott Hess's office. Hess was out so I asked for his supervisor.

Eventually a Mr. Ned Wright spoke to me. I introduced myself as an acquaintance of Hess's and asked if Ken Thomas was available.

"Mr. Thomas is out at the moment. May I help you? I'm his assistant."

"I had hoped to talk with Mr. Thomas personally. I doubt you could help me."

"Try me," Wright said, now sounding peeved.

I asked if Thomas might have mentioned setting up a meeting between Hess, Maxine, Thomas and me earlier in the day.

Wright said Thomas had been in earlier, but left about 11 o'clock and he was sure there were no meetings scheduled today in Thomas's appointment book. I mentioned Lu Fong and Kay Lu by name, hoping to strike a memory, and quickly regretted it.

"What's this all about?" Wright asked. His voice sounded anxious and interested.

"I wish I knew," I told him. "I think someone's been playing a joke on me. Do you know when Agent Thomas will return?"

Wright's voice grew more impatient. "No, I don't. He doesn't check in with me every time he gets a phone call or leaves the office. In fact, lately he doesn't seem to give me the time of day. But this Lu Fong you were talking about. Where does he fit into this?"

He was getting too curious. "I really don't know. I have to go now."

"Wait a minute," Wright bellowed. "I think we should meet."

"I don't have time right now, perhaps later."

I hung up the telephone and had an anxiety attack of my own. I had a line-blocking feature on my landline, so Wright didn't have my full name or phone number. But who knows what resources the FBI has? They could be at my doorstep in minutes if they wanted. Wright seemed to be very interested in Lu Fong, and I was sure someone inside the FBI had plotted to set Maxine up.

I called Joel's cell phone and reached him at home. "Are you working today?" I asked.

"No, I'm getting ready to go shopping. Gateway Books is having a 'going out of business sale.' You should meet me there."

"I can't, Joel, and neither can you. Maxine's in trouble and I need your help."

"What's happened?"

I filled him in on the events of the day and drew out a sketchy plan for him over the phone. He agreed to meet me at a Denny's Restaurant in Northeast Portland in 30 minutes with his Jeep.

I changed out of my rumpled grey suit and slipped into a pair of casual slacks and a long-sleeve Madras-style shirt. Then I dug out my gun and holster and strapped them under my arm, slipped on a light jacket, and hurried down the stairs. I was determined to get out of my apartment before the FBI showed up at the front door.

I almost made it. I opened the front door to a medium sized well-built gent in a designer blue suit. Bright blue eyes and red crew-cut hair balanced his square face.

He seemed almost as surprised to see me as I was to see him. He clumsily jabbed a lock pick into his pants pocket.

"I, ah, knocked and you didn't answer."

"I was in the back bedroom. I didn't hear you." I looked at the lock pick, still protruding from his pocket. There was no doubt about what it was. "So you were just going to help yourself to my apartment?"

"Are you Maxwell Starr?" he said, attempting to change the subject.

I looked at the natty blue suit and couldn't convince myself he wasn't an FBI agent. "Who wants to know?"

He tilted his head, sizing me up. "I'm John Steadman," he said, finally. "I believe we have some interests in common."

The name was vaguely familiar, but I had been under enough stress that I didn't make the connection. He didn't look like anyone in Lu Fong's stable, and Kay Lu couldn't already know I was running loose, could she?

"I'm sorry, but you've caught me at a very bad time. Perhaps we could chat later. I'm in a big hurry."

"Off on a big case are you?" Now he was smiling, confident. "Wonder if it could be for the client you stole from my office yesterday?"

"Steadman, oh you're that private eye over in the Morgan Building downtown."

An ugly grin followed. "And you must be the Max character whom left a Post-it note in my office for me. I called Sealy, and he said you claimed to be an associate of mine.

"I also spoke with Mr. Olsen's secretary, Pat, across the hall, and when I told her about your note, she remembered you too. She told me you had joined the world of private investigation.

"And she remembered a pretty redhead who went into my office a few minutes before you showed at the employment agency. I can put two and two together, and I don't like the answer I get."

Damn. He was good. But Maxine was waiting for me somewhere near Camas, Washington, and this guy wanted to keep yapping until the FBI showed up and hauled me away. I meant to move around him, but he cut me off.

This new job was becoming stressful.

"Look pal, it took me twenty-four hours to track you down," Steadman said. "Now I want some answers."

"Twenty four hours? You're really some shylock. My name and address is in the phone book."

"That kind of talk is going to get you a fat lip."

I love it when they telegraph their intentions. When I can't avoid a fight, my motto is to land the first punch.

"I want to know why you broke into my office, and why you stole my client. You're not even registered as a private investigator. I checked. Where do you get off stealing my client?"

This guy didn't look like the friendly P.I. I saw in the picture back at his office shaking hands with the mayor. What to do? If I slugged him, he'd probably hit me back. If I hung around trading insults, I'd be late meeting Joel, and Maxine needed me. I looked at my watch. It was one o'clock. I had two hours to get back and set the stage for Maxine's rescue.

"Look friend, I didn't break into your office; you left it open and I stumbled in. Okay, maybe I did happen upon your client, but that's okay too, because when I wrap this case up we're going to be married. To square things, I'll pay you fifty percent of whatever I get." I wasn't going to work for free on my first case. This was hard work. "Surely that's a fair offer."

Steadman squinted and I could tell the gears were turning. He clenched his fists at his sides. Trouble, if ever I saw it.

"I don't think so. I think you and I should go talk with the police. This constitutes a theft of services. I'm going to make sure you don't ever work as a private investigator again."

This guy was baiting me. Figuring I had nothing to lose, I planned on tagging him on the nose before he slugged me. It turned out that's what he wanted me to do. I swung wildly, and he stepped back and then rocked forward with a solid fist. It caught me on the jaw and knocked me flat on my back.

I got up, slowly, weighing my options. My plan now was to go through him. I charged his midsection headfirst. He sidestepped me like a matador and my head connected with a wooden post on the porch. I staggered back, holding my scrambled thoughts in my hands. Slowly, I lifted my chin and Steadman split my lip with an uppercut.

"Not much of a fighter, are you?" he taunted.

The Judo throw I'd used against Hess the night before stirred a distant childhood memory. I was fourteen, standing in a large open room filled with mats, dressed in a white robe with a white belt. I got in one good flip against a judo instructor early on and he assumed I must have been at least a brown belt, which is a step below several stages of black belts. He threw me all over that room for the next five minutes.

What moves did he use on me? Oh, yeah.

Steadman came in for the kill, and I staggered back a little. When he reached me, I grabbed his arm and threw him over my hip. He rattled the boards on the heavy wooden porch.

He slowly got to his feet. "Oh you're going to pay for that." I was afraid he was right. We circled each other. I backed away, luring him into a false sense of confidence. Mine. He stepped into my space and hit me in the gut. I bent over in pain and somehow managed to grab his ankles. I tugged at them hard, backing up and raised his heels into the air.

I remember a look of amazement on his face as he fell again onto the porch. He landed hard on his back and the air gushed from his lungs. It was difficult for me to breathe too. I released his ankles and tried to step past him, but he managed a weak grip on my leg. I shook my foot like a girl trying to shake gum from her shoe. A kick in his ribs did the trick.

I looked over my shoulder at the once mouthy private investigator, as he rolled on the porch, gasping for air. Would I ever figure out what I was doing? Any more foul-ups and Maxine and I would wind up dead.

And yet, a new confidence welled inside me. I was flying by the seat of my pants, and I was doing not real bad.

Chapter Seven

"You should have a doctor look at that," Joel said, straight-faced.

"When I see one, I will." I touched an ice bag to my jaw and it retaliated with pain. My lip also had complaints.

"Good thing I had that instant ice in my duffel bag," Joel said. His humor became forced, as if remembering something unpleasant. His brown eyes lost their luster.

I had explained my misunderstanding with Steadman and briefed Joel about how I fell in to my new line of work. We drove out of Denny's parking lot in his yellow Jeep Wrangler. The vinyl top was snapped down to warm us against the freeway breeze.

Joel seemed distracted, probably by what I had asked him to do later, but I had my own worries. With the big Chinese bodyguard, Wong, still self-actualizing at the Kwan Yin Temple, it was up to me to find Maxine. I had made the trip to Kay Lu's hideout and returned to town with a stoic steamroller, both times, without the aid of sight.

"I have to close my eyes and concentrate on our route," I said.

Joel turned to me, his smile gradually returning. "This should be interesting."

Once on the freeway, I closed my eyes and relaxed at the familiar rhythm of tires spinning on cement pavement.

I sank into a near meditative state, concentrating on sounds and smells. Joel had his initial instructions, which would take us as far as the bridge between Oregon and Washington. After that it was up to me.

When a familiar foul odor drifted into my nostrils, I shouted over the freeway noise, "We're on the right track. We should be coming up to an exit pretty soon."

"The Camas-Vancouver exit is up ahead," Joel said. "Would that be it?'

I nodded and returned to my contemplative state. "Turn right and veer left soon afterwards," I said.

Joel made the necessary maneuver and I could feel the sounds of the freeway again. But the humming became a harsher vibration, which rattled us. I had forgotten about the grooved pavement and the sensation we had felt in the van. The four-wheel Jeep pounded the pavement like a low drum roll.

I remained silent, counting in my head as I had on the way back to Portland with Wong, approaching the awaited number . . . five hundred eighty-five, five hundred eighty-six . . . "Joel, is there an exit coming up, or have we recently passed one?"

"There are two exits. The first one is Fisher's Landing and the next is another couple miles ahead . . . Camas."

"Let me know when we approach the Camas exit." I was counting again, and was about five numbers from my target when Joel interrupted.

"Camas coming up."

We made the exit, drove under the freeway and approached a fork in the road.

"Do we go left or right?" Joel asked.

"I'm not sure. I know we climbed a hill. I couldn't see through the window."

"There are some hills to the right," Joel said.

He turned toward the hills and I cranked my window down. Joel slowed, and I listened for clues. The Jeep's tires softened on the country road, much like the ride earlier in the day. I heard a few birds squawking, followed by pounding sounds, like somebody hammering, and a train whistle in the distance. Nothing was familiar.

The further we went the more desperate I became. Not only were the sounds foreign, the hill didn't seem steep enough. "I think we're going the wrong way," I said. "Are you sure we're going toward the hills? They don't seem as steep."

"I took the road that paralleled the freeway and then we drifted north," Joel said. "It had a few small hills ahead and the other road seemed to lead into a valley so I took the one with the small hills."

I fumed, worrying we wouldn't be able to find Maxine before the three o'clock deadline. I opened my eyes and focused on my watch. It was almost two o'clock. We had an hour and fifteen minutes before Kay Lu had threatened to kill Maxine, and we needed some extra time to set up her escape.

"Let's go a little further," I said, not wanting to turn back prematurely. We heard some construction noises that grew louder until a shrill whining buzz saw pierced my head, and I asked Joel to stop.

I jumped out of the Jeep, ran across the street and up an asphalt driveway. A few minutes later I returned to the car, satisfied. "Go back and take the other road," I snapped. "The farmer and his brother have been working on his house all morning. He said one of them has been hammering or sawing non-stop."

Joel gave me a puzzled look. "So?"

"Neither Maxine nor I heard any construction noises. I've been listening to the hammering echo across the fields for a couple of minutes. Turn around."

Ten minutes later we were heading into the valley on the other road, and I tried not to worry about time running out. Suddenly the Jeep rumbled and lurched as a whistling sound permeated the protective skin around us.

"Darned wind," Joel cried.

I opened my eyes. We were on a road in the middle of a small valley and I could see Cottonwood trees bending as the wind swept down from the mountains across a meadow. I remembered gusts of wind blowing when the Sumo boys drove Maxine and me to Kay Lu's hideout earlier.

"This might be it," I shouted over the building wind gusts.

I closed my eyes again and minutes later we began a steep accent. The wind gusts ceased, so I rolled my window down and listened. Another minute passed and I heard a sweet cacophony of croaks as male frogs called to their elusive mates. It was a sound Maxine had heard earlier.

A few minutes later we traveled over a short wooden structure, bridging a drainage ditch. Ahead, the Jeep's tires slushed through puddles of water on a dirt road. I opened my eyes and saw a series of dips in the road where snow runoff had drained from the hills and spilt across the road. We were on the right track.

"We should turn off somewhere up here around this next turn," I said.

"Which way?" Joel asked.

There were two driveways. One veered right, the other left. I closed my eyes. "We went up a road, lightly graveled, with a slight incline."

Joel punched my shoulder, and I opened my eyes. He pointed to the two driveways. The one on the right had two inches of fresh gravel. The one on the left was half dirt and half gravel. Potholes were filled with the river rock.

I pointed left and we and chugged slowly up a small hill, stopping at the top. I opened my eyes again and saw a large two-story farmhouse several hundred yards ahead of us, to the left of a long driveway. A huge maple tree wrestled a white weather-beaten farmhouse for occupancy. On the opposite side of the house was the same golden grassy field I'd glimpsed earlier, seconds before a bag was thrust over my head.

"This is it," I said, excitedly.

A slight seldom-used path descended from the driveway just in front of us. The driveway to the house leveled out about 50 yards ahead, next to a stand of Douglas Fir trees.

I stared at Joel. He was flushed and sweat beaded up on his forehead, and I knew why.

"About this plan of yours," he said. "I'm not too keen on it. I brought the propane torch you asked for, but there's got to be another way."

"There isn't time to come up with another way, Joel. I'm afraid the torch is the only option. I want you take the Jeep and drive off the road right here. Then using those trees for cover, go to the other side of the house where you won't be seen."

"And then what?"

"Okay, see that old dilapidated red barn across from the house? That's your target." I looked at my watch. "Do it in fifteen minutes, no longer."

"You want me to set the barn on fire?" Joel was incredulous. "I don't think I can do that, Max. Remember who you're talking to. Have you forgotten I'm pyrophobic?"

"I'm sorry, Joel, we don't have any choice. I need someone to create a distraction so I can get to Maxine. This is the only practical way that will give us a clear shot at escaping."

I put my hand on his shoulder. "I know you can do this. I doubt there are any animals inside, but check. If there are, get them out. Remember, we're talking about Maxine's life here."

"What are you going to do?"

I looked again at the immense tree next to the farmhouse. "I'm going to climb up that old tree and see if I can slip into a second-story window and find Maxine. Hopefully everyone will be distracted by the fire."

"And if they aren't?"

"After you light the fire, use your cell phone to call the fire department. Give them the location and tell them it looks like the house might be on fire. If we don't meet up with you by the time they arrive, go to the firefighters and tell them you saw someone suspicious lurking around and possibly inside the house. That might give us a second chance to get out."

Joel didn't like my plan, but I didn't stick around to argue. I jumped out of the Jeep and disappeared into some brush at the edge of a large open field, using a string of wild bushes for cover as far as they could lead me to the house. I stopped to watch Joel, still sitting at the top of the driveway. He must have seen me looking at him because a few seconds later he was four-wheeling off the driveway and down a slope, heading around the far side of the property.

What I had asked of him was unfair. When he was thirteen, his parents died in a hotel fire. He was rescued by an alert firefighter, but both parents succumbed to smoke inhalation. Our families were close friends. He lived with an aunt for a while and eventually moved in with my family. We had become like brothers, and I knew the fracture lines of his psyche well.

Asking him to torch the barn would bring nightmarish memories roaring back to him. But I could see no other way to distract Kay Lu long enough to free Maxine. If I'd had more experience, I might have been able to come up with a better idea-- like calling the police. I just hoped Joel could do it. I was pretty sure our lives depended on him.

I looked back toward the weathered house. I would be exposed to scrutiny until I reached the maple tree at the rear of the two-story farmhouse. Oddly, I didn't see any suspicious characters lurking outside.

I guessed they wouldn't be expecting me to come back alone or to even find this place by myself. Wong would bring me back so there would be no perceived danger in their minds.

I looked at my watch. In 25 minutes Kay Lu's deadline would expire. The tree was a long way to run without cover. What if someone was looking out the window, watching for Wong to come up the driveway?

I focused on my immediate task of getting to the tree. I noticed a limb pushing against the house. It seemed within reach of one of the windows. I bounced through the tall grass bent-over like a charging mountain goat, trying not to be seen and stumbling in pot holes along the way. My lungs felt like they were on fire by the time I reached the tree. I was too out-of-shape to be in this business.

So far, I was still alive and normal breathing would return eventually. No one had seen or shot at me and this was good news. I leaned against the Maple tree and my eyes followed the monolith's steep trunk to its branches, one of which reached to a window.

I hadn't climbed a tree in 20 years. The base of the Maple was the size of a stout elephant. Its monstrous arms extended to the heavens. I forced myself to climb without thinking about it. I gripped the bark with my delicate fingers and dug my slippery rubber-soled dress shoes into the trunk.

It was more of a jump than a climb and what goes up awkwardly usually goes splat. Lying prostrate on terra firma, I rolled over and considered my options.

Hmm, I thought. Maybe I should jot down some ideas for my memoirs when I'm famous. A tip for beginners: When things get you down, try lying on your back in midst of wet, spongy leaves. It may help you articulate where things went wrong and the oxygen nearer the earth seems to help stimulate your little gray brain cells.

Looking up, I could see the nearest branch was a few feet out of my reach. I got up off my back and looked around for something to stand on. A rusticated bicycle leaned against the side of the house.

The tires were flat, but I reasoned this would offer more

stability. I leaned the tired frame against the tree and tried to wedge the seat under the bark. I had time to articulate another plan soon after I inserted my foot onto the crossbar. I lay contorted and yelping in pain from a supine position, my twisted ankle still jammed in the bicycle, which was on top of me.

A second tip for my memoir? Where's a ladder when you need one?

I limped furtively around the side of the house again and scavenged through a pile of debris, made up primarily of lumber and tire rims. Underneath the lumber, I found an old, muddy, frayed, thick rope. I pulled it from the mess hand-over-hand, shaking off the mud as I tugged. Its twenty-foot length would do the job.

I tied a piece of two-by-four to the end of the rope, knotting the line at one-foot intervals and went back to the tree. On the fifth attempt I managed to heave the plank far enough over a limb to reach it. I tugged at it and the board wedged between two limbs at the trunk of the tree. My hands were mud-caked and cold and the climb was difficult, but tying the knots in the rope been a good idea.

I hugged the first limb and kicked my foot up over another limb in a ridiculous fashion, dangling between the two branches, committed to going upward but unsure how to proceed. My gun, holstered under my arm, dug into my side as I tried to get over the hump.

What's that they say about riding a bicycle? Once you learn, you never forget? You may not forget, but your body does. Tree climbing requires spry twelve-year-old elastic muscles and fearlessness, or at least lack of knowledge of one's own mortality. Thirty-five-year-olds are too heavy and know all too damn well about their own mortality.

Eventually I righted myself and commenced fighting my own Don Quixote windmill, steadily inching toward the window on increasingly narrower limbs. Fortunately two branches offered passage to the window. I walked a jittery path on the lower limb, hugging the upper branch with zeal.

A stuck window, however, presented another problem. It was probably locked, nailed, or painted shut. I thought about kicking through the pane of glass with my foot, but in my mind I could see my leg sliced open.

I removed my gun from its holster while balancing between the two limbs, bit my sore lip, and smashed the window with the butt of the gun.

The noise was louder than expected, and I waited for the telltale thumping sounds on the stairs. I grew bolder, after a minute of silence, methodically tapping at the remaining glass pieces clinging to the frame.

Unfortunately, I'd held the gun in kind of loosey-goosey fashion as I jostled for a better position on the lower branch. My foot slipped and, at that point, I could either grab the tree with both hands or hold onto the gun and fall. I opted for the tree and the gun spiraled end over end into a pile of rotted leaves.

I cursed my ineptness and glared at the gun. Well, what could I do? I couldn't take the time to go back down the tree after it. I shrugged and climbed through the window. The room was dark and smelled musty. I stepped on the broken shards of window glass on the floor and then maneuvered around several boxes of old newspapers, stopping at the door to listen.

I put my ear to the door and heard sounds of labored breathing. It turned out to be my own. I peeked through a keyhole into total darkness, listened to the quiet again, and finally opened the door. It was another in a series of wrong moves made by an inexperienced investigator.

Standing in front of me was a wide-bodied Asian, with a gun in his hand.

Chapter Eight

I had two things going for me. First, the door didn't make a creak when I opened it. And second, Kay Lu's bodyguard had his back to me. He was reaching toward the door across the hall and knocking on it.

"Miss Andrews," he said. "It is time for you to come downstairs. Miss Lu is unhappy. Your friend has not returned."

There was a pause before he opened the door and stepped swiftly into the Maxine's room. I had hesitated, trying to figure out how to handle the situation, and lost the advantage as he had walked away from me. I tiptoed into the hall, hugged the wall and waited for him to come out with Maxine, figuring I'd jump him or something. I had no real plan.

But he didn't come out. Inside, disjointed grunting noises erupted, followed by a low groan. As I was considering what to make of the situation, Maxine stepped through the doorway and ran the opposite direction toward the staircase.

"Maxine," I called. "Come back."

She turned and adopted a fighting stance. Slowly, the recognition in her eyes lighted the dim hallway. "Max, you made it. That creep said you hadn't." She ran up and embraced me, and for some reason I felt much better.

"You're not mad at me?" I said.

"I was for a while. But I knew you were doing it for me. I just got frustrated. Because of me, innocent people are going to die."

"Not yet, they aren't."

"What happened? They didn't they get the computer disk did they?"

"All Wong got was a Buddha-sized headache. Which reminds me, what happened to his little brother? He went into your room and didn't come out." I turned toward the bedroom in alarm.

"He won't be bothering us for a while," she said.

I walked through the doorway and found the poor guy stretched out over a major portion of the floor. "What did you do to him?"

"Well, I couldn't wait for you forever. But now that you're here, I would like to leave. How did you arrive?"

"I pointed through the open door to the broken window and we made for it. But outside the window two of Kay Lu's boys were tugging at the rope I used to climb up. One of them started chattering in Chinese as he picked up my revolver.

"I guess we can't go that way," I said, pulling her away from the window before they saw us. "How many of these guys are we up against?"

"Not counting junior in the bedroom? I would say about five," Maxine said.

We ran back into the hallway, and I looked around for a hiding place. Those two nosy guys outside would doubtless report the rope, gun, and broken window to Kay Lu. I opened two louvered doors, revealing an empty closet with shelves. The shelves lifted out, and I stacked them against one side of the closet. Maxine and I stepped in, pulled the doors shut tight against us and waited.

The sweet strawberry perfume from Maxine's hair tantalized my nose as we scrunched together in the compact darkness. I felt her heart pounding in anticipation and realized mine was in synch. Again, I felt this sense that I should be afraid, but somehow I wasn't.

We didn't have long to wait. Footsteps tramped up the stairs, and through the louvers we could see shadows bouncing off the walls in the hallway. Voices shook the walls in truncated speech, alternating between English and Chinese.

"He's in here on the floor," someone said. Another thug, from the direction of the broken bedroom window, cursed in Chinese. More shadows ran up and down the hallway and searched the two other bedrooms.

"Where is she?" Kay Lu said. "She couldn't have gotten very far. She must have gone out the window and down the tree."

Kay Lu stood inches from us in the hallway. My eyes were now accustomed to the darkness, and I could see her silky black hair flowing behind her head and glimpses of her long green dress. Her exotic perfume swept away the memories of sweet strawberries. I clutched Maxine's hand and tried to control my rapid breathing.

I watched Maxine peering intently through the vented opening in the closet doors and knew what she was thinking. If we could see Kay Lu through the downward slits of the doors, would she see us once her eyes became used to the dimness?

Kay Lu went into the room with the broken window for a moment and returned to the hallway. "Maxine is not alone," she said. "The window has been smashed from the outside. Most of the glass is on the floor. I suspect her friend must have somehow returned without Wong."

"That is impossible," a guard said.

"Perhaps. But it is the only logical explanation." Kay Lu turned her head toward the stairs. "Where can they be?"

She stopped in front of the closet doors again and the odor of Jasmine penetrated my nose. I wondered if Kay Lu could smell our scents and prayed that her perfume was too strong. She seemed to stare obliquely at me and it felt like she was looking into my heart.

"I think they must still be near," she finally said. "I feel it. They are hiding somewhere nearby."

Maxine must have felt my desire to push through the doors and charge through the menagerie of crooks to freedom, because she put her finger to her lips and shook her head.

"Huǒ! Huǒ!," an excited voice shouted up the stairs. "Táifēng, Huǒ!"

"Fire?" Kay Lu said. "What is he talking about? Tell him to speak slower—in English."

"He says there is a great wind of fire," said one of the guards.

There was movement toward the stairs and men talked excitedly in Chinese. "Miss Lu! Come quick! He says a great wind of fire is on the barn!"

"That's where they are," Kay Lu said. "I knew it. Spread out over the property and take a car out to the highway to look for them."

Kay Lu hesitated at the top of the steps and looked back

toward us. "I will kill them for this. I will kill them." Then she ran down the stairs.

My eyes locked on Maxine. We were nose-to-nose and embracing each other in that tight space. Impulsively I kissed her. It was a long, slow kiss and one that she returned with equal passion.

As quickly as it happened, the kiss ended. "That was close," I said.

"We need to get going," she said.

I pushed the closet doors open, and we stepped into the hallway and smiled timidly at each other.

"I thought Joel would never get that fire going."

"Joel's here?" Maxine asked. "What fire?"

"I planned a little diversion to help us get away."

"Nice thinking," she said. "I'll owe Joel a kiss too. I was sure Kay Lu could see us in that closet."

I turned toward the louvered door and pointed to the slats. "They're facing downward. We could see out, but they couldn't see in."

Worry lines stretched across Maxine's face. "But she was standing right in front of us. I was afraid if we moved, she would sense we were here. In fact, I think she just about did. Joel's timing was a little too close."

We decided to escape via the tree, hoping everyone would be on the front side of the house. Going down was easier than coming up. Even so, Maxine, in high-heel shoes, easily beat me.

I watched her on the ground, mocking me as the wind blew her bright red hair against her face. She brushed it back with long fingers, revealing a few scattered freckles and a mischievous smirk. "Let go of the limb."

"Move out from under me and I will." She let go of my feet and backed away, and I tumbled onto the ground.

"You're not much of a tree climber," she said.

""I climbed up it, didn't I?"

From the corner of the house we witnessed the complete chaos of Kay Lu's army. Her men were scattered across the property as flames soared upwards of 60 feet above the barn. Two of her men hauled a hose toward the fire, but it didn't stretch far enough. Kay Lu stood halfway between the house and the barn and flailed her arms in the air in disgust.

"We're going to have to run to the top of the driveway," I said. "You'll need to do something about those heels."

She handed me one of her shoes. "This escapade of ours has been pretty hard on my wardrobe."

I tugged at the heel, loosening it gradually. The second shoe broke easily in my grip. "I forgot about your head wound. How are you feeling?"

"I had a major headache earlier, but it seems to have gone away during our stint in the closet."

We scrambled along the exposed yardage, hoping to reach the bushes before being seen, but Kay Lu turned and caught us at the halfway point.

"Run," Maxine said.

"I'm running. It's not as easy as it looks."

We bobbed like Cossack dancers through waist-high grass. It was thick and wet and we couldn't see the ruts and gopher holes until we were in them. I looked over my shoulder and saw Kay Lu waving at someone in a blue pickup truck. Two gunmen in the pickup were trying to beat us to the crest of the driveway. We were in a grouse hunt and we were the grouse.

The terrain improved as we approached the bushes. We had less distance to cover than the truck to get up to the driveway, but I calculated it would be close. "If Joel is where he's supposed to be, we might make it," I shouted, over the approaching engine roar.

"If he isn't, he won't be getting that kiss."

We ran along the cover of the bushes and high grass, angling to the right, toward the top of the winding driveway. The truck's engine howled and its tires spit gravel, as it dashed closer and closer, until it sounded like it was just above us on the road. I was about to pull Maxine back when a cloud of dust exploded above.

I grabbed Maxine's hand. "Let's go." We were barely ahead of the truck, hidden in a ravine, and we'd be sitting targets if the gunmen saw us.

"I can't," she cried. "Go without me."

I stopped and pushed her down in the grass. We lie flat feeling the coldness stabbing at our lungs, helpless, impatiently waiting for the end listening to the pickup truck's engine idling menacingly overhead.

I glanced above the top of the weeds, but I saw no Asian men with guns beating the bushes. In the distance, a siren shrieked. Closer to us, the truck's engine quieted ominously.

"Listen," Maxine said. "It's getting louder. Do you hear it?"

The shrill siren filled the air.

"It's Joel's fire truck," I said. "They'll be afraid to shoot at us with witnesses. Let's go."

The siren grew louder and I looked up to see it creeping down the road. We staggered along the ravine below with renewed stamina and climbed up to the spot on the path where Joel had dropped me off.

Further down the driveway, the blue truck was backing up toward the soaring flames as a brick-red fire engine followed along the narrow strip. We could see Kay Lu's twisted face staring at us.

"Wave," I said.

"She won't like it." Maxine waved and smiled through clenched teeth. "I hope we find Joel before that truck gets around the fire engine."

As if on cue, a yellow, four-wheel Jeep climbed up the other side of the driveway and Joel beamed. "I'm sure glad to see you two. I saw that pickup coming lickety-split, and I knew it was trouble."

I jumped into the Jeep with Maxine. I sat in the back and she sat next to Joel.

"Just get this thing out of here," I said. "What took you so long?"

"I'm sorry." He revved the engine and aimed the tires toward the main road. "I was hiding on the other side, waiting. When I heard the pickup coming, I was afraid we weren't going to get out of here. The darn fire department must have gotten lost."

"You did just fine." I swatted his head from behind.

We got to the main road and traveled a few miles before Joel pulled off to the roadside near the freeway entrance. He cocked his neck to look into his side-view mirror. "I don't see anybody back there. They didn't even try to follow us."

"I'm sorry it took so long to get the fire going. There were hens and goats inside the barn, and I couldn't get them out."

"Oh no!" Maxine said. "You didn't . . ."

"I really hated it, Max," Joel said, ignoring the question. "It brought back bad memories."

"I'm sorry, Joel."

"Well, I forced myself—knowing Maxine's life was at stake."

She smiled her thanks and turned to give me a puzzled look. I patted her shoulder and she remained silent, sensing Joel needed to talk.

"I tried lighting the grass with my propane torch, but it was too damp so I knew I had to burn the barn." Joel's face became pale as he recalled the events. "The animals wouldn't leave. I tried to shoo them out, but they wouldn't go.

"I didn't want to, but I lit some of the dry hay on fire inside and prayed the animals were smarter than they looked. The flames roared up and caught me off-guard. I retreated to a back window and waited to see if the dumb clucks would leave. The flames came up so fast. It was awful."

Maxine could hold back no longer. "Did they get away?"

"Yeah, they weren't nearly as stupid as me. I nearly singed my eyebrows. Darn building burned five or six minutes, after I called the fire department, before anyone noticed it. I nearly had a stroke. I was about to throw a rock through the front window of the farmhouse."

Maxine reached over and took his head in her hands. She kissed him squarely on the lips.

"I don't know what brought that on, but I'm not complaining," Joel said. He put the Jeep in gear, and we started toward the freeway ramp.

"You were magnificent, "Maxine said. "We were seconds away from being caught when they saw the fire."

"Maxine's right," I said. "I know how hard it was for you, Joel. If you weren't driving, I'd kiss you too."

"I think I'll pass on that unless you want to make Maxine your designated kisser."

I smiled at him, trying not to let on how their kiss affected me. It brought up some unpleasant memories of my own I thought I had buried long ago.

Chapter Nine

Going to an old friend for help seemed like a good idea at the time. My place wasn't safe since Kay Lu knew where to find me, so Joel and I dropped Maxine off at his apartment. We went to the Buddhist church and I retrieved Maxine's envelope while Joel waited in the Jeep. Jon told me Wong had left an hour ago after waking up with a headache.

Next we drove to the Multnomah County Sheriff's Office to visit with Captain Jim 'Hollywood' Henderson.

Hollywood, a passive-aggressive kind of guy, played poker at our regular Wednesday night game. Our timing wasn't great. He was miffed because we both had forgotten the poker game the night before while helping Maxine.

People call him Hollywood--although never to his face-- because he starred in a few COPS television episodes in Portland and never lets anyone forget it. I wasn't sure whom I could trust at the FBI and, because we didn't know anyone at the Portland Police Bureau, we decided Hollywood was our best bet since I was pretty sure we were in over our heads.

"Are you guys yanking my chain?" Hollywood boomed. "This is far from believable. Let me see if I have this straight. Max, you misrepresented yourself as a private investigator. Then you took on a case as such. A woman was shot and you didn't report it to police. Joel, you know better than that. Max, you and your alleged client were kidnapped, and again you failed to report it to the police. Instead, you two bozos take it upon yourself to try and rescue a woman and burn down a barn in the process. Am I missing anything? Oh yeah, Max assaults an FBI agent. That ought to look good on your resume."

I tried not to snicker while he bawled us out. He was attired in the department's new official uniform, a murky olive camouflage outfit. He looked more like an army reserve than a cop. He hates it because he thinks it makes him look drab. It does.

"Between the two of you, you're facing probably twenty-odd charges ranging from assault to arson," he said. "Nice of you boys to turn yourselves in."

He brought a keen glance over us, as we slumped into the old oak chairs opposite his desk, and the corners of his lips lifted slightly. He raked his fingers along both sides of his head, combing through his sparsely salted black hair. His dilated brown eyes danced below crinkled brows as he leaned over his desk.

A tinge of alcohol stung my nostrils with each question. "Okay, Max. Why did you tell this supposed client of yours that you were a private investigator?"

"You won't like the answer."

"Why don't you try humoring me?"

I squirmed on the wooden chair. "I was trying to impress her."

"That's all I need! I'm trying to stem a flood of Chinese villains from assaulting our citizenry, but first I have to stop and babysit a love-struck fool and his friend, cupid."

He rolled his shirtsleeves up his arms, displaying taught muscles and a tattoo of a Harley on his right forearm. "Okay, here's the killer question, Max. The answer to this question decides whether you get to go home or have to start raising money for bail. Are you ready?"

I nodded meekly, knowing what was coming.

"Have you got a license to carry a concealed weapon?"

I gave another nod, but it wasn't the one he wanted. Note to self: In the future, leave out details about any gun I might carry.

"Damn it, Max. You're not making it easy for me. Okay, in the course of your investigation, did you have cause to discharge your weapon?"

I smiled awkwardly. "No?"

"Well, that's something. Hand it over to me, Max."

"I, ah, I lost it."

Hollywood raised his arms in a dramatic fashion as if to ask God to take him now.

"Jim, can I say something?" Joel asked.

"I'll get to you in a minute. Just clam up for now."

The telephone rang and Hollywood reached across his desk to answer it.

"What? Oh, hello Jane. I can't talk right now. I'm interrogating a couple of perps.

"I don't care what you say. I did not go out and leave the kids alone the other night. No, I didn't have any friends over either. I put them to bed at about nine o'clock and watched some of my COPS episodes on DVD— the ones I guest-hosted. Look, just because Brianna woke up in the middle of the night and I wasn't in bed, doesn't mean I snuck out. Crap, Jane, she's only five-years-old. Whose word are you going to take? Hers or mine?

"I did NOT have a party . . . Ian said WHAT? I was listening to some jazz CDs. Listen, Jane, we aren't married anymore, so quit riding me, okay? . . . I know the kids are your responsibility. In all the years we were married, did I ever mistreat them? Did I ever leave them alone? No, I didn't . . . Just because you feel that way, doesn't mean I have or ever will abandon Ian or Brianna, Okay?

"Jane, I can't talk now. How about I come over this weekend, and we sit down and talk all this out? I'll explain to the kids that I was watching television and listening to music . . . Jane? Damn, she hung up on me. How about that? She calls me and hangs up."

Hollywood looked over at us, his eyes cold as steel. The cleft on his chin quivered. Slowly, his booming voice slipped down into a smooth baritone business tone.

"Where were we?" he said. "Oh, yeah. Listen, Max, sorry for the hassle. It's my job, you know. I'll make some inquiries with the Feds and the Camas authorities and get back to you as soon as I hear anything. Until then, you guys just lie low and don't do anything. The gun thing will just be our little secret for now. You think your friend, Maxine, needs any protection?"

He amazed me. We're sitting there listening to him argue with his ex-wife, his blood pressure elevating by the second, and he switches back to his professional cool tone that got him where he is today. People think he's called Hollywood because he's been on television a few times. Not entirely true. Hollywood is smooth and cool, and when you think you've got him figured, he shows you another nuance. Hollywood is always evolving. That's why his marriage failed. He was just too smooth for Jane. She started doubting him because he had changed from the simple, eager boy she married.

We decided to get out of his office before he changed his mind and threw us into a damp jail cell. Friendship only goes so far. I told him Maxine was safe for the time being, and we'd call him if we needed any protection. He told me to check back the following day to see if he had learned anything.

Joel snickered as we left Hollywood's office. "Did you see that big vein bulging in his neck? Jane sure knows how to get to him."

"I think she wants to get back together," I said.

"Really?"

"Just a hunch."

Joel was silent as we sped from the parking lot in his Jeep and headed to my place. Both of us remained deep in thought until we reached my driveway.

"Going in?" Joel asked, motioning to the apartment.

"I just remembered. My Mustang's still at Denny's," I said.

Joel rolled his eyes. "Nobody's going to steal that piece of junk."

"It's a classic." I shifted in the seat and looked over my shoulder. "It's got slant six engine and a . . ."

"What is it?" Joel said, following my gaze to the street.

"Wong's white van is gone," I said. "He must have come back for it."

Joel switched the Jeep's motor off and we got out. I should have been worrying about my house. The front door was left slightly ajar. I opened it a bit wider and peeked in.

I motioned for Joel to be quiet, and we entered the room. Books and toppled furniture were strewn across the living room. Framed pictures had been ripped from the walls and lay smashed on the floor. In the kitchen, food from the refrigerator was spread across the floor and the cabinets had been stripped of dishes and food tins.

It didn't take long to determine my uninvited guest was no

longer here. As we walked through my apartment, it was obvious nothing had been ignored. This was an equal opportunity ransacking. Clothes had been torn from my closets, mattresses stripped from the bed frames, and even the contents from my medicine cabinet were ejected. Pills were scattered across the floor and a snail's trail of white toothpaste meandered from the medicine cabinet to the doorway.

"You must have really pissed off this *Wong* character," Joel said. A frightened look came across his face. He ran from the bathroom and returned later to find me in my den. "I called Maxine, she's okay," he said.

"So is your apartment, from the relieved look on your face," I said.

He offered an ironic grin. "I was more concerned about Maxine."

I looked over at the bare desk in the corner of the room. "So am I. I'm just a little distracted."

"What's wrong?"

"They've taken my laptop, my stack of recordable CD's and movie DVD's, my computer software program boxes, and even my mouse.

"This is going to set you back a pretty penny," Joel said.

I reached into my jacket pocket. "They didn't get what they were after."

"I'm going to need to borrow your computer," I said. Joel looked at the yellow envelope in my hand. I withdrew the funny money and the flash drive Maxine had entrusted to me.

"Is that what everyone is after?" Joel asked.

I nodded. "I'd like to take a closer look at it. I didn't have time to do much searching when I made a copy earlier."

"You made a copy? Did they get it?"

"No. I didn't leave it laying around."

"Then, is that the copy in your hand? I'm confused."

"This is the flash drive Maxine gave me to give to the FBI. I hid it in the Buddhist temple and retrieved it on the way to see Hollywood.

"Where is the copy?"

"It's safe for the time being. I would appreciate you not telling Maxine about the backup though."

He screwed up his face at me. "You must have your reasons."

"I do." I'm a coward.

"Okay, I won't say anything. You'd better pack some clothes for Maxine and yourself. It's not safe to stay here."

I repacked Maxine's suitcases as best as I could and gathered up some clothes for myself. Looking at the scattered mess I was leaving behind, I wondered if it might be the right time to hire a housekeeper.

Joel drove me to Denny's, and as I followed him to his house in my Mustang, a thought haunted me. I had started worrying about the copy of Maxine's data flash drive I mailed the night before. It could be in Joel's mailbox by now. I maneuvered my Mustang in front of Joel's Jeep as we approached his house and pulled into the driveway ahead of him. I grabbed our suitcases from the trunk, deposited them on the porch, and sifted through his mailbox on the front porch. There was no envelope addressed to me.

I handed Joel a stack of junk mail. "What time do you get mail delivered here?"

"She usually delivers in the morning," he said.

"What time in the morning?"

"Between eleven and noon, I think. Why?"

"I need to mail a letter." It was a white lie, and I felt guilty when I said it, but I figured Joel would be happier not knowing I mailed the second flash drive to his address.

Inside, we huddled around a pizza Maxine had ordered and I switched on Joel's computer.

"How did things go with your friend, Mr. Hollywood?" she asked.

"Well, he didn't arrest us," Joel deadpanned.

"Not yet, anyway," I said.

Chapter 10

Sometimes I hate Joel. Especially when he plays matchmaker. Maxine had changed her clothes and wore casual black slacks and a loose-looped knitted blue sweater. Her face, with very little makeup, was animated and friendly, especially after I returned her flash drive.

"I'm so happy to have this little stick back," she said. "I was so worried it would get into the wrong hands. You did a great job, Max."

I gave a mock bow, but I felt guilty because I wasn't going to let her keep it.

"I called Jon at the Kwan Yin Temple," Maxine said. "He said my car was still parked on the street in a No Parking zone. He was going to call the towing service and have it towed away."

"I'd forgotten about your car," I said.

"Well, I hadn't. It's only a rental, and I bought all kinds of supplemental insurance so I wasn't too worried. Still, I'll need to pick it up tomorrow. We can bring it back here."

"I think I should call Hollywood. He told me to report anything of importance, and I'd say someone breaking into my home warrants his attention. After being screamed at once, I don't want to give him a second chance."

Maxine's face went flush at this news. "Your place was robbed?

Joel launched into a narrative of our exploits, including how Hollywood chewed us out, with elaborate detail about how the veins in his neck seemed ready to explode.

Unfortunately, I already had dialed Hollywood and was trying to report the break-in. Joel was so boisterous, I was worried

Hollywood could hear parts of his story and the laughter that followed. I retreated into the kitchen and finished the conversation as quickly as possible.

When I returned, Joel had collapsed in a heap in a chair by the computer. Tears streaked his face as he told Maxine his light-hearted version of a story about how someone had redecorated my apartment.

Maxine wiped a tear from her cheek. "I guess it was a good idea to stay here after all. I hope you don't use the same decorator Max has." She laughed as I took it on the chin.

"Hollywood is going to send a pair of deputies over to my place to check things out," I said.

Joel wiped tears from his face and sat up. "Do you have to go back and let them in?"

"No, I told him where I hide a spare key. We won't have to go anywhere tonight."

"Good," Maxine said. "After today, I'd prefer a quiet evening with as much company as I can get."

Joel's house featured a bulky entertainment center which filled one wall of Joel's small living room. Two overstuffed chairs were sited strategically to get Maximum benefit from a giant television screen and an elaborate stereo system.

An oval dinette table and a pine desk were in the adjoining dining room. The walls were covered with nature pictures Joel had photographed and framed. Maxine shifted her chair to a desktop computer and stared at the monitor. She nibbled at a slice of pizza we had ordered and inserted her flash drive in a USB port on Joel's computer, clicking it open with a mouse.

"What do you make of this file?" she said to Joel, pointing with the slice of pizza.

Joel bent over her shoulder and peered at the screen. "It has mostly numbers and crude molecule type drawings—it looks like some kind of math formula. "It looks familiar. The pictures indicate simulate cell reproduction of some kind. The medical formula is a little more complicated. I'll have to dig out my old textbooks and see if I can decipher it. Maybe I could make a copy and take it to work tomorrow. I think Dr. Sullivan could help us make sense of this thing."

Maxine's eyes dilated. "I don't want any copies of this

floating around. There are too many people who would love to get their hands on this information. The less chances they have the better."

"Oh, sure." Joel tapped his foot nervously at being remonstrated by Maxine.

She seemed to realize she had been too harsh and patted him on the arm. "If you want to print out a few pages with the formulas that interest you, I suppose it would be all right."

"Why keep this stuff at all, if it can only hurt people?" I said.

"Because it can be helpful to my contacts in Hong Kong to see what their enemies have learned and reveal who might need protection. Also this medical research, or whatever it is, might be of help to our country, according to Scott."

"Hess again." I rolled my eyes. "I think you would do well to stay away from him and his ideas."

A quiet tenseness filled the room, and we watched silently as Joel scrolled through the pages for a while, squinting at the flashing screen in the darkened room. Joel finally turned off the computer and opened a bottle of wine. We relaxed and exchanged lies. Maxine began to pry about my ex-wife, and I decided to look for another bottle of wine.

"It's kind of a touchy topic for him," Joel said, as I drifted into the kitchen. "Max met Barbara in college. They were married shortly after graduation. Both were newspaper reporters."

"Oh, he was a writer?" Maxine said.

"A good one. An investigative journalist with lots of awards," Joel said.

I had meant to get out of earshot, but I could still hear Joel. It was easier for me to let him tell Maxine about my past. She would have to know eventually, if we were ever to become serious about each other. I hovered at the open refrigerator door looking for a bottle of wine that wasn't there.

"Max was crazy about Barbara," Joel said. "But they were only married about a year when he began to hear rumors that she was fooling around. They worked at the same newspaper. She worked days and he worked the swing shift. Max had the police beats, so he made friends with a lot of the cops. That's how he met Hollywood.

"One night, he decided to go home and surprise his wife on

his dinner break."

Maxine let out a slow whistling sound. "Uh oh. Don't tell me he caught her fooling around."

"Almost. Someone had apparently run out the back door when he saw Max coming. There was enough circumstantial evidence to make a case against Barbara.

"They had a heated confrontation and separated for a while. Then one day Max showed up during the day shift and caught Barbara and the desk editor playing 'spin the bottle' in the break room."

"What happened?" Maxine asked.

"The editor got the hell out of the break room and ran for his desk. Max caught up with him in the Living and Entertainment department and knocked two teeth out."

"No."

"Yes. Security held him for the police. He was arrested and charged with assault before the amorous editor agreed to drop the charges. The newspaper management didn't want the embarrassing publicity."

"Did he quit the newspaper? Is that why he became a private investigator? Did he want to catch other cheating spouses?"

"I'll let Max tell you how he decided to become a private eye, but he was fired from the newspaper for punching the editor out. He and Barbara got a divorce, and she married the editor, Dennis O'Keefe. The guy had pretended to be his friend, but he was the one responsible for keeping Max on the night shift.

"O'Keefe kept Max from being promoted by taking credit for some of his work. He told his superiors it took major re-writing of Max's copy to make it palatable to readers even though a couple of Max's stories won awards."

"How long ago did all this happen?" Maxine asked.

"It's been about two years, now. He really took it hard. He was in love with Barbara--as much as anyone could be in love--and he hasn't given any girl a serious tumble since, until now."

"Until now?" she asked.

"Well, yeah. I sort of thought you too were . . ."

I re-entered the dining room in time to see Maxine blushing. "Are you two still gossiping about me?"

"I'm done," Joel said. "Except, Maxine was asking how you

decided to become a private eye. Why don't you tell us? Uh, I mean tell her."

Maxine gave me a little pixie smile. "Yes, I'm dying to hear all about it."

"Perhaps another time. I'm not feeling up to it at the moment."

Joel wasn't going to let me get off that easily. "Oh come on, Max. Throw us a bone. Unless you'd rather I tell her about it."

It was the moment of truth. Well, semi-truth anyhow. "There's not much to tell. It was a while back. I had just lost my job with an insurance company as a claims adjuster."

Joel squirmed in his chair. "Oh yeah. Tell her how you lost that job, Max."

"You might say I lost my temper. My boss, Charles Norman, and I had different viewpoints on how to handle a claim. So I quit."

"What kind of a difference of opinion?" Maxine said.

"Norman wanted me to doctor a claim so we wouldn't have to pay out a hundred thousand dollars, and I refused. He was up for a promotion and felt screwing a poor lady out of her insurance money was the way to get it."

"Tell her about your resignation letter," Joel said, chuckling to himself.

"It was verbal," I said.

"And physical. He punched Norman out. Do you see a pattern here, Maxine?"

"Yes, he doesn't like injustice." She smiled at me.

"I reported Norman to the state insurance commissioner's office. The lady got her money without any problem. But I was done in the insurance business. They don't like whistleblowers."

"Or pugilists," Joel said.

"So you decided to become a private investigator?" she said.

"Sort of."

"How did you decide?"

I paused a moment. "It happened almost by accident. I was supposed to be going in for an interview with a personnel company and I went through the wrong door. It was Steadman's office.

"As it turned out, he was in need of some help. The day I entered his office he had an appointment across town and a client was expected. I offered my services for the day to help him out.

Later we discussed my role with his agency. He played hardball at first about wages and such, but eventually I softened him up. It's been a rocky relationship, and I've been thinking lately about opening my own office."

"How long have you worked for him?" Maxine asked.

"Longer than I care to remember. We should get back to business. Joel, can I take a look at the flash drive, now?"

Joel's countenance displayed a sort of admiration. He had done the mental gymnastics necessary to put the puzzle pieces together from the half-truths I had recited.

I knew what he was thinking: That's not exactly the way you explained it in the car, today.

Maxine continued looking at me as if contemplating something. Her brow was intense and her tongue caressed her lips.

"Max, there's something I need to tell you. Things have been happening so quickly we haven't had much chance to talk."

"What's on your lovely mind?"

"Tomorrow is Friday night, and I've promised to be at a charity fundraiser. It's being held to raise money to free Tibet from Chinese influence."

"Where?"

"At the downtown Hilton. It's very important to me. You see, I'm one of the speakers, and I promised some people I would be there."

"And?"

"It could be dangerous. Lu Fong might be there. He's aware of the event and of my loyalties to the cause."

I thought it over for a moment. "It might be safe. Will there be a good-sized crowd?"

"Oh, yes. Several hundred people. And someone very dear to me."

I narrowed my eyes at her. "And who might this special person be?"

"You're going to get a chance to meet my father. Remember, I said he'd be around soon. I convinced him to attend the event and even make a donation. But, please don't tell him what I'm involved in. He wouldn't like it."

I couldn't blame him. I didn't like the idea of her being in danger either. "You mean I'm invited?"

"Of course. So is Joel."

"I won't be able to make it," Joel said. "I have to work at the clinic. Friday's our busy night. I'll be seeing patients in Urgent Care until at least midnight."

"I think we can manage without you," I said. "Is it okay if we stay here for a few nights?"

"Sure. You can put Maxine's clothes in the spare bedroom. You and I can share my bedroom."

"I'll sleep on the floor in the living room. I don't want to put you out."

Later, as I lay on the floor with pillow and blankets, I thought about Friday night. It would be the closest thing to a real date I would have with Maxine during our short relationship. I imagined holding her in my arms as we danced. I imagined a lot of other things too.

But my pleasant fantasies eventually found themselves caught in a tug-of-war with nightmarish realities. I recalled the earlier conversation with Maxine in which I had avoided certain significant facts about how I had become a private investigator, and by Friday night I would regret it.

Chapter 11

Friday morning I awoke later than Joel and Maxine after tossing and turning on Joel's living room floor all night.

I sat up, adjusted my neck a few times and crawled out of the sleeping bag in wrinkled khakis and a sleeveless T-shirt.

"Morning," Maxine said. She eyed me thoughtfully from the kitchen table, and I figured she was admiring my rugged frame.

"Your hair looks like an Andy Warhol project." She was sitting at the kitchen table, drinking orange juice. The smell of burn toast was in the air.

"Go ahead and laugh," I said, through a thick mouth. "Sooner or later I'll catch you looking like an unmade bed."

"That will never happen. I never look unmade."

I believed her. She looked stunning in an Op Art print dress with hues of green, red and yellow and a questionable neckline that made me want to know the answer. She wore a golden mesh necklace with three golden cords simply knotted at the center. Two matching gold earrings played on her ears as she turned her head. Her green eyes sparkled and her red hair glistened in the morning sunlight entering through a kitchen window. In short, her beauty took my breath away.

"Are you making breakfast?" I asked.

"Are you kidding?" she said. There's something you need to know about me up front. I was raised in a privileged household where cooks and maids waited on me. I could have rebelled and learned to cook for myself, but I kind of liked the attention.

"The truth is I would burn coffee. Joel stuck some refrigerated rolls into the oven, and we're waiting for them to bake. Why don't you get dressed and join us for a gourmet experience."

Joel appeared from behind a newspaper at the other end of the table. "Say, Maxine, did you see this article about the abduction of Edward George? He's one of the top innovative types at Apple."

Maxine turned toward the rumpled newspaper Joel held in front of him. "No. What happened to him?"

"No one really knows," Joel said. "He was found drugged less than twenty-four hours after he was taken. Someone whacked him over the head when he walked out of a pharmacy in Los Angeles. They found puncture wounds in his arms, but otherwise he was all right. From the description of the wounds, it sounds like they drugged him and took blood."

Bubbles of a memory slowly surfaced into my consciousness. "I read something in The Washington Post about Steve Jasper being kidnapped a couple of days ago. He was an arms developer for the Pentagon. Then there was a Harvard professor who won a Nobel Prize in physics. In each case they were abducted and released within twenty-four hours and each had blood drawn.

"It's a great story," I said. "I wish I was covering it. Do the police have any leads?"

Joel studied the newspaper for a minute. "No. Apparently he was released before anyone knew he was missing. The FBI is offering a two-hundred-thousand dollar reward."

Maxine was no longer listening to Joel. Her face was taught and expressionless and her eyes had a faraway look.

""Earth to Maxine," I said. "Are you with us?"

"I was just wondering what this world is coming to. There are so many crackpots out there."

I ran my fingers through my stringy hair and realized Maxine wasn't kidding about my appearance. I wondered if she thought I was a crackpot too. We'd all been through a lot the last couple of days, and I'd certainly been at my wits' end.

I grabbed my suitcase and ran toward the bathroom to make myself look presentable. When I returned to the table, there were remnants of two sticky buns. I picked one up and started nibbling at it.

"So what do you want to do today?" I asked.

"Joel's going to give me a ride to my car on the way to the hospital," Maxine said.

"I don't know if that's a good idea. Lu Fong might have his

henchmen staking it out. They could be waiting for you."

"They wouldn't even know it's my car. Besides, if they want to find me, they probably know I'll be at the charity event tonight."

"I just think you should be careful," I said.

Joel put the newspaper down. "I'll watch her back."

"You want to come?" Maxine said. "I'm going shopping for a new dress for tonight."

"I'd love to, but I have a few errands I have to take care of myself."

"Well then, we're going to get going. It's nine o'clock and Joel has to be at work by ten."

Joel picked up three sheets of paper from the table. "I printed out some pages from the flash drive last night to take to work with me, Maxine. Is that okay?"

"I said it would be. Just don't tell anyone where you got them. I'm going to call Scott and have him meet me at the charity event tonight."

"Do you think that's wise?" I asked.

"You said earlier that it should be a safe place with all the people around. I want to find out why he has been acting so strange."

"What if he tries to take it by force?" I suggested.

"Just let him try it," she said.

And that was that. She tucked the flash drive in her purse and we agreed to meet back at Joel's house at four o'clock. I watched them from the porch as they drove off and decided to make some phone calls--one to a shop that rented tuxedos and another to Hollywood at his home. We made an appointment to meet at his office at two o'clock.

I spent the rest of the morning at city and state licensing offices. Along with the application forms and requirements to becoming a private investigator, there are many regulations surrounding owning a business and registering it. I walked out of the two buildings armed with sheaves of paperwork that would fill a warehouse.

Next, I had lunch and was fitted for a Tuxedo. The tailor was apologetic, claiming it was an ill fit, but it was the best he could do on such short notice. I thought he did fine. It was a classic black and white job once worn by Kevin Kline on a film shoot in

Portland, or so the clerk said. Kevin must be shorter, because the tailor had to lower the pant cuffs quite a bit.

Two o'clock found me cooling my heels outside Hollywood's office. The room was part of a tired 1960s building. The cop shop also housed local talent until they could be transferred downtown to the Justice Center jails. The lobby walls were painted an ugly olive green color, similar to the color of Multnomah County's patrol cars.

Eventually, I was ushered into Hollywood's office by a husky blonde female deputy. He was on the phone and looking much happier than my last visit.

"I have to go now, Jane. Max is here. I'll see you tonight. Me too. Bye."

"Sounds like things are looking up." I said.

"Well, sort of." He smiled tentatively. "We're going to go to a marriage counselor to see if we can patch things up. Tonight we're going out to the theater and we've agreed not to bring up past resentments. We're going to try and have a nice time together like we did in the old days."

"Good for you. I hope it works out."

"Thanks. He shuffled through some papers on his desk. "I have some information about Scott Hess. I talked with Sam Bowie, a friend of mine downtown who works with him at the FBI.

"Thanks for doing this for me," I said.

'Sure." He squinted at a notepad on his desk. "According to my friend, Hess was considered a golden boy. He could do no wrong in his short time he's been assigned in Portland. He moved up through the ranks at an impressive pace. Then, a few weeks ago he got into a bit of trouble. This is all unofficial. Sam doesn't know all of the details. He said Hess tended go off on his own on some investigations. He eschewed partners. He wants to be a star in the department. You know what I mean?"

Of course I knew what he meant. Hollywood was describing himself and apparently didn't see the irony of the situation.

"Yeah," I said. "He was in a hurry to get to the top and didn't want to share his success. He probably didn't like going by the book and probably bent the rules on a regular basis."

"That's about it," Hollywood said. "Apparently he was working on some undercover sting in the Chinese district at one of the downtown nightclubs. Somehow the club owner got wind and took his operation out of town overnight, leaving Hess with quite a bit of mud on his face."

"What was he investigating?"

"This is the confusing part. Sam said Hess was heading a team investigating some kind of animal breeding operation. You heard of those inhumane puppy mills the local authorities close down now and again?"

"I've heard of them, but don't really know much about it," I said.

"Well that's what this was. Only it wasn't dogs. It was monkeys, sheep, calves and frogs."

"The FBI is looking for frog breeders? Somebody is having fun with you, Jim."

He put a cigar in his mouth and chewed on it, not lighting it. "I thought so too, but Sam insisted it was true. The animals were raised outside city limits at several different sites. Then they were shipped across the country to undisclosed locations."

"Really?" I was thinking of another farm.

"It gets crazier," Hollywood said. "I called the Camas Police Department and they ran a check on the property where Maxine was held. Of course, authorities found no one living there when they checked it out, with the exception of a few goats and chickens milling about.

"The fire department filed a report, but none of the names given at the site match the ones you gave me."

I fidgeted on the edge of my chair. "They probably gave phony names," I said.

"On a hunch, I asked my friend at the FBI if one of these animal breeding facilities they were watching might have been the one you and Maxine were taken to in Camas."

I nearly fell off the chair. "What did he say?"

He leaned back in his chair, with his well-manicured fingers interlocked, and grinned.

"He said it matched one of the addresses the FBI had been watching before Lu Fong's operation shut down and left town. His daughter obviously used it for her little rendezvous yesterday."

I let out a low whistle. "So, somehow this business Maxine is involved in is related to an FBI investigation, and Hess is right in the middle of it."

Hollywood shifted in his chair. "Hess was the lead investigator, but he was demoted when the gang cleared town. Since the demotion, he's been cleaning up backlogs of mostly unimportant cases that have withered with age. My friend says he was the subject of an internal investigation because they thought he had tipped off Kay Lu's father, Lu Fong, but there was no proof."

"So maybe Hess *is* dirty," I said. "Or he might be trying to get back in good-graces by single handily solving the case. Maybe he's investigating on the sly and asking Maxine for help. Do you suppose it's Hess who burgled my apartment?"

Hollywood shrugged. "I doubt it unless Hess went rogue. The FBI would get a search warrant. The intruder gained entry by breaking a window at your back door. I think the FBI would have been more discreet. If it was the FBI, they might have left a few listening devices behind. We didn't find any."

I leaned back in the rickety oak chair. "It could have been Kay Lu or Lu Fong. I think they're working independently of each other. Kay Lu has some kind of separation issues with her dad. She wants to get away from her father in the worst way.

"I just remembered. The day of the burglary, I caught Steadman at my front door with lock picks in his hands. He could have gone around back and broke in after I left. Except, why would he have wanted to break in in the first place. I mean, sure I stole his client. But does that warrant a possible B and E charge?"

"Uh, Max, I'm afraid there's more," Hollywood said. He sat there in his chair, looking serious and waiting for me to respond. I was still putting pieces of the puzzle together. "You're kind of sweet on this Maxine, aren't you?"

"She's great, Jim. She's beautiful, sexy, funny and smart, and she can pack a punch. You wouldn't want to mess with her."

"Yes . . ." he said. "I ran a background check on Maxine and she has a bit of a file."

"Are you saying she's a criminal? I don't believe it."

"I didn't get much from stateside authorities. She had a few arrests for disorderly conduct in Los Angeles several years back. It had something to do with demonstrating over cruelty to animals. Charges were dropped each time.

"She was recently living in Hong Kong so I launched an

information request with Interpol. Her name cropped up more than a politician's during election time. The U.S. Custom's Department, the Treasury Department, and the Economic Fraud Division of Interpol all have issued arrest warrants on her. If I knew where she was, I'd have to arrest her on the spot. But because something seems fishy to me—especially with this Scott Hess character—I'm going to give her the benefit of the doubt for now. I'm not going to ask you where she is, and I don't want to know."

"I appreciate that." My head was spinning dangerously out of control with the knowledge the woman I loved might have to go to prison. "Doesn't this racket ever get easier?"

"Look, Max, don't get too upset. From what I've heard, you seem to have some good instincts and you've handled yourself fairly well. Just be careful."

"I don't believe any of this. It doesn't fit. Maxine is as honest as you or I."

"People don't have warrants issued for their arrest by these types of agencies without some kind of evidence. I want you to be careful."

"Okay," I said, sourly.

"And if Maxine does anything illegal, you're to call me at once. I don't care what time of day. Do you understand?"

"Yes," I said."

"You'd better. If you aren't careful, you'll take the fall with her. I'm your only chance, Max. Is that clear?"

I sighed and left his office. My problems were beginning to pile up. I wasn't worried about Maxine at the moment, although I should have been. The sheer volume of this line of work was getting to me.

I had no idea what was going on. I had a feeling I didn't know all of the players, and I didn't even know if I would live long enough to meet all of the players. My only two allies appeared to dwindle to one, Joel. I couldn't even trust Maxine, if I believed what Hollywood told me.

Yet I did trust her. I wasn't too sure about some of her associates, many of whom I would likely meet later in the evening. Her father, Scott Hess, and Lu Fong, among others, all were formidable personalities. All were used to dealing with major problems like me.

On the other hand, I hadn't dealt with society types like Maxine's father, or major criminals in the caliber of Lü Fong. I'd had some dealings with law enforcement on the crime beat as a reporter. But most cops have an attitude, and I was going to be on the wrong end of this attitude very soon. I felt like I was drowning in a sea of mud. I didn't know how I'd survived this long, fooling myself as well as bluffing the cast of characters surrounding me.

The trick, I guess, was not to let them know I'm a fraud. People call it confidence, when actually it's pure fear. Fear of being found out, fear of failure, and fear Maxine would think I'm a bad person. And if I'm not the person I'm trying to be, then what? All I know is, not taking the risk is failure by default. So, I'd continue to pretend I know what I'm doing until someone catches me at my deception—and then I'd deny it.

Except for Maxine. I couldn't continue to lie to her. Somehow I would have to tell her the truth. But how?

Chapter 12

On the drive back to Joel's apartment a growing uneasiness crept up on me like old age on a former beauty queen. At first I attributed my anxiety to the news Hollywood shared with me about Maxine's past. But that wasn't it. I did a mental inventory about the facts of the case thus far. It had nothing to do with the big night we faced in a few hours. I had done my fretting and let go of that business.

No, it was something I forgot to do, or something in the case I overlooked. A growing anxiety churned inside me, what was I forgetting?

Then, I remembered.

The damn copy of Maxine's flash drive. Two days had passed since I mailed it. I checked the mail Thursday and it wasn't there. I figured it sat overnight in the blue mailbox on the corner the night I rescued Maxine and wasn't picked up until Thursday morning.

Today was Friday and the letter was sure to have been delivered. Almost immediately after I mailed it, I'd agonized over my rash decision. At the time, I thought I was being smart by taking a page out of the book of some hard-boiled detective novel. But I was too smart. I hadn't mailed it to myself, but to Joel.

I started thinking of worst case scenarios. The flash drive might be ripped out of the envelope by a mail-sorting machine and found by somebody. Or maybe it would be destroyed? These were minor issues because Maxine still had the original.

What if I failed to put enough postage on the letter? It would be returned to my home address and could fall into the hands of Lu Fong, Kay Lu, Scott Hess, the FBI, or even Steadman, hoping to get a rematch.

I looked at my watch. It was almost 3:30 and the flash drive could have been in Joel's mailbox for four or five hours. If anyone had followed us or otherwise tracked us down, they could have gotten to it by now.

I gunned the Mustang and felt the reassuring vibration of its big V-8 engine. I was 15 minutes away from Joe's apartment. I tried telling myself everything would be all right, but I didn't believe it.

Zipping along at 20 miles-per-hour over the speed limit, I remembered how the cops love to ticket red sports cars and made myself slow down. When I finally reached Joel's house, he was on the front porch and ran to greet me as I steered into the driveway. He was excited and waving his arms.

I stepped out of the Mustang and could feel the adrenaline pulsing though me. "What happened, Joel? Did they get the flash drive? Is Maxine okay?"

"Maxine's fine. I tried to call you on your cell phone. Did you turn it off again? Dr. Sullivan knew what the formula was. You won't believe it. This whole thing is gigantic. He wanted to know where I got it, but I wouldn't tell him."

"Joel, take a breath and give me a minute. Has the mail come?"

"I don't know. I haven't been thinking about mail."

I ran up to the porch and looked in the mailbox. It was empty. "Did you get the mail?"

"No, I just got back." He looked at the mailbox on his front porch. "It usually comes in the morning."

"It's nearly four o'clock," I said. "Maybe someone took it."

"Sometimes it comes in the afternoon. I think she does her route backwards for variety."

"But what someone stole your mail?"

"For crying out loud, the mail will come. Will you relax and listen to me for a minute? I have some important news."

"I'm sorry, Joel. But maybe we should sit out here on the front steps so I can watch for the mailman."

"She's a mail lady and it's too cold. With the wind chill factor, I'll bet it's only forty degrees."

I sat on the porch steps and waited as Joel reluctantly joined me. He pulled sheets of folded paper from his shirt pocket.

"I don't have much time. I have to be back at work in thirty minutes. When I first the saw the artwork and the list of chemicals listed in these conditioning solutions, it was obvious to me this formula was about cell production of some kind. And while I don't know much about cloning, I do know an embryo when I see one."

"Cloning? What are you babbling about?"

"That's what was on the flash drive. It's a formula to clone humans. Ever since Dolly, a Finn Dorset sheep was cloned in 1996, scientists have been cloning animals."

"I read about a monkey being cloned here in town at Oregon Health Sciences University recently," I said.

"There is a lot of legitimate cloning going on by scientists. It's assumed that cloning tissue cells will speed development of cures for Parkinson's disease, spinal cord injuries . . . the list is endless. If you can duplicate the body's own cells and replace damaged cells with new cells, the sky's the limit.

"But so far no one has cloned a human embryo," Joel said.

"Do you think it could ever happen?" I asked, trying to seem interested.

"Up until today, I would have said no. But after what we've seen on this flash drive, well I just don't know. It could be happening as we speak."

"What?"

"It's a revolutionary idea to the cloning process. According to Dr. Sullivan, "The formula replaces two essential spindle proteins that are usually destroyed when removing the nucleus from a human host egg. It's something scientists have not been able to do."

Well, how did they clone Dolly?" I asked.

"Animals are different," Joel said. "They have spindle proteins throughout the egg. It's easier to save them when removing the nucleus.

"This process is unique," Joel says. "It involves a nuclear transfer by cloning the proteins and introducing them into the egg after the donor nucleus is injected. The formula shows the procedure."

"You mean this whole kidnapping thing with crime lords and the FBI is all about getting a formula that may or may not enable someone to clone a human being," I said.

I was feeling somewhere between pissed off and ready to wring Maxine's neck for bringing me into a mess that likely involved people chasing after a fictional McGuffin.

This case reminded me of Dashiell Hammett's The Maltese Falcon with Sam Spade trying to beat three crooks and a gorgeous liar to a solid gold Falcon statuette.

Maxine was playing the part of, Miss Wonderly, who tried to use Sam Spade to find the McGuffin. Kay Lu and Lu Fong were filling in for thugs Kasper Gutman and Wilmer Cook, and Ken Hess acting the role of Cairo.

That made me . . . Sam Spade? I wish.

In the movie, the golden statue turned out to be lead and the beautiful Miss Wonderly went to prison, where Maxine and I would probably wind up too.

When I came out of my mystery novel coma, Joel was still yakking.

"What kind of animals would they test this formula on?" I asked.

"I was curious about that too," he said. "Dr. Sullivan said cattle, sheep, mice, cats, dogs . . . let me see . . . deer, horses, mules, and rabbits. Oh and a rhesus monkey has been cloned by embryo splitting."

"What about frogs," I asked.

"Sure. They would be ideal."

"Has anyone successfully cloned any of these animals, other than Dolly?"

Joel chuckled. "Of course. They've been doing it for years. The Food and Drug Administration has done tests and ruled that cloned animals are safe for consumption."

"WHAT?" You mean I might be eating cloned beef and chicken without even being told?"

"Relax," Joel said. "It's highly unlikely that you will see meat from clones at the supermarket any time soon. Clones are used as elite breeding animals rather than as food themselves.

"Some of the researchers are using animal eggs to try and clone humans," he said. "The government has shut down such experiments in the U.S. on moral grounds, but it looks like Lu Fong's is pursuing the practice on his own.

"His formula relies on taking empty eggs from animals to activate human genes for successful human cloning. Animal eggs are much easier to obtain than human eggs, and Dr. Sullivan says this would create huge risks of abnormalities and mutations in human-cloning experiments.

"One percent of the genetic makeup of human clones comes from animals, according to Dr. Sullivan at the hospital. Technically, these human clones made from animal eggs would have one-percent animal DNA."

I shuddered. "So cloning humans could result in mutants. We could have humans walking around with pig tails or deformed brains?"

"Who knows? It's never been done successfully. Failure rates average eighty-eight percent in animals. But according to Lu Fong's notes, his scientists have documented a ninety-seven percent success rate of creating human embryos."

"Is that bad?" I said.

"It's terrible," Joel said. "If it's true, they might already be trying to clone humans."

"And somehow, Lu Fong has gotten hold of this information," I said. "Or perhaps he's funding it. A closer look at his financial records might provide the answer about how deeply he's involved."

"But why would he be interested in a cloning formula?" Joel said.

"I would imagine he could sell it to the highest bidder."

"Who might that be?"

I thought about it for a minute. "Maybe he plans to sell it to one of these labs looking to develop clones of organs or stem cells."

"I doubt it. Cloning is not the same as genetic engineering."

Some facts were beginning to fall into place. Among them, the FBI's curious interest in local farms that raised frogs, sheep and calves.

"Let's not tell Maxine of this."

Joel smiled incredulously. "Why are you suddenly being so secretive with her?"

"I think she may already know about this. I'd like to see if she plans on taking me into her confidence. Until then, the less said the better."

He looked at me harshly for a moment and chuckled. "The mail lady is here." He bounced up from the wooden step and walked to the sidewalk to greet her.

I followed him and looked over his shoulder. "Is that all?" I hollered to the retreating mail courier. She stopped and gave a disapproving look. Her brown locks sprang over the tips of her eyeglasses, and her blue eyes reluctantly dropped to the mailbag.

I figured she was giving me the courtesy search designed to put me off until tomorrow. She probably thought so too, but appeared surprised at finding something.

"Oh! Here's one for this address, but it isn't in your name Mister Powell. It's addressed to a Max Starr."

I stretched an outward hand. "That's me."

She handed me a crumpled envelope, with two-thirds of the end ripped open. Inside the envelope, wrapped in notebook paper, was a not-worse-for-the-wear flash drive.

I breathed a huge sigh of relief. There would be no extra copy of a possible cloning formula kicking around for Lu Fong or anyone else to stumble upon.

I didn't stop to thank her. In the next minute I was in Joel's dining room, starting up his computer. Joel, apparently forgetting he would be late for work, followed me inside.

"It works." I cried, "Everything is still here." On the monitor, I counted twelve document files. Joel, either underwhelmed by my happiness or disapproving of his oath to keep Maxine in the dark, made a noise like a bull snorting at a matador and slammed the door on his way out.

Chapter 13

Maxine didn't return to Joel's apartment until five o'clock, a scant two hours before she was due at the charity ball. Apparently, it wasn't enough time for her to get ready so she pretty much ignored me.

I was beginning to become concerned about our relationship. There seemed to be a wall slowly rising between us. Its foundation was laid when I left her at Kay Lu's farmhouse in Camas when she thought I was going to turn over the flash drive to Wong. Then she kissed Joel on the way home. That was followed by her proclamation to hold onto the original flash drive and the look she had given me when I suggested otherwise.

Of course, part of it was my fault. I had become somewhat distant since Hollywood had told me of her surreptitious past. We needed to sit down and clear the air. I had a confession to make, and I was sure she did too. The charitable function wasn't the best time to talk of such subjects, but the way this case seemed to propel us back and forth like snowflakes in a crosswind, I felt I should grab the first chance. The two of us alone on the dance floor would provide a pleasant opportunity.

A few minutes before the appointed hour, Maxine emerged from her bedroom in a breathtakingly sexy, black evening dress. It flowed graciously over the contours of her figure. Thin straps crisscrossed her alabaster back and shoulders and converged in the front, held together by dazzling rhinestone broach.

"Do you like it?" She performed a playful pirouette and the full-length evening gown revealed daring hints of thighs through accented slits. "It's a Jones New York Strappy Evening Dress. I bought it at Nordstrom."

I gave her with my best dirty old man leer, and she laughed playfully.

"This is the first time I've felt like a woman in quite a while," she said. "I've been on the run for so long it feels like I've been living out of suitcases forever. I've felt so frumpy in all of my wrinkled clothes."

"You haven't looked frumpy since the first day I met you. How do I look?" I did a slow turn and let her take in Kevin Kline's hand-me-down tuxedo.

"Mmm. Come here." She pulled me toward her by the lapels and tugged at my tie. Then she adjusted my cummerbund, patted my hips and stepped back. "You look handsome, although I think it's a little large in the shoulders. But the tux brings out the dreaminess of your brown hair, and it sure looks sexy."

I moved toward her, put my arms around her slim waist and pulled her into me. "Stop it," she said. "We're late already. There will be plenty of time for that later."

There will? That's a good sign. Any little crumb is appreciated.

"Have you got the cloning formula?" I enquired.

"It's inside my pocketbook," she said. "Oh, I left it in the bathroom."

"I'll get it for you," I said. I picked up her black clutch and opened it. She had placed the flash drive in a zippered pocket. I closed the bathroom door for privacy and dropped the flash drive into the toilet. I swished it around for a minute or so, retrieved it and washed it, and my hands, with soap and water. I read somewhere that although water might not completely destroy its data, plugging into any electrical circuit while still wet, would fry everything. I knew Hess would plug it in the first chance he got. Would he be in for a surprise!

We arrived at the Hilton Hotel 30 minutes later, and a uniformed man ushered us through the glass doors to an escalator, which he said would take us to the ballroom. We descended into a darkened area and followed signs down lush red carpeted hallway to a solid oak door.

Inside, was a cavernous multifunction meeting room made to

look like a ballroom with a temporary stainless steel floor near the band for dancing. An aging crystal ball looming from the ceiling illuminated the circular tables, adorned with maroon tablecloths.

The dance floor separated the guest speakers and a band stage from the rest of the audience. Maxine was part of the planning committee and, although we were late, the festivities weren't scheduled to begin for another 30 minutes.

"Let me take your coat." I eased the black suede jacket from her shoulders. It was splattered with raindrops from our brief one-block jaunt from a nearby parking lot.

I walked her coat to a check-in booth and returned to find her in a dialogue with one of the technicians preparing for the evening's gala activities. "After your father speaks, he will introduce you. You will have five minutes to talk and then you will introduce the Mayor."

I smiled at Maxine after the technician left. "I'm impressed. You know the Mayor?"

'I've never met him, but it's who you know that counts. The coordinator of this event knows me. I roped in my father. His connections and power within the movie industry are enough to convince the Mayor's office he should attend. After all, they all want to keep those big budget movies coming to Portland to be made."

That was true enough. Ever since Rachel Welch filmed the movie Kansas City Bomber in a North Portland neighborhood in the '60's, Portland has proven fertile ground for movie producers looking to eradicate themselves from the ubiquitous L.A. scenery. Portland offers wet Northwest locales for gloomy films, spectacular Fall foliage for educational backdrops, snow-covered mountains for winter setting, Eastern Oregon's desert for westerns, and even the Max train light-rail has been featured on film. And because of Portland's film fame, everyone has moved here, along with urban sprawl and all of its associated problems. Still, if Portland's popularity attracted Maxine, it might be worth all the growing pains.

"Maxine, honey, how about a hug for your tired old dad?" A tall distinguished gentleman had walked at a quickened pace across the large expanse of floor toward us. He was dressed in an outdated monkey suit and looked like something out of a vintage movie. His salt and pepper hair favored mostly salt tones, and he was clean-shaven, except for a pert white mustache. His face was plump, but not obese, and his green eyes showed alertness.

Maxine hugged her dad and pushed him back a step to size him up. "Father, you're wearing tails. How avant-garde. And a top hat too. La de Dah!"

"I've had this tuxedo for fifty-some years. I wore it as a dancer in Gentleman Prefer Blondes with Marilyn Monroe, and it looks as good today as the first day I put it on."

"Father's a little sentimental and somewhat old- fashioned." Then she whispered to me: "He was 12-years-old when the movie was made, but he loves to tell people he worked with Marilyn Monroe."

"What's the matter with being old-fashioned?" he boomed. "Got to remember where you came from. I get tired of all the stuffiness in this business. You'd be surprised at how serious people get these days." He winked at me. "Is this the new friend you were telling me about this afternoon?"

"Yes, father, this is Max Starr. Max, this is my father, George Andrews. Max has been helping me out with the Lu Fong business."

"Gads, you're at it again are you? Glad to meet you, Max." He shook my hand with unexpected firmness and fervor. "What's she been up to now? It's always something horrendous, you know. My daughter seems to have a knack for getting herself into trouble. Tried to hire a bodyguard for her once, but she kept ditching him. It wasn't worth the trouble."

Hello. Sir," I managed.

He sized me up with a serious glance. "You look like you can take care of yourself. Perhaps you'd like to take a stab at protecting my baby."

I didn't know what to say. His eyes seemed to plead with me in earnest. I looked to Maxine, puzzled, and took my hand back from her energetic father.

"As you've said already, she seems to be able to take care of herself."

"Maybe so, maybe not. She asked you for help didn't she?"

"Father, why don't we sit down? You're probably tired after your flight."

"I'm not tired." He sat at a table near the dance floor and propped his hat on the corner of a nearby chair. Maxine and I sat on each side of him. His sharp eyes surveyed me before he turned them to his daughter. "Say, what's going on here? Maxine, you have a color to your face that I haven't seen in quite a while. Are you in danger?"

"It's nothing I can't handle, honest."

"Max, maybe you should know this about Maxine. My little girl is sort of an adventuress. She flits from one cause to another. First it was Save the Whales, next it was Animal Rights, then The Homeless. Before I knew it, she was flying around the world and getting involved in all kinds of human rights causes. Now, whenever I hear about a dictatorship being overthrown or a coup in a foreign country, I wonder if Maxine is involved."

"Oh father, you're so funny. Just because I happen to get involved in a political cause once in a while, it doesn't mean I'm overthrowing governments."

"I wonder." I had spoken my thought aloud.

"So do I," her father said. He studied me keenly and a grin evolved on his face. "Say, you're kind of stuck on my girl, aren't you." I could feel my face heating up and imagined how it was betraying me. He turned his gaze to Maxine, who was wearing a modest Who me? expression. "And judging by the guilty look on her face, I'd say the feeling is mutual," he said.

A hint of blush colored her face, and she smiled in a carefree manner. "Oh father, you're being silly. Trying to embarrass me again. Max and I are just friends. But he's been marvelous. He's very sharp and a very good detective. He has great instincts and in this business that's very important."

"What business?" Her father was serious for a moment, but the tension in his face relaxed as Maxine spun a tale of wanting to help the Dalai Lama return from exile to Tibet. She talked about Lu Fong's politics and how they sometimes led him to extremes. She told her father that Lu Fong had gotten a bit rough with her, but backed off when he saw I was by her side.

I watched her eyes, and they seemed to want me to go along with this half-baked story she was spewing to soothe her father. I watched his reaction and it was that of someone trying not to doze off during an extremely boring recitation. He doubtless had heard these wild tales before and suffered her grievous accounts, knowing it would be fruitless to pursue a straight line of inquiry.

Eventually, Maxine was called away to greet some Tibetan dignitaries. She had given me a brief history lesson on the way to the Hilton. It seems Tibet had long tried to assert its independence. The monks provided a spiritual government after becoming independent of British rule. Mao Zedong pushed the Tibetans, headed by the then 18-year-old Dalai Lama, into gradual submission, claiming a delegation sent by the Dalai Lama had agreed to a 17-point declaration asking China to bring Tibet under China's rule. The Dalai Lama, who had tried to protect his people from the Red Force, was forced to flee Tibet with the hopes he would someday return.

George Andrews tugged at my wrist, drawing me out of my thoughts. "I want to have a word with you, young man." The movie mogul was all business now. Gone was the happy and carefree father who appeared to play matchmaker minutes earlier. Now he was grim and determined. He displayed a magnified persona of charismatic power and intimidation, and I was appropriately awed.

"Look, Max. The most important thing in my life just walked across that floor. I love her dearly and will do anything in my power to protect her. I won't have her taken advantage of or harmed in any way. Do I make myself clear?"

"Crystalline," I said.

He looked at me skeptically. "You have a familiar attitude about you. One I raised in Maxine. You two are very much alike, I think. I may put up with her insolence, but I won't tolerate it in you."

"Then it looks like we're in for a rocky relationship," I said coolly. "I can't change my personality to suit you. As for Maxine, I'll put you on notice now that I'm in love with her and will do everything humanly possible to entice her to marry me. I would appreciate your permission to do so, but if that's not possible, well . . ."

"Just a minute. I didn't say—I didn't mean—you'd have to excuse an old man. I've been overly stressed lately by my daughter's behavior. I'm sorry if I offended you."

"Apology accepted," I said.

He looked at me thoughtfully for a minute and created a broad smile across his face. "You know, I've had you checked out."

"Checked out? What do you mean checked out?"

"Maxine called me last night before I flew up. I had my man in L.A. make some inquiries about you this afternoon before I caught my plane. He turned up your credit history, subpar by the way, and your record as a private investigator. After all the glowing things my Maxine said about you, I wanted to make sure you weren't conning my little girl. I must say, of all the people I've run checks on in the past none were as interesting as yours." He raised his eyebrows in mock surprise and waited for a response.

I hesitated, feeling what I said next was a make-or-break situation. An air of doom seemed to flutter over my next sentence. "You can't believe everything people tell you. I think action speaks better than any words."

He leaned back in his chair and gave me an irreverent wave with his hand. "You may be right. But in this case, I don't think so. I was blown away when I saw your dossier."

I started to protest, but he waved me off again. "Don't give me that modesty routine. What you've accomplished in such a short time is miraculous. In three short years you've risen from a beginning investigator to a top-notch operative. Everyone my man talked with raved about you.

"I must say, I was surprised to learn about your work with the FBI. That agent at the FBI actually said you were the best he's ever worked with. Said you'd helped him on two important cases in the last year alone."

"Who did you talk with?"

"My man talked with the state licensing board. A clerk there gave him a list of references from your file."

"My file?"

"Yes, and what a list it was. Portland Police Chief, District Attorney, Captain with the State Police, Captain with Multnomah County Sheriff's Office, Thomas at the FBI and a few others. Reads like a 'Who's Who' of criminal investigation."

He paused to look at my confused and tired face. "I hope you don't mind. I didn't know you were such a notorious bird up here. Hope my little inquiry hasn't offended you."

What could I do? I played along. "No, no. I am surprised a bit

at the enthusiasm these fellows have shown, but I'm not offended."
A worrying thought occurred to me. "Have you told Maxine about
this?"

"Oh, I wouldn't do that. She wouldn't like it, I'm sure. I
would hope you might keep it to yourself for a while."

"I think it's best if stays our secret," I said. "I wouldn't want
her to think I'm something I'm not. Those people in your report
probably meant well, but I'm sure they exaggerated a bit."

Dad slapped me on the back. "You're all right. I have a
proposition for you, Max. I'm worried about Maxine. You see, her
mother died when she was young and it's been up to me to raise
her. Unfortunately, I raised a spunky, spoiled tomboy who gets
into one jam after another and won't listen to me. I know that yarn
she spun earlier hasn't one iota of truth to it. She's in some kind of
danger." He looked to me for acknowledgment, but I remained
poker-faced.

"Anyway, I'd feel a lot better if there were someone like you
watching over her. I'll pay you double whatever your normal rate
is. What do you say?"

I looked at his face and counted the worry lines in it. "I'm
sorry. I can't accept your offer. I'm working for Maxine and it
wouldn't be ethical for me to accept money from you. Besides, I
have a feeling Maxine would kill me if I did.

"But, rest assured, Maxine is very important to me, too. I'll do
anything necessary to keep her safe. I should be honest and tell you
that she does a pretty good job of taking care of herself."

He looked at me and managed a smile. "I'm sure she does. I
appreciate the position I just put you in. But a father has to do
whatever he can to protect his little girl even if she isn't so little
anymore."

The old producer pushed himself up from the table and waved
toward Maxine. "I think they want me for something. I'll see you
later, I'm sure."

As he walked purposefully toward a throng of event planners,
my thoughts returned to an earlier portion of the conversation. Was
he putting me on when he said he had me checked out? How could
the state licensing bureau even know about me? I hadn't mailed
any paperwork to them yet.

I gained some comfort from watching a pretty redhead across

the room talking with five men. Her face was animated and beautiful and every few minutes she would look at me and smile. She was the only constant thing about this business. Each time I solved a piece of the puzzle a new load of questions was dumped in my lap. Luckily for me, Maxine was the answer.

Chapter 14

I sat at an empty table in the corner as Maxine and her father sat among dignitaries at the head table. The highlight was Maxine's speech. She was enthusiastic about her cause, emphatic about the need for change, and forceful in her urgency for action. And I thought I was an idealist.

After about an hour of speeches and dinner, the orators left the head tables and mingled with the audience. The band played a slow tune and the spectators gradually became participants on the dance floor.

A soft hand touched my shoulder. "Hello, handsome. I believe our dance is long overdue." I looked up a long alabaster arm to Maxine's sparkling turquoise eyes and bold red lips.

"I'd almost given up on you," I said.

"Don't ever do that. I shouldn't like it. Shall we?"

We swept out onto the floor. I put my arm around her slender waist and held her hand in mine, trying to remember some of the dance steps I learned in grade school. The only thing I could remember was the Waltz.

"You know, we need to talk about your fee," she said. "The money I gave you Wednesday isn't going to cover all you've done for me since."

"I don't want your money."

"Why not?"

"I don't believe in mixing business and pleasure."

"But I may still need your help. This affair isn't over yet, although it may be later tonight if I turn the flash drive over to Scott."

I wasn't ready to discuss business. "Listen, I think we should talk about our relationship first."

She looked at me in mock surprise. "What relationship?"

"Up to now, I've been joking about my feelings for you, and you've been taking it in stride and coming back with the appropriate romantic repartee. We've been trying to have fun under some pretty tough circumstances."

"Yes, well it has been fun—working with you, I mean."

"Maxine, I have a confession to make."

"Oh Max, you're acting so serious. I don't like this side of you."

"I'll try not to show it often, but there are a few times in a man's life when he has to be serious. I think professing your love for a woman is one of them. Maxine, I wasn't kidding when I said I thought we should become engaged."

"Neither was I."

"You mean you do like me?"

"Max, I never kid when I'm kidding. You have a certain flair for life, a certain sameness with my lifestyle. You're bold and not afraid to take chances. The night you carried me out of the Kwan Yin Temple was the first time I ever really needed a man's help. It felt good. I'm not sure I'm ready for marriage yet, but I am crazy about you."

She brought her lips to mine and for a moment time was suspended as we kissed in the center of the floor, oblivious to the other dancers. We continued to dance and whispered our feelings. I was caught up in the romance and forgot my mental outline of things to discuss. I was concentrating on Roman Numcral One.

That turned out to be a mistake. At one point in our lengthy dance card, a hand tapped me on the shoulder, and I was greeted with a crooked smile. Behind the smile stood a tall, somewhat muscular gent with slick, black hair. It was Scott Hess, of the FBI.

"Mind if I cut in?"

"This is a private dance," I said.

Maxine put her finger to my lips. "It's okay, Max, I need to talk with him. I won't be too long."

I locked my arm tighter around her waist and pulled her closer to me. "At least let us finish this dance," I said. "I have something I need to tell you, Maxine."

"Like how you are nothing but a fraud?" Hess said.

I froze. There was that word I feared. "What are you talking about?"

"I did a check on you, mister. There is no Max Starr licensed as a P.I. in the state of Oregon. I checked with some local trade associations and they've never heard of you either. I don't know how you conned Maxine, but it's over. Come on, Maxine, I'll tell you all about it."

"Max, what's he talking about?"

"I was going to tell you tonight," I said. She pulled away from me. "Maxine, I meant to tell you—let me explain."

"I think I'll get a less biased explanation from Scott. Why is it that every man I've ever been close to has lied to me?"

She gave me a dramatic look, grabbed Hess by the arm and walked off in a huff. Three steps away, she looked back at me. "I can't believe I ever cared for you," she said. Then, she winked.

I blinked at her. This was the second time in two days she had said that to me. But this time it was as if she was trying to tell me something. And that wink . . . I stumbled over to my table and sat next to Mr. Andrews, whom was in a glib conversation with a silver-haired, round-faced, octogenarian woman. After a few minutes they excused themselves and walked to another table, heavily populated with middle-aged women.

I observed Hess waving his arms at a table across the room, likely telling Maxine what a liar I was. Occasionally she would look up in my direction and shake her head. Once when Hess wasn't paying attention, I thought she smiled at me.

"Is anyone sitting here?" A charismatic, older Chinese man, dressed in a dapper light-gray tuxedo, pointed his cane to an empty chair. He had a full head of black hair and spectacles properly perched on the bridge of his nose. He was thin and agile for his age and used the cane more as a prop than for reassurance.

"No, please sit down," I said.

"Perhaps I should introduce myself, first." I sized him up, curiously. "My name is Lu Fong. I am the former employer of Maxine Andrews."

I stared in disbelief. Maxine said he might show up at the event, but I hadn't expected him to be so brazen.

"Please sit down," I said, a little shakily this time. I looked over at Maxine and watched her hand the computer flash drive to

Hess. He smiled, stood up, said something to her, and walked away. Distracted, I tried to focus on Lu Fong. "I've heard of you, I think."

"You should not believe everything that is said about me," he said. "My reputation is sometimes exaggerated as that of the ferocious tiger. In truth, I am more of a domestic cat."

"Either way, you have sharp claws."

"That may be, but I wish no harm to Maxine. She is a sweet and endearing person, if not a little too overzealous. I merely want back what she has taken from me."

"I don't know how I can help."

"You can convince her to return what she has taken from me. My sources tell me she has it stored on a flash drive. It is for her safety. There are many people who would kill for the information she has in her possession. My daughter, Kay Lu, might be one of them."

"Maxine and I ran into your sweet little daughter. I wouldn't doubt it for a minute."

"Alas, she has turned away from me. She believes me to be old and obsolete. Kay Lu is of the generation that needs instant gratification. I have slowly worked toward amassing a fortune, and I am not going to let her or Maxine try to steal it from me."

"Try to?"

"Yes. Maxine has the numbers of my private bank accounts, and if she would have turned them over to the authorities immediately, they may have frozen my assets. But many of the accounts are part of my memory. I simply transferred my funds to new accounts.

"What she has now is a list of names the Chinese government would dearly love to have. Other than that, there are a few items, which only would interest me. Yet, my enemies may not know I have moved my money, and they would kill to get what she has."

"What about the list of Tibetan loyalists the Chinese government considers traitors?"

"It is true the list might be worth a tidy sum, but it is not of interest to me. She may keep the list if she would then return my property, I would let it be known I have it, she would then be out of danger and everyone would be happy."

"You seem pretty anxious to get this information back, for

someone who supposedly has all his bases covered."

"You are very astute. Yes, there are other items on the flash drive that are of importance to me. But I am the only one to whom they are important. I will pay you, to get it for me, the sum of fifty thousand dollars."

"Would this item of importance be the cloning formula?"

Lu Fong's facial expression remained unchanged. If I had surprised him, he wasn't going to show me. He smiled and rested his hand upon mine on the table. "It is one of the items that are of interest to me, but there are others. Here is my card. You may reach me at this mobile number. I will be driving to a conference in Hood River tomorrow afternoon. It would be well to hear from you before then."

I looked over at Maxine's table. It was empty. I glanced furtively in all directions for her. I spied her walking toward an exit at the far end of the ballroom. "What time will you be leaving?"

"Approximately two or three p.m."

My thoughts were with Maxine. There was a man with her. A waiter. He seemed to be shoving something against her back. A maroon towel concealed the something in his hand.

"I've got to go now, excuse me."

Lu Fong grabbed my arm with an iron grip. My arm ached and I turned toward the pain. "What are you doing?"

"Oh, I am sorry. Sometimes I don't realize my strength. I only wanted to know—are you going to help me?"

"I don't know. I'll have to talk with Maxine. She's leaving now. I have to catch her."

He held onto my arm. "I think she will be available to you in a minute. But now I need your assurance. I will pay you one hundred thousand dollars. You may split it with Maxine, or keep it for yourself. I do not care. But you must tell me now. Will you get it for me?"

Maxine was gone and I had a feeling of impending doom. It was like a dream where you are running in slow motion, trying to get somewhere, yet unable to advance. But unlike a dream this was real, and I knew what was keeping me from getting where I wanted to go. It was this seemingly fragile old man who actually had the strength of a bull. I turned on him and tried to pry his fingers from my forearm.

"I'll do what I can. I'll call you tomorrow and let you know," I said. "Right now I have to go." I stared at him for several seconds, not afraid now, and he released his grip, slowly bringing his lips to a grin.

"I will await your call."

I turned and pushed my way through couples on the dance floor. I hit the exit door hard and ran into a darkened hall. To the right was a longer hallway that emptied into a series of other hallways. To my left was an office. I ran to the maze of hallways. We were in the basement level of the hotel, so it was conceivable one might lead to a parking garage.

I followed one hallway into the kitchen and retreated and followed another hallway to the bathrooms. I checked out the men's room and the ladies lounge, much to the chagrin of two middle-aged women in stardust gowns.

I dashed back to a third hallway and followed it to a green exit sign over a metal door. The door was jammed, but it gave a bit and an arm was visible through the opening. I pushed harder and the body gave way, revealing an unconscious waiter—the one I had seen ushering Maxine from the ballroom a moment earlier.

I stepped into the parking lot and looked in both directions. There were indecipherable sounds coming from around the corner to the right. I ran toward the noises and plummeted to the ground, skinning my hands on the asphalt. I had tripped over another body, groaning in the shadows. This one wasn't Chinese. He was dressed in blue jeans and a black sweatshirt and had a milky white complexion and short brown hair. I jumped to my feet and continued running.

Around the corner, four men, dressed in black and wearing stocking masks, were struggling to shove Maxine into a blue van. Two of them were holding her arms from behind and dragging her toward the van. A third attacker was grabbing at her feet.

My oversized rented dress shoes clopped on the concrete as I pursued them, about 100 feet away. My undersized pant-legs rode up my shins during my long strides the result of the tailor being unable to lengthen the legs further on Kevin Kline's tuxedo.

I grabbed the guy with the foot fetish by the collar and smacked him in the nose. Something wet and warm splattered my hand.

Maxine was on her feet now and pulling away from her attackers. She did this marvelous back flip, while being held by each arm and wound up behind her assailants, still in their grasp. She kicked one in the foreleg as he turned. He let go of her arm to grab his leg, and she planted a karate chop into the throat of the other thug, who fell to the ground gasping for air. She turned back to her hopping friend and hit him with a karate chop to the back of the neck.

The fourth guy, who had been fumbling with the van's sliding door, stumbled through it and maneuvered his bulky frame into the driver's seat. The engine fired up and the tires burned rubber in the opposite direction. The other three attackers lay helplessly on the asphalt waiting for sweet dreams to come.

I stopped behind her as she watched the van speed off. Breathing hard, I managed to blurt out: "Who are you, lady?" She turned and came at me in the dark.

"Maxine, it's me." I was too late. I vaguely remember an artful karate chop striking me on the side of my neck. I woke up a few minutes later, lying on my back on the hard concrete.

"Are you okay?" Maxine said. "I'm sorry, honey."

I groaned. "I tried to tell you it was me. The last thing I remember is you accidentally slamming me with a karate chop."

Maxine turned her face toward the shadows.

"You did hit me by accident, didn't you?"

The shadows continued to play upon her face.

Maxine?"

She turned back and offered me a sorrowful smile. "My adrenaline was still pumping from the fight, and when I saw you it just carried over. I tried not to be upset about your fibs, but I'm just not very good at controlling my feelings I guess."

"Or your hands. So, you are mad at me."

She stood and primped her hair. "Not any more. I think that last karate chop helped immensely."

"That's right, you called me honey. Or was that a dream?"

"No dream, darling. I was just playing along with Scott to see how far he would go."

"You aren't upset with me for deceiving you?"

"How can I be? You're the goods, darling. So what if you

aren't a licensed private investigator. You've saved my life twice, saved my little computer flash drive from getting into the wrong hands, and kept us ahead of the competition. I got more than I ever bargained for with you."

She helped me to my feet and I wobbled back to the exit door. The three guys I had joined on the pavement were gone now. They probably figured an expedient exit was better than running into Maxine again.

We went back to the ballroom with our dignity intact—even if our attire wasn't. I had grease stains on my tux and a hem had come loose on my pants, making one pant leg longer than the other. Maxine still looked stylish, even with a run in one stocking and a longer than intended slit up the side of her dress.

"Looks like your waiter didn't like his tip," I said, opening the door for her. He had vamoosed too.

Nobody in the ballroom seemed to be paying attention to us, so we joined George Andrews at a table. He noticed our ragged attire right away. "What in the heck have you two been doing?"

I put my fingers to a tender spot on my neck. At this point, it seemed conceivable that George's sponsoring of his daughter's self-defense classes could have been a ploy to keep her suitors at bay.

"Maxine was showing me a couple of her martial arts moves in the parking garage," I said. "I guess we got carried away."

He looked at me in disbelief and sighed. "Never mind, I don't want to know. I have to leave soon to catch a plane back to L.A." We talked for another hour before her father excused himself for the evening.

The orchestra played a slow tune, and I asked my dream girl for a dance. I had a million questions to ask her, but I liked the way she felt in my arms. The questions could wait. They might result in arguments. I looked around the ballroom and Lu Fong was gone.

Maxine brought her head up from my shoulder. "Max, why do you think . . .?"

I leaned into her. "No more business tonight. We can talk about it tomorrow. Our heads will be clearer."

She smiled and put her head back on my shoulder. We danced and talked and got to know each other better.

Tomorrow would come soon enough.

Chapter 15

"So what happened between you and Scott last night?" I asked.

The tone in my question leaned toward accusatory. I didn't like the familiar way he acted around Maxine or his arrogance. We were sitting at the dining table, having finished a breakfast of bagels and tea. Joel had disappeared into his bedroom to give us some privacy.

She apparently didn't catch the jealousy in my voice because she didn't rise to the bait.

"He spent most of the time badmouthing you, Max. Scott has a complete dossier on you put together by the FBI during the last two days. He said you worked a variety of jobs over the last few years, but didn't stay very long at any of them. Is that true?"

I nodded meekly.

"Oh." It was a short word, but it just left her disappointment dangling for what seemed like forever.

"He said you were arrested once for assault, but Joel already told me about that. I think it was probably justified. I mean punching out that editor. I'd like to think my husband would fight for me."

She paused as if in thought. Maybe she was imagining me slaying some dragon for her because she smiled.

"I saw you give Scott the flash drive," I said. "He must have made a convincing case."

Maxine looked up from her teacup and grinned. "He was a little too assertive for my taste. He wanted the flash drive real bad. If he hadn't attacked you so vehemently, I might have given it to him."

"You did give it to him. I saw you."

"I gave him a blank flash device I picked up at Office Depot yesterday. I bought it just in case I didn't want to give it to him. It saved me arguing with him.

I hadn't figured on this. She had the original flash drive but it was corrupted, and eventually I would have to explain my part in it. Or would I? Maybe it just went bad. Or with luck, maybe someone else would steal it. Or maybe I could switch it with my good copy. I was getting that stress headache again.

I told her about Lu Fong's appearance and his offer of $100,000. I explained how he tried to act nonchalant about the flash drive and about his steel grip when I tried to follow her.

Maxine brushed a bagel crumb from her crème colored pantsuit. "I wonder who sent those guys to kidnap me. Do you suppose it was Lu Fong? I don't think Kay Lu knew I was there last night, unless she's still talking with her father. Scott was acting so odd I'm beginning to suspect him, now."

"I don't think he's behind it," I said. "He thought he had the flash drive, so he should have been happy. Lu Fong seemed genuine about paying for it, but he did try to stop me from going after you."

Maxine sipped her tea. "Who else could be after me?"

"I don't know. Have you ever seen those guys in the parking garage before?"

"Never. But Lu Fong has a lot of people working for him."

"Maybe, but I've got a hunch there's someone else involved that we don't know about."

Maxine didn't look like she was buying that idea. "You're just guessing, aren't you? How long have you been doing this, Max?"

"You mean, sleuthing? Since the minute you walked into Steadman's office."

Her mouth dropped. "What? Then what were you doing there?"

"Looking for an employment agency. Turns out it was across the hall."

"But why? I mean, how did you come to represent yourself as a private investigator."

I cleared my throat. "Um, you inspired me. I wanted to be whatever you wanted me to be. No, that's not really true. I wanted to be with you, to help you, for you to believe in me."

She jabbed her finger at me. "So you just bluffed your way through the whole thing? You'd never worked as a private investigator? Not even one day?"

"That's right."

She leaned against the chair's backrest and tilted her head, running her hands through her hair. "I can't believe this. You seemed so sure of yourself. You had this air of confidence. I thought you were something straight out of a crime novel."

"I have read a few of them. I tend to identify with the tough hard-boiled P.I.'s in some of those books. They had a code of ethics, a moral outlook on life. It was good versus evil. Even if they sometimes had to break the rules to make things come out right."

"I can't fathom how you so completely fooled me into believing you were a private eye."

My back stiffened. "That's private investigator. Let's just say, I'm interning at the moment. I'm thinking of opening an office when things settle down. I do like this kind of work, and people tell me I have good instincts for the job."

"Hmm. Well, I guess I wouldn't bet against you."

"Are we square? I mean, are you disappointed in me?"

"I'm surprised. I feel a bit letdown, but I wouldn't call it disappointment. It's just, well, I wonder what we're going to do now? Someone's still after the formula and me too. Where do we go from here?"

"I think I might have a few ideas. But first, I need you to answer some questions for me."

"Like what?"

"Like, why do you have arrest warrants put out by such agencies as Interpol, the Treasury Department and the FBI?"

"WHAT? Where did you hear that?"

"Hollywood told me. Now, would you mind answering the question?"

She looked around the room for help, but there was no one but me. She stood up and walked into the living room, pacing out an answer.

"You have quite a few surprises up your sleeves, don't you? You must feel like you're a pretty smart guy, checking up on me like that."

"I didn't check up on you. That was Hollywood's idea."

"Oh." Her face pouted, and she came back to the table and perched on a chair across from me. "I've been involved in quite a few causes over the years. My father likes to joke about me overthrowing governments. Well, he isn't too far off base. I've been involved in causes in different countries, and not all were about human rights.

"What I learned is that there are agents scattered in every country, and they are ruthless, following up on bureaucratic government missions that often have been obsolete for years.

"So it might surprise you to know that some of those spies might approach a free agent, like me, to help them with some of their dirty work. I must admit, I was surprised the first time."

"Are you saying you're a spy?"

She scowled. "Nothing so droll, dear. I work only for myself. But once or twice I agreed to help them out. There were a few times we shared mutual goals. Then they wanted to enlist me full-time.

"When I wouldn't sign up, they put out those obscene warrants to harass me. A few times our paths have crossed, those agents and mine, and they've picked me up for questioning using those warrants as a premise. They'll hold me for a few days until whatever they're working on blows over."

"How can they do that? They have no legal right."

She looked at me cynically. "Yes they do. There have been a few times when, as you would say, I bent the rules."

"Hollywood calls it's breaking the law."

She didn't laugh. "I broke International laws. I've never been charged because I was acting as an agent for some of these people—The FBI, The Treasury Department."

"The CIA?"

"Them too. Anyway, they won't take me to court. This is the way they keep me in tow. Get me to do things for them." She looked directly at me and pouted. "And you know, Max, it's getting to be a real pain."

"So, are you working for them against Lu Fong?"

"No, Max. I got a job with him at his office in Hong Kong because I heard he was working with the Chinese Government on some special project involving inhumane treatment of animals. I learned Lu Fong was breeding farm animals for laboratory experiments in Hong Kong, Seattle and Portland.

"Some of my sources told me he had a list of Tibetan loyalists living in Hong Kong that he was planning to peddle to the Chinese. Some of these people were feeding information to the United States about the Chinese interests in Hong King. I got a job as Lu Fong's bookkeeping assistant and waited and watched. It didn't take long for me to realize others were watching him too."

I leaned forward on my chair. "Who?"

"I don't know."

"Then how do you know someone was watching him?"

"I kept hearing clicks on the phone line in his office. From experience, I guessed the phone was tapped. So I looked around the office and I found three bugs. I told Lu Fong about it, thinking it might ingratiate him toward me.

"He laughed at me. He said in Hong Kong everyone is watched. Apparently the Chinese spy on local businesses looking for foreign agents planted by the CIA and other countries. Lu Fong said he would be offended if someone wasn't watching him."

I looked at her wide-eyed. "So did your ruse work? Did you gain his trust?"

"To a certain degree, I think. But I might have overplayed my hand. He seemed to keep me at arm's length. Still, I was close enough to see anything strange that went on."

"Such as?"

Maxine thought for a minute. "Sudden visits from emissaries of the Chinese government. They were supposed to be ambassadors of some kind from the Republic of China working on a plan to stimulate commerce. First, the visits occurred about once a month. Then it was every few weeks. Before I left, I would see one of them almost weekly. They were careless, assuming because I was American, I didn't speak Chinese."

My breathing quickened and my face flushed. I was in love with a woman who should be out of my league. "You speak Chinese?"

"A little bit. I was taking some classes in Mandarin. I knew enough to realize that Lu Fong's visitors were actually government spies. It sounded like they were plotting something they didn't want the Communist Party to know about.

I scratched my head, trying to figure how this might fit into the puzzle. "And?"

"That's about all I know. One of my co-workers ratted me out. She caught me eavesdropping at the door during one of those official visits and went to Lu Fong. After that, I wasn't privy to any of his activities. Everyone in the office watched me from the time I entered the office until the time I left. I think they even followed me home a few times.

"I panicked and made the mistake of sending an email to Scott in Portland. After that, things really got dicey. The next day Lu Fong called an emergency meeting with everyone in the office except me."

Joel's phone rang, but I ignored it. "I wonder if they were tracking your email activity. Did you contact Scott on the office computer?"

Her cynical look returned. I had the feeling my credibility with her had taken a steep dive. Her face seemed to question my every action. She peered up toward the ceiling as if reconstructing the event.

"Yes, that's possible. Anyway, during one of their secret meetings in his conference room I slipped into Lu Fong's office and accessed his computer. I cracked his password with a software program left over from a CIA job I once helped on and downloaded everything that looked interesting onto a flash drive. The next day I got an email from Scott telling me to get the hell out of Hong Kong.

"Before I left Hong Kong, I returned to Lu Fong's office after working hours and uploaded a particularly nasty computer virus to his computer network system. Then I broke into his safe and found a stack of computer USB memory drives and some CD's. I dropped them into a trashcan and had a little bonfire. I found some flash drives in a box on his desk, so I threw them in the burning basket too. Then the darn fire alarm went off.

"My belongings were packed and in my car so I made a hasty retreat to the airport and boarded the first flight to Seattle. I drove to Portland to meet with Scott, and you know the rest. For some reason, Scott didn't want to meet me at his office, and he suggested I have someone act as a go-between. I still don't know why."

As her story unfolded, I watched for a tell: a nervous facial tic or other body language that might show me she was lying. I know, I read too many mysteries. But her story was so incredible I was having a hard time believing it. I didn't notice any signs of her lying to me though.

"Maxine, about the files you copied. Why did you select the one on cloning?'

She looked at me blankly. "Cloning? What are you talking about?"

Crap. I hadn't had time to tell her about Joel's theory. I filled her in on what Joel had told me about the formula which might be effective on cloning people."

You're putting me on," she said. "But if that's true, we can't let Lu Fong or Kay Lu get the formula. They would sell it to China and who knows what the Chinese government would do with it."

"I don't think they have a shortage of people," I suggested.

"I just thought of something Lu Fong said one day back in Hong Kong," Maxine said. "He said, 'wouldn't it be something if there was a way to create a super race.' I thought he was crazy and told him the Nazi's tried to do that during World War Two at the expense of millions of people. We had quite a conversation about it, but I couldn't sway him from his thoughts that someday someone might create a perfect race of people."

"Do you think that's what the Chinese want to do?" I asked.

"Five minutes ago I would have said no, but now?"

"How did you happen to copy the cloning formula in the first place," I asked.

She bit her lip as she considered my question. "I'm trying to remember. There was a phrase I saw when I scanned the files. I heard one of Lu Fong's ambassadors use it. Nuclear transfer. That was how it translated into English. It sounded ominous, so I copied it.

It sounded ominous to me too. Joel said something about nuclear transfer in the cloning procedure.

At that point Joel walked into the dining room. He wore an off-white Berber sweater with tan chinos. His brown eyes were excited as he spoke.

"Max, Hollywood called. He wants us down at his office. Now!"

Maxine shifted in the chair. "What's happened?"

"He says the FBI wants to meet with us."

My first thought was for my new client. "Do they want Maxine?"

Joel nodded. "Hollywood says they want to speak with everyone associated with the kidnapping."

I didn't like the idea of them browbeating Maxine again. "What if we don't want to meet with the FBI?"

"Hollywood says he'll send out some deputies to pick us up. We'd better go, Max."

Maxine stood up and smoothed her tan slacks with her hands. "Scott's probably mad because I gave him the phony flash drive. We'd better go."

"It's not your friend, Hess, that wants to meet us," Joel said. "It's some guy named Ken Thomas."

"I think we should go," I said. "Maybe he can shed some light on Agent Hess."

But first I updated Joel on what had happened the previous night, including Lu Fong's offer for the flash drive. Then I called the number Lu Fong had given me and arranged for us to meet him at a hotel in the Columbia Gorge for dinner. Joel and Maxine stood by and nodded their agreement to this meeting.

I hung up the phone and looked at my two partners. Lu Fong suggested I bring Maxine's purloined flash drive, and I was vague about whether or not we even had it, accusing him of the attack on Maxine the previous night at the Hilton. I frowned into the phone receiver and hung up.

"He said he didn't know anything about the attack on Maxine, and the surprise in his voice and his concern about the flash drive made me want to believe him."

But then again, I was new at this racket.

Chapter 16

Hollywood's office was a fifteen-minute drive from Joel's apartment, and Maxine suggested we go in her rented blue sedan. She said it was too cold to go in the Jeep and there was no room for the three of us in my Mustang. But when she loaded myriad suitcases for an overnight stay at the Columbia Gorge Hotel, I suspected she had wanted to go in her car because it had more trunk space.

"Where did you get all of this stuff? I asked. "I've done a little shopping the last few days here and there," she said. I had to leave Hong Kong so quickly I practically had nothing to wear."

"Practically?" I said.

She ignored me and slid into the driver's seat.

I sat in the front and Joel crowded into the back seat with the luggage that wouldn't fit in the trunk. We were greeted on the second Saturday in March with a cloudless sky. The sun awakened sleepy plants, and a man with cabin fever was outside in his tee shirt and shorts, washing an orange Pontiac in the 40-degree weather.

The morning summed up how I felt about myself. It was a new beginning. Maxine and I were starting over with nothing to hide. Well, almost nothing. I omitted the part about sabotaging her flash drive with the cloning formula.

But she finally knew about my other indiscretions and apparently had forgiven me. In turn, I was relieved to learn she wasn't a notorious criminal mastermind wanted by U.S. and International law enforcement agencies for treason. Now I only had to worry about how to come clean about my latest deception.

And a darker cloud loomed over us. This case was muddled

because there were too many potential adversaries around us. They seemed to be coming at me from all direction so we never knew what to expect.

Lu Fong, Kay Lu, Scott Hess, Steadman, Hollywood Henderson, and now the FBI. I didn't know when they would show up or what they would do. I had a feeling I didn't even know all of the players.

So far, Lu Fong hadn't shown much of his hand. His men had shot Maxine, and he may have been responsible for the second kidnapping attempt at the Hilton. But if he had transferred his bank accounts, why was he so frantic to get Maxine's flash drive? What was it he wanted that drove him to such extremes? He had to be after the cloning formula. He must have put a lot of money and resources into it.

I saw a clearer picture of Kay Lu. Here was a spoiled little rich girl who couldn't wait for her freedom, and she was kept her under her father's flash by him controlling the purse strings. Kay Lu was ambitious and wanted to strike out on her own. Whatever was on the flash drive was her ticket to independence and financial freedom. She scared me more than her father, because I had seen the greed in her dark sinister eyes.

Scott Hess was the other unknown quantity. Was he a free agent, looking to fatten his bank account by taking kickbacks from Lu Fong, or an unjustly accused scapegoat working on his own to clear his name? I couldn't help feel there might be others, working behind the scenes, planning to relieve Maxine of her prize.

I also questioned the wisdom of my carrying around the only copy of the cloning formula. I felt guilty, letting Maxine be the target and wished I had told her about my complicity. I was afraid telling her now might be the fatal blow to our relationship. I carried the good flash drive with me because I couldn't think of a safer place.

Mailing it to Joel had been a stupid idea, and I couldn't leave it in his apartment. What if the someone stumbled upon Joel's apartment? We easily could have been followed from the Hilton after the charity event.

I didn't know of any banks open on a Saturday that might rent a safe deposit box, and there was no way I could discreetly break away from the others now that Hollywood had summoned us. So I carried it inside my jacket pocket as I had done the night before in my tuxedo.

It was doubly dangerous since we were meeting with the law and could be subject to search, and we also would be meeting with Lu Fong later.

"Max, you're awfully quiet, what are you thinking about?" Maxine turned the radio down and her beautiful smile finally returned. "There's that serious side of you again. I don't think I can take too much of that."

"Turn here, Maxine," Joel said. "It's that pea-green building."

I looked up at the ugly building's facade, realizing we had arrived. "Sorry, I was doing a jigsaw puzzle in my head. The pieces are still a bit jumbled."

A few minutes later we were standing in Hollywood's office, surrounded again by a less than elegant array of tired oak furniture. Hollywood abruptly rose from his chair and reached a hand across his desk.

"You must be Maxine. I'm Captain Henderson. I've heard so much about you."

She rolled her eyes at me. "I can imagine. I assure you, Max exaggerates things."

"Not this time he didn't," Hollywood said. "You are as charming and beautiful as he said."

She blushed and turned toward another man, also quick to rise from his chair. "And this must be Ken Thomas."

Hollywood released her hand. "No, this is Ned Wright. He's with the FBI."

"Pleased to meet you," he said. "I'm sorry, Agent Thomas was unable to make it. He got called into the field and asked me to take his place."

"I'm starting to wonder if this Agent Thomas even exists," I said, shaking his hand.

"I'm beginning to wonder about that myself." Wright was thin and tall, clean-shaven and wore smaller round-lens glasses, which perched neatly upon his nose. His suit was a dark shade of blue.

Hollywood introduced Joel and me, and we all sat down on hard oak chairs in a semi-circle around his desk. Hollywood doesn't work Saturdays, and he had traded his new camouflage uniform for casual slacks and a charcoal sweater.

"I believe this is Mr. Wright's show," he said. "My job was to bring you all together. However, since a great deal of these goings on have happened in my county, Mr. Wright agrees I should be here for the meeting, both to be informed and of assistance if needed.

"Mr. Wright . . ."

"Thank you, Captain Henderson. I believe our first contact with Mr. Starr here was a few days ago. Mr. Starr, you called Agent Thomas in reference to a meeting you supposed had been set up with a subordinate of ours, Agent Scott Hess. That was you, wasn't it?"

He was all business now. He knew it was me whom had called. I looked at him intently and nodded.

Mr. Starr, you have no idea what anxiety this has caused us. Agent Hess has been the subject of quite a bit of scrutiny lately. He's been suspected of compromising an investigation and now we get a call from you, indicating he's been working on something on the side of which we have no knowledge. And you say he was supposed to set up a meeting between you and his supervisor. Something he never did."

I simply smiled at Wright who had stopped talking and seemed pensive. He was debating something, almost to the point of talking to himself.

Finally he spoke again. "Look, in order to proceed, I'm going to have to give you all some background information on something I think is related to what you all have been mixed up in. I'm reluctant to do this unless I feel what I say will remain confidential."

"We're here on a fact-finding mission," I said. "None of us are gossips. We can keep our mouths shut." I looked around and saw Maxine and Joel nodding in agreement.

"Okay, then I'll lay it out for you. Several weeks ago, we had been watching a local Chinese restaurant. One of the people we were watching was a woman named Kay Lu. Our information was she was fronting an operation for her old man, Lu Fong. We got a tip from the CIA that Lu Fong was involved in some scheme with the Chinese government involving cloning experiments. We suspected Kay Lu was sponsoring some special breeding farms for animals to be used in these experiments."

"Why would they breed their own animals?" Maxine asked. "Why not just buy them on the open market?"

"We don't know," Wright said. "We were just following a lead. The CIA wanted us to report anything unusual. Our man, Hess, got a job at the restaurant as a bartender. He got close to Kay Lu and began to get bits and pieces of information from her.

"It seems like her father has some kind of deal in the works with the Chinese. Apparently he had a cloning formula that was further advanced than what anyone else is working on. The Chinese are a scheming lot. Their government has joined all the other governments of the world in going on record against the cloning of human beings. Yet, they are busy cloning pigs in their own country and their government has put a ton of money into the research."

I straightened. "Do you think their government wants to clone humans?"

Wright winced. My thought was he hated giving out any information to civilians. "The Favored Nation Status the United Nations awarded China a decade ago has been a boon to their economy. The country has experienced an industrial revolution of sorts funded by corporations around the world.

"China has nearly a billion-and-a-half-people and is growing at the rate of ten million a year, and now their economy has also grown at an alarming rate. If there were a chink in their armor, it would be lack of technology. They have done their best to steal secrets from the United States, and we've given them away during the last decade by letting them build computer manufacturing plants in China in exchange for their cheap labor."

"You should be worrying about the loss of American jobs and what that is doing to our economy," Maxine said.

'That's for the politicians," Wright said. "My job is to protect the free world. Some leaders in our government are afraid China may eventually become a cold-war threat. We are increasingly concerned we are funding our own demise. Our only edge is our superiority in computer systems and nuclear technology."

"What are you saying?" Maxine asked.

"I understand you have a flash drive that has information on it from programs in Lu Fong's personal computer?"

"How did you know that?" I asked.

"We have our sources. I'm asking you, Miss Andrews, do you have such a flash drive?"

"I took a few extras with me when I left Hong Kong."

"Well, if you've taken the time to look at the flash drive, you would have noticed if there are any files on cloning. Are there?"

Wright stood up and leaned over her, practically salivating. She put her hand in his mid-section and pushed him backward a step. "You're crowding me. Max tells me there is something about cloning on the flash drive. I wouldn't know."

Wright sat down in his chair and gazed at me. Wrinkles in his forehead succumbed to a more relaxed demeanor. "Mr. Starr, would you happen to know what's on the flash drive?"

I tried to look unabashed. "I know Lu Fong wants it badly." I felt Wright wanted me to say more. Not because he needed to know what was on the flash drive. He seemed to know. He wanted to know if I knew.

I thought about this for a minute and wondered what was behind his maneuverings. If I knew what the game was about, then his secret was out. He might feel free to discuss it. If I didn't know, he wasn't going to tell me anything. He would just want the flash drive. I decided to bluff him.

"I know there's a formula on the flash drive that is eons ahead of what other researchers are working on. I also know that with this formula it's possible to clone humans. I know the success rate is nearly ninety-seven percent so if someone else has it, they may be cloning human beings as we speak."

I fitted a few more puzzle pieces together in my mind. There was only one way they could interlock. "I know the Chinese government is very interested in this cloning formula and will pay outrageous sums of money to get it."

Wright sat there somewhere between stoic and stunned. He did not move, did not twitch a muscle in his tight face.

"I also know Lu Fong was working with the Chinese government on a project to clone humans. I'm guessing Lu Fong's researchers had reached a breakthrough when Maxine destroyed all of his records and ran off with a critical portion of the formula. It must be critical or his scientists would simply replicate their experiments. There must be something they couldn't duplicate. Some unknown entity they overlooked. Lu Fong likely thinks it's in the data Maxine stole. Or at least he hopes it is."

Wright finally collapsed back into his chair, dumbfounded. He stuck a piece of gum in his mouth and chewed it furiously. Hollywood's eyebrows were raised and his eyes gleamed at me. Joel made little ticking noises at my left elbow, and Maxine had scooted to the edge of her chair.

Wright finally spoke. "You know a great deal more than I realized. How did you get all this information?"

"Joel taught me about cloning. He's a physician's assistant at the hospital. He showed a portion of the formula to a colleague, who filled us in on the specifics. Some of it I learned from Maxine's telling of her adventure in Hong Kong. You told me the rest."

Wright tugged at his ear. "You're pretty clever, Mr. Starr. More so than I would have thought. Everything you have said is true. The Chinese government wants the formula. We think they mean to clone humans, even though publicly they are on record against it.

"There are factions in their leadership that have hatched on a scheme so diabolical; nothing matches it since the Nazis' attempt to create a superhuman race during the Second World War. The Nazi's were going to create a superior race by selective genetic breeding. Of course that also included disposing of humans they felt were inferior."

Wright held up his hand and gazed absently at his fingernails. "Some factions in China appear to have the same idea, although the methods have changed in the twenty-first century. With cloning technology they could literally pick the person they want to duplicate and clone that person."

Maxine challenged him. "Why would they want to do that? They already have too many people. That's why they've taken over Tibet and Hong Kong. To export their exploding population. For years they've been trying to reduce the number of people, not add more."

Wright smiled condescendingly. "They only want to duplicate a few people, the type of people whom could help them catch up with the United States in technology. Suppose you could clone Bill Gates, or one of the top physicists in the country, or someone developing new nuclear technology. Wouldn't that inspire a country like China to develop cloning technology?"

"Cloning wouldn't ensure a duplicate of Gates or any of those other people," Joel said. "Environmental upbringing plays a significant role in a human being's development. Besides, it could take fifteen to thirty years before a clone of a person would mature enough for them to realize any scientific benefits. And there could be severe side effects in the cloning process."

"Maybe," Wright said. "But the Chinese government is capable of providing enriched environments. They also have the patience needed to pull off such an experiment. Meanwhile people may be created in a way not intended by God. China continues to grow economically and by the time some of their cloned scientists mature, the country will have the ability to fund any futuristic project. Keep in mind, the government retains the greatest amount of wealth generated by its people, many of whom practically work as slaves in their own country."

After a moment's pause, in which we all considered this idea in earnest, I leaned forward, facing Wright. "This is all very interesting. But what do you want from us."

"I want your help in stopping Lu Fong and his daughter. I have already done you a very large favor. Agent Thomas put together a dossier on you and found out you are not now, nor ever have been a private investigator. We also learned there are quite a few people trying to learn something about you."

I nodded. "Yeah, Scott Hess already shared your dossier with Maxine."

"Then, you were misleading your client. I'm sorry about that. Scott is turning out to be a loose cannon. Sticking his nose where it doesn't belong. He's the one whom we believed tipped off Kay Lu, you know. Scott had learned there was a lab of sorts in the basement of the restaurant run by Kay Lu. Agent Thomas decided we needed to get a warrant and search the lab.

"Agent Hess was against it. He said there was too much more to learn. That we would tip them off and they'd simply move their operations elsewhere. I think he got too involved with Kay Lu. She has a way of casting a net around men and towing them into her web. I'd guess Scott was hopelessly in love with her.

"Anyway, Agent Thomas overruled him and we got the warrant. By the time we got there, everything of importance, including Kay Lu, was gone. Scott tipped them off; we know he did."

"You just can't prove it," I said.

"We just can't prove it."

"Maybe Scott was right."

Wright glared at me. "What do you mean?"

"He said a raid would scare them off. If you hadn't gone ahead with the raid, maybe Scott would have learned more."

I could tell Wright didn't like that. But he went on with his agenda. I had something he needed and he wasn't going to let me rile him, no matter how hard I tried. And I was trying.

"As I was saying about your dossier. We decided to improve it. I contacted some people at the state-licensing bureau and expedited your application for your business. You've been registered as a private investigator for three years. You've been quite successful, just ask anybody in the law enforcement community. You've even helped the FBI a few times."

My eyes must have nearly popped out of their sockets. "That's how George Andrews got the false report about me being a private investigator."

Wright nodded. Senior Agent Thomas had talked to Captain Henderson and learned about you misrepresenting yourself as an investigator. Captain Henderson mentioned you were fairly eager to continue this career. When he told us about your little adventure with Kay Lu, it occurred to Thomas that you might be helpful to us.

"Thomas had me do a background check on you with the state of Oregon, and I learned someone else was inquiring about your credentials. So we decided to help you along with your career. You never know when one might be called upon to return a favor. As it stands, not only are you an accredited member of the Oregon Association of Private Investigators, but you have a pretty good reputation too."

Maxine and I looked at each other somewhat perplexed.

"So, what do you want from me?" I asked.

Wright looked down his nose. His voice was surly, but concise. "For starters, friend, we want that flash drive. You help us out, and we'll give you a leg up on your career."

Chapter 17

It was as if the seasons were playing tug-o-war as we drove up the Columbia River Highway, meandering along the cliffs high above the majestic Columbia River.

New flower buds forced themselves from dormant tree branches as birds did aerial stunts overhead. The late morning sun strained to climb above the trees enough to melt patches of ice on the road.

The scenic highway was punctuated by impromptu waterfalls sprouting over cliffs now that the temperatures had warmed and mountain snows were melting. The asphalt was rough and bordered with ornate masonry walls built along the 74-mile historic highway constructed between 1913 and 1920.

Joel sat beside me and Maxine occupied the back seat. They were joking about the interview in Hollywood's office, reliving their exploits like athletes after the big game.

"Did you see that guy's face when Lady Maxine got down and dirty with him?" Joel said.

Unruffled, she spoke matter-of-factly about her dialogue with Wright. "Sometimes you must lower yourself to their level to be understood."

Joel shrugged and laughed. "I think he got your message."

I glanced in her direction and caught a glimpse of her satisfied smile.

"Anyway, I think Max was the one who set the tone. I'm glad he didn't buckle to their demands. I like a man who can stand up to authority."

Her words of support seemed to rejuvenate me. "I don't think we can trust Mr. Wright yet. I wasn't real keen on turning over the flash drive to him. Once we give it up, there's no reason for us to be involved in this anymore."

Okay, truthfully, I didn't want to risk losing the reason to continue investigating and possibly losing access to Maxine in the process.

As Joel and Maxine continued to talk about the shades of red that had colored Wright's face, their jokes pulled me back to Hollywood's office.

Wright had been adamant. He wanted Maxine's flash drive. Fortunately Maxine supported me as I attempted to negotiate better terms. I wanted the FBI to clear Maxine's arrest warrants within National and International jurisdictions. She was to have a clean slate, I said. No more hauling her in for questioning. No more games.

When Wright said it couldn't be done, I figured we were through and motioned Maxine and Joel toward the door, so we might start our trip to the Columbia River Hotel to meet with Lu Fong.

Wright's face turned violet with anger. "I can't do what you're asking. I don't have the authority. I'd have to contact twenty different agencies. I won't do it."

I smiled at Maxine. "Then there is hope. And you thought there was no way out of your little dilemma, my dear."

She rolled her eyes at me. "I think my dilemma is about to become your dilemma, darling."

Wright puffed himself up like a tomcat preparing for battle. "Listen, smart-mouth. I'm not about to negotiate anything with you. She's the one with the flash drive. And I don't plan on making any more deals to get it. I went to great trouble to clear the slate for you, but I can undo everything I've done and make sure you never work as a private eye."

"That's private investigator," Maxine said.

I smiled at my fiancée-to-be. "Perhaps we aren't dealing at the right level. Mr. Wright, it might be a good idea for you to refer our proposed solution to Mr. Thomas. Where is he anyway? I'd think something of this importance would merit his attention."

Wright had looked flustered. I told you, Agent Thomas is in the field on a very important case. He can't deal with you right now. When the time comes, you will meet him."

"Well, maybe we should just wait until he becomes available,"

I said. "Let's go, Maxine. Joel?"

Wright's face colored again. "Who do you think you are? I'll tell you who you are. A big fat nobody, that's who. You're a plebe who couldn't detect a gas leak with a match. Why don't you just stand in the corner over there and *Go Fish*." He didn't exactly say *Go Fish*, but it was something to that effect.

I looked at Hollywood for help. He sat motionless behind his desk, except for involuntary jerks as he tried to stifle chuckles.

Maxine proved to be more helpful. She suggested Wright play some card games by himself. She apparently knew a few obscure variations of the *Go Fish* game. Joel, ever the doctor's assistant, said he thought what Maxine suggested was physically impossible. I didn't think poorly of Maxine's fixation with cards. It was Mr. Wright who first suggested the game.

Upon hearing Maxine's vast experience with the subject, Wright's whole body began trembling. Those FBI guys have no sense of humor. He stormed out of the office and I thought that was the end of it.

But Hollywood motioned for us to stay and went after him. A few minutes later Wright came back with a cell phone in his hand. He had calmed considerably and we got down to serious negotiations. Wright suggested he would ask the various agencies to consider his recommendations that Maxine be removed from the most wanted lists in exchange for me turning over the flash drive.

At this point I felt it necessary to outline the principles of our new agreement. I told him we would turn over the flash drive when he could assure us all charges would be dropped. Until then, we would keep the flash drive in hopes we could use it to lure more information from Lu Fong about the cloning experiments.

"No way," Wright said. "You are all out of it as of now. No more prying, snooping or investigating into this case. Understand? And I want that flash drive before I leave this office or I'll have a search warrant here in fifteen minutes."

"Go ahead and waste your time," I had said. "If we were in the habit of carrying it around with us, Lu Fong would have gotten it a long time ago."

Wright seemed to consider my bluff as the truth because he sat down and shut up.

Maxine turned on the charm. "Certainly it would be of interest to the FBI to find out if and where any cloning experiments are underway. We might be able to learn to what extent Lu Fong has developed his cloning operation."

Wright didn't like the idea, but he had a difficult time arguing against the logic. I could tell he was wrestling with the idea of suggesting another game of *Go Fish*. Reluctantly, he agreed to contact the multi-agency law enforcement jurisdictions and arrange to clear Maxine of all charges.

Maxine twisted the knife Wright was sure we had stuck in his heart. "I also want your assurance that Max's new credentials, created by the Bureau, will remain intact."

I swear, when he looked at me he had a tear in his eye, but he turned to Maxine and managed a smile. He agreed to her request, and she thanked him and apologized for her unladylike behavior.

I was quite impressed by her actions. Until Wright had suggested that card game, I believed Maxine was almost perfect. Now, I knew she was.

"It's a lovely drive," Maxine said, bringing me back to the present. "I didn't know Oregon was so beautiful."

"Wait until you see the hotel," I said. "It's built on the very top of a hillside overlooking the Columbia Gorge."

"The gorge looks like a big funnel cut into the rugged mountainsides," she said. "It's so large and breathtaking."

Eventually, the road began leading us downward toward Hood River and then unexpectedly we happened upon a rustic sign announcing our destination. A newer driveway took us up a long road and emptied into a dormant garden area. In the middle of the garden area, sat a European L-shaped stucco three-story building with a castle tower rising above the point where the wings intersected. Round pillars supported a square entry with French doors with green trim. Matching green window shutters on the bland yellow building balanced the Spanish rooftop with orange curved clay tiles.

I parked the car in the lot, and Joel and I toted bags toward the lobby. Maxine had gone ahead to admire the marble work in a pond on one side of the lobby. Inside, we were greeted with plush jade colored carpets and late 19th century mauve loveseats and sitting chairs.

A short, skinny man, dressed in a green uniform, struggled to be noticed behind an ornately carved walnut counter. "Do you have reservations?"

I stepped closer so I could see the Leprechaun. A brass name badge affixed to his blazer revealed his name was Lenny. "We have three rooms reserved under the name of Maxwell Starr."

"Oh yes, Mr. Starr. You called earlier this morning, didn't you? Please sign in." The little man pushed a leather-bound book with the word Guests engraved in gold letters.

Maxine selected an old quill pen, dipped it into a fountain of ink and, with a flourish, penned her name in broad strokes. "This is fun. Not many places allow guests to sign in anymore. Almost everything is done by computers."

"Oh, we have computers too." The man pointed at a lower counter behind him to a blue-screened monitor. "The guest book is just to get you into the mood. We like our guests to feel they're getting away from the city."

I took the book from Maxine and signed my name. "Does everyone sign in?"

The little man seemed surprised. "Oh, yes, they must. We won't have any party poopers staying with us."

I looked up the page and recognized two names in the book. One was barely decipherable, but I deduced it was Lu Fong. Under his name was his lovely daughter's. Realizing I might not know all the players in the game, I pushed it between Joel and Maxine.

"Look, honey. Some of our friends have already arrived."

While Maxine took the book and studied it intently, I kept our host busy with small talk about the hotel's amenities. There were some entries written in Chinese script, and I hoped she might recognize the signatures. She shook her head.

"You three wanted separate rooms?" The Lilliputian looked over his shoulder at me in a professional manner. "I have rooms' two-o-seven and two-o-eight in the west wing. The two suites have a door that opens between them. It can be locked from either side. Room two-twelve is available across the hall. Will that be okay?" He was looking at Maxine now.

She blushed and tugged at her tan suede coat. "That will be fine. Mr. Starr and I will take the adjoining rooms."

A few minutes later we entered our rooms. My digs turned out to be the least feminine of the bunch. The carpet was lush with strong hues of pink. A floral design accentuated the pink ceiling. White sponged paint tried to subdue the pink walls. A rugged black fireplace anchored the room with two blue floral wingback chairs on either side. The queen-size bed had a full silk canopy to match the sky-blue floral silk bedspread. After I put my clothes away, I knocked on the partition door and Maxine greeted me.

"Isn't it grand?" she said.

I almost laughed out loud. In the center of her room was a four-poster arched canopy bed. The ornate walnut sideboards matched the headboard and rear-board, which featured a pink velvet embroidered center. The four bedposts twisted awkwardly inward to support a small wood-carved canopy, with more of the pink velvet stuff sewn inside.

It was as gaudy as it was feminine.

"Look at the curved wooden rocking chairs with the floral pads," Maxine said. "And look at the walnut-trimmed tall mirror sitting on arched wooden legs. Isn't it old worldish?"

I sighed. My gaze was frozen on a monstrous looking white marble tabletop, holding a silver coffee setting. The table had pink curved legs with a swirl at the feet. It looked like something from a nursery rhyme. I expected it to run away with the fork and the spoon.

This is just the type of place Lu Fong would pick to stay," Maxine said. "He's very old-fashioned. If he couldn't find a place with an Asian décor, he would settle for the European influence."

A knock rattled the door, and Maxine admitted Joel, who looked sheepish. He glanced around her room and snickered. "Don't get me wrong. This hotel is beautiful, but it's kind of like going to a chick flick. You would only come here because your girl would like it."

Maxine acted hurt. "I don't think it's that bad."

Joel cringed. "If I had a date, it would one thing. But my room is so pink I might as well be stuck holding a woman's purse in the lobby downstairs in front of all those detective types. I couldn't feel more out of place."

I smiled at his awkwardness. "I think if we had made reservations earlier, we could have gotten you a more manly room. But the desk manager said that there are two conventions scheduled here this weekend. We're lucky to get three rooms."

Maxine twisted a swath of hair around her finger. "Did you boys happen to notice what kind of a convention it was?"

Joel's face lightened. "One was called something like the Collective Lecturers Organization of Nature Embryologists."

Maxine chuckled. "I don't think Max saw the placard in the hallway. He was busy dragging my suitcases. If he had seen the name of the other organization, he may have wanted to go home."

It was my turn to take a ribbing again. "I'll bite. What was the other organization?"

Her green eyes glowed. Her cheeks flushed slightly, and she smiled broadly. "It was the Northwest Private Investigator's Annual Conference."

I fell backward onto Maxine's bed, stunned, but she wasn't going to let me off easy. "Gee, Max. Maybe you could sign-up while we're here. I'll bet your friend Mr. Steadman is around somewhere. He could sponsor you."

She laughed a loud and hearty laugh as Joel managed a feeble smile.

"What's wrong Joel?" she asked.

"It just occurred to me. The other organization that's here for a conference?"

"Yes?"

"The one word wasn't Nature, it was Nuclear. The Collective Lecturer's Organization of Nuclear Embryology. And I just realized the acronym would be C.L.O.N.E."

"Clone?" I said.

Maxine plopped onto the bed beside me. Nobody spoke as we gaped at each other.

Chapter 18

It was one o'clock when Joel and I decided to go to the hotel restaurant for lunch. Maxine wanted to visit the gym for a workout, claiming she hadn't worked up a sweat for weeks. I wondered what she called the events of the last few days. Isometrics?

I had a knot in my stomach that needed to be released before I could think of food. "Go ahead and get us a table, Joel. I want to stop by the desk for a minute."

"I may not wait for you," he said. "I'm starving."

I nodded and walked toward the lobby. There was no one at the desk when I arrived. The leather-bound book was open to the page Maxine and I had signed. I flashed back a page and then another. It looked as if more than 100 new people had checked in on the previous day.

Many of the guests were of foreign nationalities. There were signatures in French, German, Italian and Chinese. Interspersed with the odd nationalities were the periodic Tom Dent, Jack Spaulding, and Lisa Roberts. I stumbled upon a Lew Archer, Lindsey Kilhone, and a couple of Sam Spades.

Instead of Smith or Jones, some of the private investigators used a literary alias. As others checked in, some of them noticed the joke and added their own crime fighting alias. If the desk clerk were to scrutinize the guest book he would find a Who's Who of crime-fighting derivatives staying at the hotel.

This didn't help me. I was looking for a particular name. And although Steadman wasn't listed, he could have used one of the pseudonyms, although I doubted he read much. I sighed and turned away from the book.

"Can I help you?" I turned and saw the tiny desk clerk, who

seemed to appear out of nowhere. He might have been there all along when you considered his size.

"Ah, I'm looking for one of your guests. His name is John Steadman, but I didn't see his signature in the book."

Lenny the Leprechaun seemed indignant. "Everyone signs in. I make sure of that."

"That may be, Lenny, but don't any of your guests wish to remain discreet?"

He huffed. "Well, they must sign in."

His lack of imagination assured me he wouldn't recognize any of the fictitious celebrities he had staying at the hotel. "Do you remember a man checking in yesterday? He was well built, medium sized, square head, red crew cut hair, winning smile?"

"Yes, I do. That would be Mr. Spade."

I smiled to myself. "That figures. Could you give me his room number?"

The little man's smile turned sarcastic. "I could. But maybe you'd rather turn around and ask him yourself."

A thickness closed in on me. It was like I was standing in the middle of a high-pressure storm system. I turned slowly to see Steadman's square face, his sparkling blue eyes and his enormous smile.

"Well, isn't this a small world," he said. "Have you been avoiding me? I stopped back at your place yesterday. What a mess. You should fire that housekeeper of yours."

My legs became unsteady as I prepared for the worst. "Hello, Steadman. Let's not make a fuss here in the hotel lobby."

"I don't plan on making a fuss," he said. "At least, not at the moment. I'd like to. I'd really like to. But I have to give a speech in a few minutes. Maybe later."

My chin dropped as I watched Sam Spade walk down the hall. I turned toward Lenny, who was still grinning. "Where are the conference rooms?"

"They're in the east wing on the first floor. We try to segregate our conference guests from our other patrons. Most of the conference attendees' rooms are also in the east wing. It's a shorter commute to the meeting rooms for them and the parties don't wake our guests in the west wing."

"I'm in the west wing," I said.

"Yes, you are. Would you like me to see if I can find a room in the east wing, closer to Mr. Spade?"

I looked at him suspiciously. "No thanks. I'm not much of a party person." I turned and walked toward the restaurant.

"Mr. Starr, if you change your mind . . ."

I kept walking into the restaurant where I wound up on the end of another surprise. A young black-haired woman in a sexy long black dress was engaged in an animated discussion with Joel. I could tell he was enjoying himself. The girl playfully stroked his arm in an intimate gesture as she laughed. She turned as I approached and gave me a warm smile.

My knees wobbled as I crossed the floor. "Hello, Kay Lu. I see you've met Joel."

"Max, darling, we were just talking about you. I remembered him as that dashing young man who appeared out of nowhere at my farmhouse and whisked you and Maxine away. He's simply delicious. I hope you aren't going to make me give him back."

"He's old enough to make his own decisions."

Joel grinned. "Hi, Max. Say, Kay Lu's not such a bad egg. She was just telling me how she was acting on her father's orders. She says he's holding her inheritance over her head to get her to do his dirty work."

Kay Lu flipped a portion of her silky long hair off her face with the back of her hand and pouted. "It's true, Max. I must have been mad. I could have been arrested for that stunt. I hope you will forgive me. I have been under so much stress. Father will do anything to get that flash drive back from Maxine. Even to the point of putting his own daughter into jail."

I smiled sardonically. "That's not exactly the way I remember it. It seems to me you wanted to get out from under his flash, all right. But I remember you had some very definite plans about striking out on your own."

"I was so confused. I was afraid of what would happen to me if I failed Father. I might have misspoken, but I am telling you now that I wish you no harm."

"Are you working with your father now?"

"Yes. But he said he would not ask me to do anything illegal again. He just wants to try to persuade Maxine to give the flash drive back. I told him he has my loyalty, but I will not help him if he tries to hurt you or Maxine."

"That's a relief. I feel so much better."

"Come on, Max, you're not giving her a chance," Joel said. "I believe her."

"Okay, Kay Lu. Everyone deserves a second chance."

Joel's face seemed relieved. I noticed he was holding her hand now. They were gazing into each other's eyes. I looked around the room to see if I fit in with the rest of the furniture. When they remembered I was still there, I asked Kay Lu if she knew her father's plans toward Maxine. She said she didn't.

"I've got to join him at his conference, Kay Lu said. "Joel, are we on for dinner and drinks tonight?"

"You bet. What time?"

"Meet me at my room at a quarter to seven. Room three-twenty in the east wing. Max, you and Maxine will come to dinner too? Father said he was meeting with you tonight."

"We'll be here. Seven o'clock?"

"Yes, darling." She flipped her hair once more for good measure, kissed Joel's hand and walked gracefully out of the restaurant.

"How did you manage to hook up with Kay Lu?"

"I didn't hook up with her. She was sitting at a table over there." He pointed to a table near the window overlooking the hotel gardens. A short young Chinese man at the table turned away when I looked toward him.

"She was sitting with that guy in the brown suit," Joel said. "I was watching her--she's so pretty—and she caught me, I guess. Without a word she got up and walked over and asked to join me. I said sure and then wondered if her friend was going to come over and make a scene. But he acted like he didn't care."

I looked back toward the window in time to see the man in the brown suit leaving a tip for the waitress. In the next instant he was gone. "Did Kay Lu tell you the name of her friend?"

"No, she said he was a business associate of hers from Hong Kong who was here for the convention."

"Did she say what the convention was about?"

Joel looked down at his menu. "I told the waitress I was waiting for a friend. She must have gone on a break or something."

"Joel?"

"I meant to ask her as soon as she told me who she was," Joel said. "I guess I got distracted."

"Did you learn anything?"

"Not really. She went into this big explanation about what happened in Camas, and I guess I forgot why we were here. She did most of the talking. I just listened."

I lifted my eyebrows in a mock reprimand. "She works fast. We were apart for five minutes and sparks were flying all over the place when I got here."

"She smiled at me, and we flirted a little," Joel said. "I don't believe everything she told me, but I'd like to give her the benefit of the doubt until I catch her lying."

I let it go. Joel hadn't criticized me for my sudden choice of professions or my wanting to pursue a woman who was so out-of-my-league. Kay Lu was pretty, charming and displayed sincerity in her apology for what happened with Maxine and me. I would wait and talk with Maxine, who knew her much better than I did. I wanted her opinion before I got into an argument with my best friend. What harm could come of it? Besides, nothing I was going to say would change his mind.

Eventually the waitress made an appearance and we ordered soup and salad for lunch. Periodically I looked over at the window table the Chinese gentleman occupied earlier, wondering what he and Kay Lu were talking about.

After lunch, Joel talked me into a brisk walk around the grounds. I figured Maxine would need time to get dressed after her workout, so I agreed. We were standing under the west wing of the building when I happened to glance up at a figure inside a window on the second floor.

"Joel, look up there." I pointed to the window as the lace curtains closed ranks around the man I'd seen standing inside.

Joel squinted into the sunlight. "What? I don't see anything."

"I saw a man close the drapes in the window above us on the second floor."

"So?"

"I think that's Maxine's room. Why would a man be inside her room?"

Joel squinted again. "It could be her room, I guess. I don't see anyone now."

"I think we should go and make sure she's all right," I said, and hurried toward the entrance.

Joel quickened his pace while trying to look at his watch. "It's a quarter after two. She might not have finished her workout yet."

"All the more reason to go up there. Someone could be lying in wait for her."

"Yeah," Joel said. "She could be in real danger here. She's been a kidnapping target twice already."

"It'll be my fault if she gets hurt because she's carrying that bad flash drive."

Joel was trying to keep up. "What do you mean bad flash drive?"

I didn't answer him because I was busy concentrating on what to do when we got to her room. Joel grabbed my arm as we entered the elevator.

"Max, what's this about Maxine having a phony flash drive?"

I avoided looking him in the eye. "Last night I was worried she might give the it to Scott Hess. I didn't trust him so I sort of dropped it into the toilet before we left your place."

"But she told me she gave Scott a blank flash drive. So she knew?

"No. She's smarter than I thought. I didn't expect her to slip him an empty store-bought flash drive, and during our little talk this morning I forgot to tell her about my little deception last night."

"You mean you chickened out."

I smiled feebly. "Joel, do you think I'm afraid of a pretty little redhead after facing the likes of Steadman and Kay Lu's friend, Wong?"

"Scared to death," he said.

And he was right.

"You've really fallen for her," he said.

I watched the light on the door panel as the elevator finally approached the second floor. "I guess I have. I've never known anyone like her before."

"What about Barbara?"

"Who?"

"Barbara, your ex-wife. The one you still carry the torch for even though she cheated on you? Oh, you *do* have it bad."

The elevator door opened and we ran down the hall toward Maxine's room. I listened at her door for sounds, but heard nothing. We stepped back to my room door, and I slid a card key into a brass slot mounted on the door. It clicked and I quietly turned the handle and pushed the door open.

Joel followed me inside and discreetly closed the door as I approached the adjoining entrance to her room. We stood motionless and strained our ears against the mahogany passageway.

"I don't hear anything," Joel whispered.

"Quiet, just listen."

We listened so hard I forgot to breathe from time-to-time. I thought I heard a rustling inside the room, followed by a distinct thud as if something fell to the floor.

"Maxine might be in trouble," Joel said.

I motioned him away from the door and gestured toward the phone. "Call her room. Maybe we can avoid making fools of ourselves."

"What if she doesn't answer? Or what if someone else answers?"

I shrugged. "I suppose nobody's going to be surprised if I burst in, guns blazing."

"Do you have a gun?"

"Are you kidding? Not after the way Hollywood screamed at me. Guns blazing was just a figure of speech. Now, make the call."

I put my ear to the door as Joel called the desk. The phone in Maxine's room rang relentlessly until I couldn't distinguish it from the ringing in my ears. Joel hung up the receiver and walked back toward me, and we looked at each other in anticipation. My side of the door was unlatched. I hoped Maxine trusted me enough to leave her side unlocked.

I turned the doorknob slowly and pushed. The hinges creaked loud enough to be heard at the bell desk. The door had opened about half an inch when I heard the distinct noise of a bedspring recoiling. Images of a stranger having his way with Maxine shot through my mind.

I bashed against the door with both hands and charged into the room with Joel on my heels. Lying on the bed in a blue suit, sans jacket and shoes, and wearing a broad smile and a gun holster over his unbuttoned vest, was Agent Scott Hess. At the exact same moment, Maxine, wearing nothing but a large white hotel towel, was ushered from the bathroom by a gust of steam.

"Scott, dear . . ." She stopped, realizing someone else was in the room. Hess took her vision in and smiled. His stupid grin lasted well into the time it took her to notice me.

"Max, Joel, what are you two doing here?" Maxine said.

Joel made an annoying ticking noise with his tongue he does when he gets excited or nervous. Maxine stood dripping wet and revealing more about herself than a girl should.

I draped my arms across my chest. "I might ask the same question. We came to check on your safety, but apparently you're in good hands."

Chapter 19

Maxine summed up the situation quickly, and just as adroitly, she handled it.

"Good. You're all together and you've all seen more than is good for you. So why don't you go next door and give a girl a chance to get dressed. Go on, shoo."

I was still waiting for an explanation.

Instead, she offered an indifferent look. "I don't know what you're so startled about, Max. You must know by now how uninhibited I am. Remember Wednesday night at your house when Joel came over? Same attire as I'm wearing now. A real fashion blunder, I know, to be caught wearing the same outfit twice in four days. Now, get out of here so I can get dressed. I'll be over in a few minutes, and we can talk."

Hess chuckled to himself as he gathered his shoes and jacket. Joel was grinning too. My sour mood followed us out of her room. We sat down in chairs around a table near my bedroom window.

Hess shook hands with Joel. "I'm FBI Agent Scott Hess."

"Oh," Joel said, not trying too hard to avert a snicker.

"What are you laughing at?" I said.

Joel erupted. "You. Your eyes almost bugged out when you saw Maxine in that towel and him on her bed."

Hess's penetrating eyes summed up the situation immediately. "So *there is* something between them."

"Oh yeah," Joel said.

"That explains why she hit me so hard that night in the Buddhist temple. She was cross because I hit you."

I managed a feeble smile at his belated conclusion. "What were you doing in her room anyway?"

"Look pal, I just came to ask for her help. I'm at a dead-end, and I have a feeling my boss is about get me fired over this business with Kay Lu and her father. I need to get that flash drive from her to clear myself. The one she gave me last night was blank."

"She must not trust you," I said. "So, did you show it to Thomas?"

"Thankfully no. That was a rotten thing to do. I would have been dead meat if I'd given it to him without previewing it."

"How did Thomas find out that Maxine has the drive?"

"Does he know? I haven't told anybody. I don't trust anyone in the Bureau right now. Besides, I don't even know what's on the damn thing. All I know is, it's something Lu Fong must want pretty bad because he's been chasing after it ever since Maxine left Hong Kong."

So what I'm wondering about now is not why everyone is chasing us, nor where the mysterious agent Thomas fits in, not even if we're going to be able rescue Maxine from the big bad Feds who wanted to put her in jail. No, I'm wondering if this guy's interest in Maxine is more than professional or, worse, if Maxine has a crush on this agitated, quick tempered, athletic looking jerk.

After a few minutes of awkward silence, Joel spoke. "So, where did you and Maxine meet?"

Hess leaned back in a chair. "We were high school sweethearts. She was this flighty daughter of some big-time movie producer, and I was planning a career with the FBI. We dated for a year into college, and I was thinking about marriage."

The revelation that he almost asked her to marry him made me more resentful and jealous. I suspected there may still have been a romantic spark between them, but had discounted it after meeting him at the Buddhist temple. He was too straight-laced and serious. Maxine's carefree attitude was a mismatch.

Hess grinned at the memory. "She kept getting into trouble. She was a big activist for animal rights causes. She was arrested a couple of times for breaking into cosmetic labs in the Los Angeles area."

"Right in character for our Maxine," Joel said. That must have been tough on you, an FBI agent in the making."

"Exactly," Hess said. "I went through a series of background checks just to get into the training academy. Maxine's forays into crime were jeopardizing my career."

"I'll bet you guys fought a lot." Joel seemed to be enjoying this.

"Yeah, but we had our good times too." Hess's eyes darted to my sour expression.

I stood up and walked over to the hospitality bar. Was three o'clock too early in the day for a drink? I bought a bottle of rum and a coke. After several minutes of awkward silence and another drink, Maxine appeared at the door in a simple bluish dress wearing a gold chain with a heart-shaped diamond pendant.

"Are you all friends, yet? If not, I'm leaving."

"They haven't come to blows," Joel said. "Come back in a few minutes."

She walked over to my bed and sat on it, carefully crossing her legs. "No more fighting boys. Scott, I'm curious. How did you find us here?"

"I followed Ned Wright to the Sheriff's Office," he said. "I heard Thomas telling Ned he was to take his place in a meeting he set up with you and Maxine. I didn't realize we were going away for the weekend or I would have brought a change of clothes."

"So why did you follow us?" Joel asked.

"I figured she might still have the flash drive. I'm here to ask you guys to help me."

"Look, Starr, I'm sorry about my tough-guy routine with you" Hess said. "I've been frustrated and edgy. Someone has set me up to take the fall on the Lu Fong investigation, and I've gotten nowhere in the last couple of weeks."

I listened to the tone of his voice as he spoke. It sounded gravelly and jagged, and his appearance had suffered too. His tie was uneven, and the wrinkles in his blue suit jacket blended with the worry lines in his face. He caught me observing him and sat up suddenly and straightened his coat.

"Wright says he thinks you tipped off Kay Lu that he was going to raid her father's restaurant," I said.

Hess stood up and banged his palms on the table. "Thomas told him that? They're wrong; I didn't tell her anything."

Maxine put her hands over his. "Calm down, Scott. Tell us what happened."

Hess flinched at Maxine's touch and looked at me. "Did Wright tell you I was against the raid?"

I nodded.

"We knew there was a lab of sorts in the basement. And that they were performing experiments with animals somewhere, but they never brought animals to the restaurant or to the lab in the basement. All I ever saw were men in white coats standing in front of test tubes or microscopes.

"I asked Kay Lu what they were doing. She said they were working on new low-fat recipes that would revolutionize the Chinese food industry. It was lame, but it was hard to refute. They had dried noodles and canned food stacked on shelves to dress it up, but I never heard of using petri dishes to culture recipes."

"Tell us about the raid," Maxine said. "How do you think were they tipped off?"

"Well, someone told them, but it wasn't me. I was the fall guy because I was the only one who spoke against the raid. I tended bar the night before we planned to hit the club with a search warrant.

"We were closing up and Kay Lu came down and started chatting me up. She poured me a drink and started flirting. She hadn't done that before. I thought it might be the break we were looking for. I thought if I could get closer to Kay Lu I might really learn something."

I looked over at Joel and noticed his formerly impish face now appeared gloomy.

Hess picked up a hotel pen and tapped at the table. "All I could think about was what a mistake it was to raid the place. I thought maybe I could talk my superior, Ken Thomas, out of the raid. I thought maybe I could cultivate a romantic relationship with Kay Lu.

"We had a few more drinks and talked. She wanted to know about my family, my schooling, and why I was tending bar. I had a cover story, but for some reason I had a hard time focusing in her presence. I tried to switch the conversation toward her, but she didn't want to talk anymore. She wanted to dance."

Joel stiffened. "So you guys danced? Then what?"

Hess smiled lightly. "She smelled like Jasmine. She wore a sexy, short black dress with slits up her hips. I just went along with her. We danced and had another drink. I don't remember what happened next."

"Why not?" Joel snapped.

Hess responded to the tone of Joel's voice. "Because I passed out. I woke up to shouts of 'Freeze, we're the FBI.' I looked up through a stupor and said, 'so am I.' The next thing I knew Thomas was looming over me. 'What are you doing here?' he says. 'Why weren't you at the briefing this morning? Where have you been?'

"When I told him about my drinking with Kay Lu and passing out, he hit the roof. He said I must have tipped her off. I told him I didn't tell her anything. He said I must have blabbed while we were drinking.

"What could I do, Maxine? She might have become suspicious if I refused to drink with her. I only had two drinks and I was sober. She must have put something in my glass."

"It's more likely, you just couldn't handle your liquor," Joel said.

"Joel, why don't you go downstairs and get the agendas for the conference tomorrow," I suggested. "I think we should attend a few sessions to see if we can learn anything." I was aware of my friend's feelings, but he was getting in the way of our investigation.

Joel didn't say a word. He stood up and walked out of the room.

"What was that all about?" Hess asked.

"Joel has a crush on Kay Lu," I said.

"What?" Maxine said. "That's crazy. Why would he have a crush on Kay Lu?"

"He met her in the restaurant at lunch before I joined him. She told him a sob story about how her father made her kidnap you. She gave us this gushy apology and begged forgiveness. Joel forgave her."

Maxine's look cut through me. "And did you forgive her too?"

"I gave her the benefit of the doubt until I could talk with you."

"You gave her too much," Maxine said. "She's the devil, Max. She can't be trusted. Do you hear me?"

I couldn't resist the urge to tease. "I didn't think she was that bad. She seemed sincere."

Maxine appeared at a momentary loss for words.

"She seemed fairly decent to me too, at first," Hess said. "If she hadn't been the subject of our investigation, I never would have suspected her of anything more than coming on a little too strong with men."

"You guys are idiots," Maxine sputtered. "A pretty girl smiles and flips her hair, and you all melt like ice cream on a hot sidewalk. This woman is evil, and she must be stopped. Don't let her innocent smile, push-up bra, and revealing legs fool you. She'll do anything to get what she wants."

"I was kidding." I took her hand and stroked it. "I know she's not to be trusted. Joel seems to have fallen under her spell, and I didn't have the heart to confront him."

"I'll take care of that," she said. "When he gets back, I'll sit him down and have a talk with him."

"While you are figuring out how to deal with the love-struck boy, why don't you let me take a look at your flash drive?" Hess said. "Maybe I can figure out what's going on if I could look at it."

"I'm not ready to turn it over yet," Maxine said.

"Shit, Maxine. Give me a fuckin' break. You passed off a blank drive for me to take back to my boss. Do you know what would have happened to me if I'd given it to him? I'd be teaching recruits at Quantico."

"I'm sorry, Scott, but I'm not ready to give it up, just yet. Something just doesn't feel right."

Call me a softy, but I felt sorry for Hess, and I believed him. I decided to take a chance and told him most of what we had learned. I explained our theory that Lu Fong might be at the center of a plot to pass on new technology that could lead to cloning of humans. I told to him we were at the hotel to try to learn if and where Lu Fong's cloning experiments were being conducted. I told him and Maxine about the Chinese guy, in the brown suit, I saw in the restaurant who had been talking with Kay Lu, and I briefed Hess about the cloning formula on the flash drive and how it may be the only copy of the formula in existence.

Each time I parted with one of these gems, Hess's expression became more amazed. Thomas had told him nothing. Hess leaned back in the chair when I was done and reflected on what I'd said.

His face displayed nervous energy in the form of active brows and facial tics. His eyes glistened as the machinery behind them worked. Finally he sat up, and for the first time he seemed at ease.

"This all starts to make sense," he said. "The stakes are higher than I imagined. Thomas didn't tell us anything about cloning. According to him, our investigation was about illegal experiments with animals that crossed state lines. The cloning angle opens up a whole new world.

"You've been quite successful, Max. I underestimated you, I think. So where do we go from here?"

"Yes, Max, where?" Maxine said. "You said you might have an idea."

I cracked my knuckles. "We've been kept in the dark through all of this while Lu Fong and his daughter have held all of the cards. I think it's time we dealt ourselves in.

"Tonight Maxine and I will have dinner with Lu Fong. Our story will be that we don't have the cloning formula with us, but we can get it. The implication being it's back in Portland.

"I'd like to let him think we're going to make a deal. We'll tell him the FBI and the cops are threatening us with jail time, and we'd just as soon get rid of the damn thing and be rewarded for it. Maxine, do you think they'd buy that story?"

"Perhaps," she said. "It might be more believable if I insisted on keeping the list of so-called traitors. He's aware of my views on human rights. My wanting to keep the list might move him into believing your yarn."

"Good," I said. "Hess, you'd better stay out of sight. Kay Lu might see you. You can room with me tonight and tomorrow we can put you to work. I'm thinking both father and daughter are attending the convention. I'd like to check their rooms tomorrow."

"Maybe Scott could do that tonight during dinner," Maxine said.

"I'm not sure that would be a good idea," Hess said. "If I get caught without a search warrant, all hell could break loose for me and the bureau."

"I think it's best to wait until tomorrow," I said. "We'll have a better lay of the land, and I'll have some time to corrupt Hess. I have a few ideas."

Hess nodded.

Maxine stood up, walked to the door, opened it and stepped

into the hallway. In a minute she returned. "I knocked on Joel's door, but there was no answer. I need to set him straight about Kay Lu when he comes back."

But Joel didn't come back. We didn't see him again until dinner and by then it was too late.

Chapter 20

"You shouldn't have told him everything," she said.

"Why not?" I said.

Maxine made a sour face. "I used to love him dearly, but I don't know if I can trust him anymore. You shouldn't have told him everything."

"If he's on the level, he needs to know what's going on. Obviously Thomas has kept him in the dark. If he isn't legit, he probably knows everything already."

"Maybe Thomas has a reason for not telling him. You shouldn't have told him everything."

"I thought Scott was a long lost boyfriend of yours. Suddenly you don't trust him?"

"I haven't seen him for years. There are too many things I don't know about him anymore. He's changed and . . ."

I looked around Maxine's ultra-feminine room. She had asked me in for this private talk, and now she wasn't making sense. "And what?"

"He says he still loves me. He wants to marry me. I told him I don't have feelings anymore for him." Her eyes flashed with excitement. "I told him there was someone else."

"Who? I mean what did he say?"

"He said he would solve this case and prove himself to me. He won't give up, Max, and I wouldn't put it past him to try to implicate you in something to give himself a clear path."

"I shouldn't have told him everything."

It occurred to me that I might need some help in the next 24 hours. I picked up the phone and dialed a Portland number. "Hello, this is Max. I've got a proposition for you."

It was nearly seven o'clock as I primped before the bathroom mirror. My suite was large enough that it offered me enough privacy to dress while Hess flipped channels on the television. I adjusted a busy gold silk tie and retrieved my Harris Tweed sports jacket from its hanger. The coat exaggerated my physique. I ditched the tie. Maxine would be impressed.

Earlier, she and I tried to track down Joel in the hotel, but he was not to be found. Maxine knocked at his door several times without success. We guessed he was sulking because of our comments about Kay Lu and figured he would join us for dinner since she would be there.

After dressing, I left my room by the hallway door because I didn't want Scott following me into Maxine's room. I rapped on her door and waited. The peephole clouded and the door opened slowly, revealing a statuesque model in a bright red evening gown. Her crimson hair cascaded on bare white shoulders and a simple gold necklace hugged her long neck. A nervous titter betrayed her as she spoke. "Hi, I'm almost ready."

She retreated, and I followed. The room seemed different. Clothes were strewn over chairs, the bed and the dresser. She caught me looking at the mess.

"I'm sorry. I had a difficult time deciding what to wear."

"Understandable. You pack a lot of luggage."

"I wanted to look carefree, yet assertive when we meet Lu Fong tonight. It's not too bold is it?"

I was distracted by her boldness. "You look great."

As I watched her run her hands over her hips in front of the mirror, it occurred to me she had something on her mind. And for some reason I wasn't in a hurry to find out what.

"Max, we're straight with each other, aren't we? I mean, there's nothing else you haven't told me, is there?"

I hate it when my intuition is right. I looked at her questioning green eyes and held her hands. It was time to come clean. "There is one thing I haven't told you. The, ah, flash drive you have? Well, ah, it's probably not good anymore."

"What are you talking about? What's wrong with it?"

"I sort of dropped it in the toilet the other night. I was afraid you might give it to Scott. I didn't trust him."

She sized me up for a minute, saying nothing. The tension inside me nearly burst an artery while I waited for her to explode.

"Do you have another copy?"

"Yes."

More than one copy?"

'Just the one."

"Where is it?"

"I'm sorry. I should have trusted you." I opened my tweed jacket and fingered an inside pocket opening.

"I'm not the sweet, innocent, little girl I must appear to you," she said.

"I know now."

"Any other little secrets?"

"No."

"When were you going to tell me about this?"

"Now."

"Would drowning the damn thing destroy everything on it?"

I nodded. "Probably. There may be some retrievable data, but probably not enough to put together the cloning formula. If someone tries to use it before it dries, it would cook the thing.

She walked over to a laptop on a table and picked up the flash drive. She held it up to me and I could see the blackened metal plug-in receptacle.

"Uh, you tried to use it?" I asked.

"I nearly fried myself and my computer," she said. "I thought I had done something wrong, but then, knowing you, well . . ."

"Sorry?" I said.

She stared at the burnt flash drive in her fingers for a moment and a slight grin surfaced. "I can't figure you out. Why didn't you just tell me not to give it to Scott?"

"I suggested it was a bad idea."

"Okay," she said. "I know you did. But if we're going to get anywhere we have to be able to trust each other. No more secrets."

"I agree. From now on, we're a team."

And that was that. A few minutes later we strolled down the hallway arm-in-arm toward the elevator.

"I wish we could call this whole thing off, just for tonight," she said. I smiled and pushed the button. We embraced in the empty elevator, and I felt my heart pounding against hers as we descended.

"Are you going up?" a voice said. I looked over to see a smirking elderly lady in a loose-knitted yellow sweater who had stepped in unnoticed during our embrace, and we left with lightly red faces. The dark ambiance of the hotel restaurant hid my still flushed face, but it became warmer as my eyes adjusted to a sight through the restaurant window.

"I know where Joel has been all day."

"Where?" Maxine asked.

I nodded toward the table I'd seen the Chinese gentleman sitting at earlier. Kay Lu and Joel were holding hands, and Joel was saying something into her ear as they leaned into each other.

"Don't they look cute?" Maxine said, in a voice laced with venom.

I watched them paw over each other. "She's hooked him good."

I started toward their table, but Maxine grabbed my arm. "Don't. He'll only become more enamored with her. The best thing we can do for now is nothing. Besides, Lu Fong is here."

She pointed over to a large table where two men sat. One was the elderly oriental gentleman I'd met at the Hilton. He wore a dark suit with a black shirt and a solid blue tie. He seemed irritated with another man wearing a tan suit. As we walked toward them, I recognized Lu Fong's guest.

Maxine stopped in her tracks, her hand still firmly affixed to my coat sleeve. "Max that man talking to Lu Fong. Do you know who he is?"

"Yeah, he's the guy I told you about earlier. He's the one talking to Kay Lu at lunch."

"He's one of the Chinese ambassadors who visited Lu Fong regularly at his office. His name is Wei Ming. He's an awful man."

We were still 20 feet from the table as I gazed at them. "Lu Fong doesn't seem too thrilled with him either. Shall we interrupt them?"

She trembled and clung to my arm as we walked toward trouble.

The man in the tan suit scrutinized me carefully as we approached. He said something in Chinese to Lu Fong and turned back to us. "Miss Andrews, how good it is to see you again." He gestured for her to sit.

"I hope you don't mind," Lu Fong said, managing a half-hearted smile. Kay Lu and her friend will not be joining us. They seem to want to be left alone. Oh, how thoughtless of me not to introduce you to each other. This is Maxine's associate, Mr. Max Starr. Mr. Starr, this is Wei Ming. He is a colleague of mine from the Republic of China."

I nodded at the tan suit, but he dismissed me with curt eyes.

"Maxine, I've heard that you have been a nuisance to Lu Fong," he said. "You have something of his that rightfully belongs to me."

"So much for small talk," I said.

He ignored me. "I understand you have a computer flash drive that has a certain formula on it. I wish to have that flash drive. Did you bring it with you?"

This guy was already rubbing me the wrong way. "Look, Wei, She doesn't have the flash drive, and we didn't bring it with us. We can have it here within a few hours, but we came to discuss a monetary deal with Lu Fong, not you."

Wei Ming grabbed Maxine's wrist. "Miss Andrews, you had better give me the flash drive, now!"

I lunged forward and caught Wei by the arm, squeezing it for emphasis. He winced and released his grasp on Maxine. His eyes were black and ruthless. He wasn't tall, but I saw girth in his build when he stood up. We wrestled for control, his limb still firmly in my hand. Our arms trembled as he tried to break free.

Lu Fong became agitated. "Stop it, both of you. We are in a public place. We must show decorum."

I released Wei. He ignored his bruised arm, staring into my eyes, and his glare pierced me more than any blow. Anger and loathing roiled within him and for the fourth time since I entered this business, I was scared.

"Where I come from, we don't manhandle ladies," I managed to say to him.

We sat down with him still glaring maniacally at me, and I looked away to Maxine's friendly eyes for reassurance.

"We come from different cultures," Lu Fong said. "I would remind Wei Ming we are not in his country. This culture is much different."

Wei's eyes lifted a bit and his lips formed a look of superiority. It was a nasty smile and again my heart grew heavy.

"I must apologize, Miss Andrews. I have been rude. But you see, Lu Fong and I have been working together in a partnership. He has offered to sell me his formula."

I looked at Lu Fong. He was sedentary, willing to allow Wei Ming to do the talking, managing only to occasionally squirm in his chair.

"Are you saying we must deal with you?" I asked.

"You begin to grasp the situation. I understand Lu Fong has offered you money."

"One hundred thousand dollars," I said.

"Unfortunately, that deal is no longer available. However, I do have something else to offer. Perhaps worth more than the money you mentioned."

He reached into a vest pocket and fished something from it. He tucked the object in his fist and tossed a shiny metallic ring onto the table.

Maxine gasped. "Father." A man's ring wobbled on the table. I saw the gold letters C-F inset on the ring-face when it settled, and I remembered George Andrews was a producer of Climatic Films.

Lu Fong looked away from Maxine's scornful eyes and stared at his table setting. Wei Ming's sneer grew larger.

"Yes, Miss Andrews. Lu Fong and his daughter Kay Lu have made such a mess of things that I am forced to take matters into my own hands. You see, I have offered to make them both rich beyond their wildest dreams, but they continue to bungle things.

"I think someone may always offer you more money, but no one will be able to replace your father. I met him last night on his way out of the Hilton Hotel and persuaded him to join me. He is safe and in close proximity."

"You swine." Maxine stood up, walked around the table and pummeled Wei Ming's chest with her fists. He jumped to his feet to meet her onslaught and tried to repel her blows with his hands. Stunned, I managed to snap myself out of my lethargic state and join the melee. I managed to retrieve a wine bottle from her before she could christen Wei Ming's head.

"Let me go. I'll kill him. I'll kill you too, Lu Fong." She shook her fist at him. "I should have known better than to trust you to be civilized."

The crowd in the restaurant was loud, but a few patrons near us turned at the racket. Lu Fong tugged at his colleague to sit down. I dragged Maxine back to her chair and tried to soothe her.

Wei Ming spoke through clenched teeth. "I am tired of this. You will have the formula here by one o'clock tomorrow. If you don't, Mr. Andrews will not join you again in this life." He brushed by a surprised waiter, who managed to keep a tray of drinks from splattering to the floor, and tramped out of the restaurant.

The waiter turned toward us. He wore a white kitchen apron over a dress shirt and tie and a ready smile. His salt and pepper hair glistened against the candlelight. "Is everything all right here?"

Maxine gasped at the waiter and caught herself.

"We are all fine," Lu Fong said. "My friend is a little high-strung. He needs to rest."

The waiter winked at me. "We all suffer from stress from one time to another. I hope your friend wasn't upset with the service. We've been very busy tonight."

"We are in no hurry," Lu Fong said.

"Good, I'll be back in a minute with your menus."

After the waiter departed Lu Fong spoke abruptly. "I am sorry for this, Maxine. I had nothing to do with the kidnapping of your father. I would have preferred to handle this as a simple cash transaction.

"Wei Ming is under much pressure from his government. He will pay me a substantial sum of money for the formula. If I oppose him, he has told me harm will come to Kay Lu. I have no choice. I promise you I will see he keeps his word about the safe return of your father."

"I don't believe you," Maxine wiped a tear from her eye with a table napkin. "First you get your daughter to kidnap me. Now you have my father kidnapped. This game is too similar not to be yours."

Lu Fong became rigid. His brown eyes seemed tired, but earnest. "Maxine, I have not done many things in my life that would please Buddha. But I am old and wish to quit my ways. I have funded researchers in the hope of selling a formula to the highest bidder.

"The Chinese government became aware of my activities and has promised me a great amount of money. I would retire and give my daughter enough riches to keep her from the life I have lived."

"She doesn't seem to want your help," I said.

"This is true. She has become rebellious. She thinks I want to control her because I don't want her involved in a life of crime. She also seeks the formula. I suspect that is why she is being nice to your friend."

I glanced toward Joel. "Are you saying it was her idea to kidnap Maxine, not yours?"

"Yes," Lu Fong said.

"Then, who was it who shot Maxine at the Buddhist Temple?" I asked.

Maxine regained her composure.

"Yes. Who?"

Lu Fong's eyes again fell to the table. "That was my doing. But I told no one to shoot you. I told them to get the formula at any cost and bring it to me. The fools panicked when you didn't have it. They told me you made a move to attack them and the gun went off. They thought you were dead, so they hid your body and left."

I shifted in my seat. "And when you learned what happened, what did you do?"

"I returned with them to the temple, of course."

"Did you follow us home?"

"No," he said. "We were involved in an auto accident."

This caused me to smile. "Was Kay Lu with you?"

"No."

"Where was she that night?"

"I don't know. She was on her own. If you don't mind, I am growing weary. Perhaps we can talk tomorrow. I have to give a lecture at ten-thirty in the morning and I will be free afterward. You can come and listen to my lecture or meet me later."

"We'll let you know," I said.

He rose from the table and bowed. I watched him as he observed Joel and Kay Lu. They were deeply engrossed in each other and didn't notice the old man's melancholy eye.

Maxine watched after Lu Fong, who seemed much older than

the last time I'd met him, as he slowly paced out of the room. A stoic demeanor concealed her rage.

"We're going to have to do something," she said under her breath. "I won't have my father hurt."

"I know. I think we'd better give them the flash drive. Your father's safety must come first."

She mustered a smile and hugged me. "I don't know what I would do without you right now."

"But not tonight. Tomorrow will be better."

"But Max, we can't wait."

"It wouldn't be safe to try and rescue him tonight. They could kill him and escape into the night. Give me a chance to figure something out so he'll be safe."

She nodded. We stayed and ate dinner. Neither of had much of an appetite. It was eight o'clock when Joel and Kay Lu approached.

"There's a band playing in one of the convention rooms," Joel said. "Kay Lu says it's open to all hotel guests. Drinks and dancing. Want to come?"

I looked up at Kay Lu. She wore a dark blue evening dress with a plunging neckline. Her feathered bangs artfully outlined her young face. Her black earnest eyes pleaded with us not to come.

"I don't think so, Joel, but I need to talk with you tonight. It's important."

"Well, gee. I'd like to, Max, but we have a busy evening planned. Can't it wait until tomorrow morning?"

Maxine tugged at my arm. "Yes, Joel. Tomorrow will be fine. I think we might join you at the party later. Wouldn't that be fun, Max?"

"Huh. Yeah, I guess."

As Kay Lu hurried Joel along with a strong-arm hold, I turned to Maxine. "Why did you say that?"

"Say what?" Maxine asked.

"We need to get Joel away from her. The more he's with her, the more difficult it will be."

"Oh, it will be simple," she said. "I'm more worried about how he'll take it when she drops him like a hot potato."

"Why did you want to go to the dance?"

"We can't let our guard down if my father is in trouble. We

need to stick close to Kay Lu in case she leaves. She and Lu Fong are our only leads to my dad. You should call Scott and have him shadow Lu Fong tonight."

"That's a good idea. Then we'll dance?"

She eyed me wearily. "Yes, I need to work off some nervous energy."

And that was exactly what was about to happen.

Chapter 21

It was nearly nine when we joined Joel and Kay Lu in the convention hall. A band was playing loud rock and roll and the hotel's patrons were just beginning to find the party.

Joel greeted us from a small table near the edge of the dance floor situated at an angle from the stage.

"Sit down," he said. "Kay Lu went to the powder room. She'll be right back."

The band stopped playing in the middle of Joel's shouted invitation. He laughed and sipped at a glass of white wine.

"Having a good time?" Maxine said.

"Having a great time," Joel said.

I smiled graciously. "I hope you feel that way tomorrow."

"Why shouldn't I?"

"Just take it slow with Kay Lu. We just met with her father. He's kidnapped Maxine's father to get the cloning formula from her."

"What? That's incredible." Joel fell back into his chair, looking defeated. "She didn't say anything to me about this. I'm sorry Maxine."

Maxine looked at him demurely, but said nothing. We watched him as he wrestled with his conscience. "I can't believe Kay Lu is involved in this. I'll talk with her. I'll demand she--"

I put my hand on his arm and shook it to get his attention. "No, Joel. You can tell her about it, but don't accuse her. The best thing you can do is to try to learn where Mr. Andrews is being held. Even if she says she doesn't know, ask her if she has an idea where her father might have him. On the off chance she isn't involved in his kidnapping, she might be of some help. Don't alienate her."

"Ha," Maxine said. "I tell you two, you don't know her. She is evil through-and-through."

Joel looked hurt at Maxine's words. However, his moodiness quickly transformed to a smile and his eyes lightened. I guessed correctly that Kay Lu must have entered the room. She stopped short of our table and smiled warily at Joel. Her icy countenance suggested it might be a good time to dance. Joel took the hint and they glided into a mix of Saturday night revelers.

A pretty blonde in an old English wench costume, full of frills, laces and leg, approached our table. "Would you 'ave a drink, sir?"

My eye lingered a little too long at her outfit's revealing bustline, and Maxine bruised my ribs with her knuckles.

"I'm just trying to get into the spirit of things."

Maxine ordered us a glass of French wine I couldn't pronounce if my life depended on it. When it came, I sipped it properly and my lip curled in respect for its vintage. That's why I prefer a mixed drink.

The wine seemed to have a calming effect on Maxine. In time, it seemed to calm me too. I felt spry and ready for anything. She asked me to dance and I obliged her. We got up and I staggered a bit for the crowd. She was more sure-footed and guided me effortlessly.

I reciprocated with some of my better dance moves, but the tune ended before I got my best stuff out. I was struggling to assimilate some new moves for the new backbeat the band had chosen, when a handful of thick fingers pinched my shoulder.

"Mind if I cut in?" It was my old buddy, Steadman. My heart skipped a beat before settling down.

"Uh, good to see you again. Maxine, this is my former associate, Mr. Steadman. I can't remember his first name for some reason. You know, he has that little office over on Front Avenue."

Maxine remembered. She was very cordial to the clod, considering what she'd been through. My former associate wasn't as nice.

I believe one should put oneself in another person's shoes before judging them. I try to give people the benefit of the doubt. For example, I don't know why Steadman is such a jerk, but it probably comes from an unhappy childhood. However, even the

Steadman's of the world should try to walk in another's shoes once in a while.

If he had, he likely wouldn't have made his fatal mistake. He leered, more than smiled, at Maxine.

"Would you like to dance, Babe?"

She looked at me.

"He's no problem," the brute said, brushing me aside with the back of his hand.

I summed up the situation quickly and realized—by putting myself in his shoes—he'd likely drunk too much. Perhaps he wanted to impress his private eye buddies over in the corner. I noticed they were all watching us.

"Listen here," I said. "You've got no call to act like that." I pushed him back.

Maxine tried to intervene. "He's had too much to drink. Don't hurt him."

She was talking at the pitiful drunk and putting herself in his shoes.

"I know he's had too much," I said. "But that doesn't excuse his rudeness to you."

She rolled her eyes. "I was talking about you."

I planned to jab him in his chest but the room moved and I was facing our table. The clod had pushed me again. I turned back to Maxine.

"I'll take care of this . . ." The words ran together because of my thick tongue.

"No, Max. I can handle it. You go and sit before you fall down. I'll be okay."

I nodded. "Suits me."

"Yeah, runt. Go sit down. The lady wants to dance with a real man."

I found my way back to our table with Joel's help. "Are you crazy?" he said. "That guy's built like a Mack truck."

"I beat him up already."

"You fought that guy? Who is he?"

"That's my partner, Steadman. He's not so tough." I rubbed my still somewhat tender jaw, a reminder of our earlier encounter.

The tension at the table was thick enough to spread on a sandwich and Kay Lu kept piling on the ingredients. "He looks like he can take care of himself," she said. "And Maxine sure seems to be enjoying herself."

I looked at the couple. It was an upbeat tempo, and they were in the clinches as he whispered something into her ear. She laughed at the joke. He pulled her tighter, and she laughed again.

"I don't know what's so funny," I said. "I think I'd better break it up. He's getting a bit too friendly."

Kay Lu winked at me. "Maxine is all right. She seems to like your friend."

I was on the edge of my chair when I saw Steadman's hand drop dangerously low on her backside and perch itself perilously. I was about to jump to her rescue when something in their rhythm stopped me.

He lurched and began jitterbugging backward with Maxine in close pursuit. Now he seemed to me trying to get away from her, and she seemed to want to be closer. She faced me as they gyrated toward us and away again.

I was standing now. "Uh oh. I've seen that look before. Grab your drinks and head for the hills." I grabbed two wineglasses from the table and retreated.

Joel looked at me, then to Maxine and Steadman. "Cripes," he said, and he grabbed his drink and Kay Lu.

Kay Lu backed away from the table in a nick of time, but her wineglass teetered on the edge of the disaster as Maxine placed her hip against Steadman's gut and tossed him aside. The bulky gumshoe sailed gracefully over the dance floor and landed profoundly on our apparent break-away-table.

She walked over to the former tough guy, who was laid out over the flattened table in his green slacks, pinstriped shirt and suspenders. She lifted Joel's plaid sport jacket from his chair's post and placed it in the middle of the floor as dancers retreated toward walls. She offered the shamus her hand and, incredibly, he took it. With some effort he struggled to his feet and started to turn away from her, looking for his lost equilibrium.

Maxine grabbed his arm and spun him toward her. She tugged at the poor guy's taut suspenders and reeled backward, planting her heels into his gut and rolling back onto Joel's coat on the floor. She pushed the lug up and over her and toward his doom.

Maxine strained her eyes from her supine position, willing his flight and descent, and seemed amused at the result. The room vibrated as Steadman struck the pine floor and a laborious expulsion of air escaped from his lungs. The deep lines on her face were gone, replaced by placid smooth alabaster skin. She was having fun, momentarily putting aside concern for her father.

She stood up and retrieved Joel's coat from the floor, smiling briefly before the tension returned to her face. She brushed any potential dirt from the jacket and handed it to Joel.

"I've never seen anything like that," Joel said.

"I have," I said. "Do you feel better now, dear?"

"A bit," she said. "It was good to work out some of my frustration. I hope I didn't hurt him too much. I'm sure his heart was in the right place even if his hands weren't." She gazed philosophically at the former immovable force resting on the floor.

"He'll be okay; he has a thick head," I said. "I'll help him up."

Kay Lu hovered over the knucklehead with an alarmed expression, but chuckled to herself as he began to stir. "Come, Maxine," she said. "Let's go to the ladies room and freshen up."

The redheaded Amazon winked at me. "Yes, I think I mussed my hair."

I walked over to the lugubrious lout and bent over him. "Can I help you up?"

One eye opened and he gasped. "Is she gone?"

"She's gone."

He offered me a hand, and I strained at it. It took a few attempts, but I managed to get him to a table where I held up three fingers for him to count while serious looking waiters ran around clearing the mess.

One of the waiters was the gent with salt-and-pepper hair, who served us in the restaurant. "You okay, fellah?"

"I'm fine," I said. "My good friend picked the wrong night to get fresh with my girl. Bring him a stout beer."

Steadman nodded at the idea of a beer. "You go with her?"

I nodded back.

"She the client you stole from me?"

"She packs quite a punch doesn't she?"

"She ever hit you like that?"

I showed him a bruise on the side of my neck. "This is what she did when I crossed her."

He flinched. "She do the eye too?"

"No, that's your work."

"Ha! That's good to know. As far as you stealing my client, you can have her, buddy. We're even."

"You're not irritated with me?"

He took a pull on the beer the waiter handed him. "I didn't say that. It's just not worth pursuing anymore."

I looked across the room for Maxine. She and Kay Lu were near the entry. Maxine was bent over a table, holding a hand to her ear over the loud music. Kay Lu, lurking behind Maxine, fingered her hair in sporadic fits. Maxine rose slightly and mouthed something to a thin, tall man with round glasses. He wasn't wearing his FBI duds, instead opting for blue jeans and a long sleeve denim shirt. Agent Ned Wright was undercover.

Maxine's face flushed. She extended her index finger and poked at the air.

Kay Lu leaned forward attempting to listen to them over the din of the band. Her eyes shone, and she turned slightly and caught me watching her. I flashed a smile, which she returned.

I jabbed Joel on the arm to get his attention. "It looks like our friend Wright has joined the party."

He looked in the direction I indicated. "What's he doing here? Do you think he followed us?"

Steadman let out a loud burp. "I know that guy. He wanted me to do a job this weekend."

I'm sure my mouth dropped. "Is that why you zeroed in on me tonight? Did Wright hire you to start trouble?"

His face snapped to attention. He rubbed his jaw with his beefy hand and coughed. "Nah. You know, there aren't too many women here. That other convention is made up of scientific types. And the female private investigators are either too taken or too ugly. That's why I asked your girl to dance. Riling you was just a bonus."

"Why did Wright approach you?" I asked.

"He cornered me this afternoon outside a workshop and wanted me to watch some guy named Lu Fong this weekend. Said he just wants to make sure he doesn't leave the hotel."

I looked at him suspiciously. "Did you agree to watch Lu Fong?"

"Hell, no. I'm here to have fun. If I wanted to work, I'd stay in Portland. He said he'd find someone else. Dude said he was with the FBI, but I thought he was kidding me. The badge looked okay though."

"I think I'll go ask Maxine to dance." I stood up, steadied myself and stepped deliberately between tables until I reached the three amigos. "Hello, Wright. Fancy meeting you here."

"Jeez, you guys are blowing my cover. Why don't you take your act elsewhere?"

"Us?" I blinked at him. "What are you doing here? Did you follow us?"

"I just told your friend that I'm here to keep an eye on Lu Fong and his daughter. We've had them under surveillance since they returned to Portland." His eyes darted to Kay Lu who stood a few paces away and tried her best to seem disinterested. He looked back to me with steel blue eyes.

"Now would you two kindly walk away?"

I turned toward Maxine for help, and she took my hand and guided me toward the erupting resonance some refer to as music. Three songs and five less-pounds later, the band segued into a tune requiring touch between dance partners.

"What were you talking to Wright about?" I asked.

"Mostly he was trying to convince me to give him the cloning formula."

"Did he tell you anything?"

"He claimed he had planned to be here before he talked with us today. He said it was part of the FBI's surveillance on Lu Fong. Then, he spotted Kay Lu and clammed up. I hadn't realized she'd followed me in from the powder room."

"Did you tell him about your dad being kidnapped?"

"Not with Kay Lu standing right there. She tried to pump me for information in the ladies room about Dad's kidnapping. She pretended she didn't know anything about it. I told her to ask her father."

"Did she tell you anything helpful?"

"She said there were a few warehouses nearby her father used a few years ago. She said she'd check around and get back to me."

"Well, that's something. Maybe she will be of some help."

"It's all double talk. She wouldn't say anything that would

help us."

"Anything else?"

Maxine sighed. "No."

"Well, we know we might be looking for a warehouse. There can't be that many warehouses in this small community. I'll check it out tomorrow."

Maxine nestled comfortably in my arms and touched my chin with a finger. "Say, are you really as tipsy as you've been putting on?"

I looked around the room at Steadman and his buddies, then to Wright and over to Joel and Kay Lu, dancing nearby. "I'm not tipsy at all, dear. Haven't been all night."

She frowned. "Why the act?"

"People tend to let their guard down when their adversary appears plastered. I let Kay Lu think I'm here to have a good time and she doesn't take me seriously. Then I see Steadman and he lets it slip that Wright has been talking to him."

"What? Why?"

"He said Wright wanted him to watch Lu Fong. He also told me he was here to have fun, not work, so he told Wright he wasn't interested. Maybe he's telling the truth, maybe he's not."

"Keep talking," she said.

"Kay Lu seemed to really enjoy it when Steadman cut in on me. She made several little digs at me during your dance. She enjoyed watching me squirm."

"Why were you squirming?"

I ignored the question. "Then I watched her when you were talking with Wright. She was trying to listen in. I caught her staring over at me. I don't know what that was about.

"I looked across the table at Steadman and he was watching her too. At first, I thought he was going to go over and ask her to dance, but he must have decided to sit out the rest of the evening after his bout with you."

"What is it about Kay Lu that vexes men so?" Maxine said.

We turned, and I dipped her dramatically for effect. My lips pecked her pointy little nose, and as I gazed over her shoulder I saw Joel and Kay Lu embroiled in a steamy kiss. Past them I saw a red-faced Steadman nursing a beer and watching them intently.

I lifted Maxine up and pulled her to me again. "This morning in Hollywood's office, Wright mentioned someone else was trying to locate me when he was checking up on my credentials with the state."

"So?" Maxine said.

"It could have been your father's investigator or it could have been Steadman after his retainer. If I was an FBI agent trying to track down my past, I'd certainly follow up on someone else looking for me, wouldn't you?"

Her eyes crossed at that. "You mean the elusive Agent Thomas called Steadman? Or had Wright call him? Why would the FBI hire a private investigator? Why not use their own people?"

"They've got us working for them, don't they? They might be concerned about a leak in their department. Maybe Wright is working this case on the side, like Hess."

She moved her toe away from my plodding foot. "This is all guesswork. Don't you have anything definite?"

I nodded toward our table. "Just the furtive glances Steadman has been shooting at Wright, when he's not making eyes at Kay Lu."

"What?"

Maxine started to turn, but I stopped her. "Don't be so obvious." I raised our hands above our heads, staggered awkwardly and spun her ridiculously into Kay Lu and Joel.

My words seemed to run together again when I spoke to them. "Sorry, I think Maxine has had too much to drink."

Chapter 22

Maxine entered my room from the adjoining door to our rooms dressed casually in black slacks and a black sleeveless blouse, which revealed her slim but semi-muscular arms.

A heavenly smell wafted through my room early Sunday morning. Scott Hess, Joel and I had raided the Columbia River Hotel's famous breakfast buffet table before the conventioneers woke from their alcoholic induced slumber. We brought tables from our respective rooms, pushed them together and sat around plates heaped with an array of pancakes, omelets, bacon, Belgian waffles, hash browns, salmon, fruit and deserts.

We could have eaten in the restaurant, but we didn't want to risk Lu Fong & Company stumbling upon our planning session. It was eight o'clock and Maxine and I had been up for two hours learning our way around the hotel and pouring over the convention schedule Joel had neglected to obtain the previous day.

I'd located the room numbers of Steadman, Lu Fong and Kay Lu. Wei Ming was also registered at the hotel. We decided to do some preliminary investigations before handing over the flash drive to Lu Fong or Wei Ming on the chance that we might locate Maxine's father before the one o'clock deadline.

"Hess, did you find out anything from your contacts?" I asked.

"Not yet. I've made some inquiries. I should hear back something later this morning."

"About Friday night?"

"Yeah. So far nobody knows anything about any special Ops orchestrated by the Bureau. Nothing on the schedule anyway. But one of my contacts said he heard my supervisor, Agent Thomas, discussing something about a special detail with one of the new recruits. He figured it was some rookie assignment like picking up his dry cleaning."

I shifted anxiously in my chair. Maxine and I discussed the possibility that Thomas might have been following Hess or us Friday night at the charity ball. It stood to reason Thomas might become interested in my activities the day I called him asking about a mysterious appointment with him and Hess.

I'd asked him to also check up on any special operations or investigations that Thomas might have scheduled the night of the charity event. If there had been an assignment that night, Hess hadn't known of it. He said he had been there on his own to try and get the flash drive from Maxine and left promptly when he thought she had given it to him.

I bit into a Danish. "Okay, see if you can find out how Thomas learned about the flash drive. Now, let's go over our day's activities again. Maxine, Joel and I will check in at the morning C.L.O.N.E. seminar. Lu Fong is supposed to speak at ten-thirty. We're hoping Kay Lu will be there. If she is, I'll visit her room while Maxine checks out Lu Fong's room. We need to find a clue as to where Lu Fong is keeping Maxine's father. We're also trying to find anything that would indicate how far along Lu Fong is in his cloning experiments.

"And I'm to attend Lu Fong's talk to try and get an idea how far his cloning process has been successful," Joel said.

"I'm hoping with your medical background you might pick up on anything significant," I said.

Hess agreed to attend the private investigator's conference to keep an eye on Steadman.

"We'll meet back at Maxine's room at eleven-thirty, I said. "Any questions?"

"How do you plan to break into the rooms?" Hess asked.

I reached behind me and opened a dresser drawer. From it I retrieved a battery-operated sonic toothbrush. Instead of a brush attachment, a thick needle was attached to the base.

"What is that?" Joel said.

"This is a pick from a set I brought along with me. It's one I used when I was a locksmith."

"You were a locksmith?" Hess said.

"For about nine months. I was helping out a friend for a

while."

"Oh, I thought you were just naturally larcenous," Maxine said.

I laughed at her barb. "In addition to the pass cards, the hotel has the old style locks that open with a key. I suspect they wanted to retain the Old World ambiance.

"I noticed Maxine's electronic toothbrush back at Joel's apartment, and it gave me an idea. I learned this trick from the guy who owned the locksmith business. He saw these electric lock picks when they came out and devised his own version using a sonic toothbrush at a fraction of the cost.

"You insert these long metal needles into the lock, in the same way as you would with a regular lock pick. By inserting this pick into the keyhole the toothbrush's vibration makes the key pins virtually bounce off of the pick, transferring their weight to the driver pins, which ricochet up into the hull of the lock. With the help of my little tension wrench here, I can turn the lock and open the door.

I walked over to the front door and opened it. "Want to see a demonstration?"

The others followed me out into the hallway and I closed the door.

"I hope this works because I left my key on my dresser," I said.

Hess rolled his eyes. "We have snap guns for this kind of thing at the Bureau. I've seen pictures in catalogues of the electric picks, but they're supposed to be unreliable. Your toothbrush contraption looks uncannily similar."

Maxine, Joel and Hess formed a stealth wall around me in the hallway as I began the process. I sprayed graphite oil into the keyway of the lock to loosen any sticky pins and inserted the pick into the lock until it touched the rear of the cylinder. I then pulled it back slightly so the picking needle would be able to vibrate freely in the key slot, and positioned it against the pins.

I carefully inserted the tension wrench into the keyway below the picking needle. The sonic toothbrush hummed, then jammed, and the needle ejected from the keyhole and pierced the hall ceiling.

"Shit," I said.

All three of them stood stunned for a millisecond and began laughing.

"I hope you have a plan "B," Joel said.

"I uh. No, I don't." Once again I screwed up, not only in front of Maxine, but Joel and the god damned FBI (Hess).

"I'll be back in a minute," Maxine said. "Wait inside until I return."

She returned five minutes later and handed me a key card.

"Where did you get this?" I asked.

"I went down to the lobby and sent the desk clerk on a short errand. While he was gone, I made us two master key cards. I've done it before in one of my, um, other adventures. It's simple, really. You just need access to the hotel's computer and the little machine that codes the cards."

I looked at her in amazement. I needed to quit reading pulp detective yarns and start reading technology books.

"Let's go over our assignments one more time," she said. "Each person can give a blow-by-blow description of their activities and their objectives."

A series of groans met her request. None of us had gotten much sleep. Hess had spent the evening calling a few trusted friends at the Bureau, trying to track down information for me. Maxine said she tossed and turned all night worrying about her father. Joel seemed more lethargic than the rest of us combined. And it was he who was most irritable this morning with dark circles under his bloodshot eyes.

"Why are you so grouchy this morning?" I asked him. "No good night kiss from Kay Lu?"

He massaged his temples with his fingers, balancing his breakfast plate in his lap. "We had a great time last night. She came to my room, and we talked late into the evening. But I must have fallen asleep or something, because I woke in the middle of the night on the loveseat and she was gone."

"She didn't wake you, or say goodnight, or anything?" I asked.

"The last thing I remember was her asking me questions about something. I can't even remember what it was. Then I seemed to drift into a terrible reoccurring dream."

Joel shuddered. "It was about an old woman, with a sour

disposition, wearing white, like a nurse. She said I had misdiagnosed a patient. The patient was very sick, but would recover. The nurse said she would protect me and help others see I meant no harm.

"Then she went into a closet and came out dressed in black. I watched her as she went behind my back telling hospital staff what I had done. She had become younger, and more attractive, almost as if her treachery had transformed her into a stunning beauty.

"When she came back to me, she said she had been out trying to help, but people were angry with me. As she spoke, I realized she had transformed back into the old woman dressed in white. But there was something different about her. Her sourness was gone, and she seemed pleased with herself."

Joel stopped and took a sip of coffee. "Man, my head is killing me. I didn't think I drank that much last night."

"What do you think your dream means?" I asked.

He grimaced. "I figured it has something to do with Kay Lu."

"It could have nothing to do with Kay Lu," Maxine said. "It could be a defensive feeling about feeling attacked or betrayed by your friends."

"I know it's not that," he said. "It could be a warning that there's something bad about to happen to us. I felt the presence of evil in that nurse."

He started working on his eggs. An ominous rapping sound filled the room. Someone was at the door.

I got up from my table and walked across the room, expecting to meet up with a distressed waiter looking for all the missing food we had purloined from the buffet downstairs. I opened my door instead to Kay Lu. She wore a khaki colored skirt held up with shoulder straps over a crème-flavored blouse. Her loose, long black hair swayed against her hips as she twisted shyly.

"Hello, Max. I just stopped by to see if you were coming down to the lecture. The subject matter should be of great interest. And I . . ."

She stopped and met my eyes with a shy smile. They were dark and mysterious and momentarily pierced my soul with their playfulness. I saw why Joel had been no match for this coy little fox.

"What do you want, Kay Lu?" I tried to block the doorway so

Maxine wouldn't see her flirting with me.

She pouted at the stern tone in my voice. "I hoped we could steal a few minutes to talk. I wanted to see if there was a way that I could help you. I know Maxine doesn't think I'm sincere, but I am. I know you would listen to me, Max. Maybe I could come in now for a few minutes."

She stood on her tiptoes and peered over my shoulder and into the room. I saw her face turn white and looked over my shoulder instinctively. There, standing next to Maxine and Joel, Hess looked at me helplessly. I'd blown his cover. Kay Lu appeared shocked to see him here. I stepped toward her and let the door close behind me.

"Oh." she said. "I see you already have company. Well, perhaps we can talk later." She started to turn away, but stopped and took my hand in a warm grip. I looked down at her long tapered fingernails. They were painted white today. "Please come to the lecture," she said. "I need to talk with you." She caressed my cheek with her other hand and I felt my face turn prickly warm.

"Maxine and I plan to attend."

"That's no good. We need to talk privately. Meet me after the lecture."

She started to walk away, and I called after her. "Don't you want to wait for Joel?"

"No, I want you."

I watched, distracted, as she glided down the hallway. I knocked on the door, and Maxine opened it.

"Kay Lu saw Scott, didn't she?" Maxine said.

"Unless she's blind. I'm sorry, Hess, I thought the door was closed more."

Hess's face had relaxed. "It's okay. I don't see what further damage it can do. They aren't going to run off without Maxine's formula."

"But she'll tell her father," Joel said. "Does Thomas know you're here?"

"No. But even if he finds out, I couldn't be in much more trouble than I am now. I think we should stick to our original plan."

"I agree," I said. "Our first priority is finding where they're holding Maxine's father. I've talked to Maxine and she's agreed to turn over her flash drive to Lu Fong today at lunch if we don't have any solid leads."

Joel looked at me sharply. "But, Max, That flash drive is a ---"

"Maxine knows everything that's on the flash drive. We talked about it yesterday. She says she's willing to trade it for her father."

"I think you should make a copy before you turn it over to Lu Fong," Hess said. "We can use one of the hotel's computers. I'll call down and ask the concierge."

"No," Maxine said. "I don't want any extra copies floating around. If I had my way, we'd destroy this one. It was a mistake to create it. It's caused me nothing but trouble."

Joel looked puzzled. He studied my face briefly and looked to Maxine. She nodded at him and smiled. He didn't know I had destroyed one of the flash drives so he probably was nervous thinking I was still keeping the secret copy from her. I'd have to fill him in later.

Hess obviously wanted possession of the memory stick to clear himself with the FBI, but Maxine was having no part of it. Neither of us wanted him to know that we would be turning over the destroyed copy and keeping the real one.

"But, Maxine, the information on that thing could put the United States light years ahead in the cloning race."

"I thought our country wasn't interested in cloning people," Maxine said. "Are you telling me that our government would try to clone a human?"

Hess shook his head. "Don't be naïve. Cloning is a frontier that scientists and nations are going to explore no matter what government officials say publicly. Most countries are opposed to human cloning. Some have even banned it. But privately they will move mountains to obtain the technology."

Maxine's eyes seemed to pierce Hess. "I'm not foolish enough to believe what you're saying isn't true. But it's not going to happen on my watch if I can help it."

Chapter 23

Maxine, Joel, and I sat at a table in the back of the convention room with two French speaking students. We were situated close to the door for an inconspicuous departure. Lu Fong had been talking for about five minutes of his scheduled forty-five-minute lecture. Kay Lu sat facing the audience from a table closest to the podium.

I listened to Lu Fong as he spoke of scholarships and grants he had awarded in previous years for the brightest up and coming research scientists in the area of cloning. He discussed futuristic lab facilities he set up in countries around the globe apparently under the oblivious eyes of these governments.

Doesn't anybody ever monitor the topics at these conventions? This hotel apparently didn't. There was one person who seemed out of character in the room. Hiding behind a ridiculous beard at a rear table on the other side of the room with researchers from Austria, was Steadman. Had he come in off a drunk the night before and landed at the cloning lecture instead of the PI forum down the hall? Or was he was watching Lu Fong for Wright.

Steadman, who seemed to be dozing off during the lecture, appeared as disinterested as Lu Fong, who seemed to be going through the motions. He talked about the brave new world of cloning, about the need to cut through red tape and skirt what he called Draconian laws being suggested by world powers. But he couldn't seem to muster enthusiasm for the cause today, and I was beginning to realize why.

Lu Fong had what he wanted. Or nearly had it. Once Maxine turned over the flash drive to him, he'll sell it to the Chinese government and ensure his wealth and place in history. He was done exploiting these young earnest scientists.

Lu Fong's lethargic speech didn't sound like it was going to go the distance. Maxine also must have realized a possible early ending because as Lu Fong turned to make some marks on an easel, she slid from her chair to the door. A few minutes later, Lu Fong turned his back on us again, and I winked at Joel and left him alone with his fellow scientific types.

I approached Kay Lu's door on the third floor of the east wing and searched the hall for possible witnesses and there were none. Lu Fong's room was located at the very end of the hall and around a corner, and I figured Maxine was at work tossing his room.

I slipped the master key card into Kay Lu's room door and pulled it out. The little red light blipped at me and the door remained locked. I tried again and got the same result. I inserted the card fast, slow, and with a multitude of speeds and flicks of the wrist, but the door remained stubborn.

I sighed. The card didn't work. What to do?

I felt a bulge in my sport coat jacket and withdrew Maxine's electronic toothbrush. I found the pick in my other pocket and carefully inserted it in the toothbrush, dropping to my knees.

Checking the hallway again, I inserted the pick into the lock. The steel cylinder hummed and I felt the pick vibrating against the mechanism. I said a short prayer consisting of God's will not being for the needle to fly out and stab me.

"What time do you think we'll reach Portland?"

I turned and saw the door open in the room directly behind me. I stood up and yanked at the toothbrush, but the pick was stick in the lock's pins and wouldn't dislodge. I switched the toothbrush off, turned and stood between the lock and an elderly man and woman who had stepped into the hallway from their room across the hall.

"About noon," the old woman said. "Oh, hello. You startled me."

I told her she startled me too.

"It's another beautiful day. Don't you agree?" she said.

"Yes, it should be a nice drive for you if you're going to Portland."

"Oh, no, were going to see my daughter in Eugene. She just had a baby, our grandson. We're so excited, aren't we, Papa?"

Papa reached into his coat pocket and brought out a stack of baby pictures.

"We got these in the mail just before we left Idaho," he said. He showed them to me, one after another. I slowly retreated from his enthusiasm and the toothbrush jabbed me in the small of the back. I winced in surprise.

"Are you all right?" the old lady asked.

"Just my back. Hotel beds never agree with me."

"I know a remedy for that," Papa said. He stepped toward me and put a hand on my shoulder. "Turn around."

"Sorry. I don't let chiropractors or amateurs touch my back. I've got a workout scheduled in the gym later. That always takes out the kinks."

Papa seemed disappointed. "Are you sure?" He started around me again.

I closed ranks on him and smiled. "You'll be late seeing the grandbaby."

Mama tugged at the old man's sleeve. "Oh yes, Papa, we mustn't be late. Goodbye, young man." I watched them slowly segue down the hallway, tugging at their luggage on wheels. "He was a strange man," the lady said to her husband.

"A real jumpy sort," the old man agreed.

I turned back toward the door, doubting they could even see me from the elevator. The toothbrush stuck out from the lock at an odd angle. The pick was bent so I tried to bend it back, but I couldn't get the kink out of it. Worse, it was jammed in the lock. I turned the switch on and the handle jerked violently, and I grabbed it with both hands and yanked. The pick came out on the third attempt.

"Oh, no." I cried.

The pick's tip was contorted beyond use. I decided to ditch the toothbrush idea and work the lock with a set of picks. I carefully inserted one and worked at making the lock do what I wanted. Panic raced through my mind as I imagined having to go back and tell the group I failed. I had taken a couple of pretty well deserved hits on my credibility in the last twenty four hours and I was desperate to prove myself to Maxine.

Perspiration seemed to flow like a river from my brow and it was streaming from other parts of my body too. I fumbled some more and finally heard a click that gave me hope. However the single success escaped me as I lost my balance while squatting at the door and pulled the pick out.

Any moment now, I imagined hotel security would come up from behind and handcuff me. I looked at my watch on my wrist. Twenty-minutes and counting. It wasn't that difficult of a lock. I just hadn't practiced this in a long time. I struggled for a few more minutes and to my surprise the stubborn lock cooperated.

I coaxed the mechanism a little with my tension wrench and the latch turned.

A breath of relief escaped my lips and I wiped the sweat from my face on a sleeve and gently nudged the door open, peeking into a room that was twice as big as mine. The furniture was not as pretentious as it was in the west wing. A Sleigh bed and more neutral designs and objects of art gave the room more vibrancy.

My search began in the closet, with me tossing the few items left in Kay Lu's suitcase and finding nothing. I went through her exotic wear hanging seamlessly from wooden hangers. Blue, green, black and yellow silk dresses all with the same slit on one side of each dress. A few skimpy negligees and a black fur coat also hung waiting for their mistress.

Fingers delicately perused through her dresser drawers next, separating skimpy lace underwear while looking for information. At the bottom of the underwear I found a nail care set, some costume jewelry and a small black notebook with phone numbers. Most of the numbers seemed to be long distance, and I guessed they were of Hong Kong origin.

I flashed through it again, more carefully this time. There was a 360 area code—that would be Washington—with the notation Cam Lab, possibly the house in Camas. A 503 area code—the Portland area—held the inscription Twin Dragon. I guessed it would be Lu Fong's downtown nightclub Hess had investigated.

A hotel notepad on Kay Lu's phone stand allowed me the opportunity to jot down some of her scribblings. I turned the pages of her directory and found another 503 area code. The phone number was assigned to TK, which meant nothing to me. I printed it on the pad. On the cover page of the booklet, I spotted a third 503 area code. The inscription said "HR." "Hood River," I muttered. The prefix was the same as the hotel's.

I wrote it down on my pad too, then walked to the phone, and dialed the local number. A throaty, heavily accented voice answered me in Chinese. I couldn't understand what he said, but I recognized the voice. It was Wong, the thick-armed, thick-necked thug who accepted my invitation to nap at the Kwan Yin Temple.

I slammed the phone down before he might guess it was me. Wong was in Hood River. I didn't particularly want to meet him after clubbing him with the statuette of a Buddha. He'd surely want to even up the score.

I tore the sheet of paper from the pad, folded it, and tucked it inside my jacket pocket next to the flash drive I carried with me. I replaced Kay Lu's phone directory under her underwear and continued my search. There was nothing much of interest. Pens, coins, name badges, and a cameo necklace cluttered a small table. The bathroom was crowded with hair sprays, perfumes, toiletries and a makeup case, which I searched to no avail.

Next, I was on my knees on the floor and jamming my hands deep between the mattresses. I waved them about with no result and went to the other side of the bed and repeated the gesture. For the second time that morning a voice came from behind me.

"Are you looking for something or putting hospital corners on my bed?"

I stood and turned around. Kay Lu was ten paces away, her hand on her hips and an incredulous look on her face.

"This is embarrassing," I said.

Her smile was sardonic. "Why? You're just doing your job. private eyes are supposed to snoop, aren't they? Did you find anything?"

"No."

"That's too bad. If I knew you were coming, I would have left something for you to stumble over. Or maybe I came too early. Do you need more time? I can come back."

I was having a hard time returning a wisecrack. She walked over to the kitchenette, filled a teapot with water and put it on a small stove. "I saw you leave the lecture and I can't blame you. Father's talk was dreadfully boring. I went to your room, but you weren't there. I even knocked on Maxine's door. She wasn't home either. Let me guess. She's visiting father's room."

"I don't know where she is." I straightened my tweed jacket and walked over to her. "She said something about going for a workout so I decided to spend my time judiciously. Your father was putting me to sleep."

"I'm making tea. Would you like some? It will energize you."

"No thanks. I'd better be going."

"Is that any way to treat me after breaking into my room? You said earlier you would meet and talk with me. The least you can do is sit down and have some tea."

"What did you want to talk about?" I asked.

"You'll see. Have a seat over by the window in the loveseat." I sat in a blue-colored cozy loveseat and waited. Kay Lu avoided any discussion until the teapot whistled. She poured the brown steaming liquid in two Victorian cups on saucers and carried them, offering me one tattooed with roses.

She pulled up a chair across from me and sat as I sipped the hot brew, balancing the saucer on my knee. The tea was strong and smooth and tasted like sweet almonds. Good. A bitter almond taste has been associated with cyanide, and I wouldn't put anything past this China doll.

She made confusing small talk, and I wondered if she was trying to work out something in her mind. Finally, she looked eagerly into my eyes.

"I think I know where Maxine's father is stashed. I can show you. Father has said he will try to meet Maxine at lunch and give her until one o'clock to hand over the cloning formula."

She took a sip of her tea, pausing to gage my reaction. I didn't give her one.

"If you turn over the cloning formula to me, I'll tell you where her father is," she said. "You can go and get him now."

"You said you thought you knew where he was. That's not the same as knowing where he is."

I watched her lower the cup to a saucer on her lap. "All right, I know where he is. I've known all along. What's the matter with you? Don't you want to be a big hero to Maxine? This is your chance."

She put her cup and saucer on a table and took mine away. Then she crowded her way onto the settee with me and draped her arms around my neck.

"Maybe you aren't that concerned about Maxine. Maybe you like petite Asian girls with milky-white complexions. I won't lie to you. I was attracted to you the first time I saw you in the farmhouse. You will find I am a very affectionate woman."

She leaned forward and pressed her dark colored lips passionately on mine. I tried to resist, but I'm only human. She went at me three or four times before coming up for air.

"Did you learn anything?" I asked.

"Mmm, I think I underestimated you," she said.

"I underestimated you too."

She came at me again, but I turned away. "What's the matter? I thought we were having a good time."

"You were right the first time. I've fallen for Maxine." My eyes were burning. They felt heavy and thick.

"You could have fooled me with that kiss."

"You caught me by surprise."

"Maybe the first time. But not after that."

I yawned. My head flailed around like it was on a circus ride." What did you put in that tea?"

She looked at me curiously. "What are you talking about? Are you okay? You look sick. I'm going to take a bath and wash my skin with floppy socks."

I know. It didn't make sense to me either. But my head was swimming in colors. Purple men danced around the room and on the walls. Kay Lu turned into a snake and hissed at me. She wound her body around my waist with a suffocating squeeze, released me, and slithered through the sleeve of my coat. And then things really got strange.

The room contorted and spun around in my head and a brown steamy liquid poured in from the ceiling, scalding me in a giant teapot. I screamed and, mercifully, passed out.

Chapter 24

I drifted back into consciousness earlier than Kay Lu had anticipated. I'm stubborn that way. However my face was still attached firmly to the floor. Next to my eyes was a hotel key. I could read the lettering on it. It said Master Key.

I wanted to go back to sleep but I knew I had to get up, although I wasn't sure why. The first time I tried to rise, my hands wouldn't work properly. They were numb. So were my legs, neck, arms and head. I tried again without success. I talked to the rubbery limbs at my side, telling them to put their hands on the floor. They finally obeyed after I repeated the message about seventy times.

Five minutes later, my body gave me the first real sign it understood what I wanted it to do. I pushed myself up from the floor and stalled in a pushup. My body asked me what to do next as I hovered over the carpet.

"Roll backward and sit on your hip," I said. We hesitated and slowly rolled backward. We sat like that for a while and I tried to remember what had happened. Kay Lu had given me a Mickey. She must have drugged my tea with some kind of hallucinogenic herbal knockout drops.

Gradually, my body responded more quickly to my wishes, and I staggered up from the floor, leaving behind coins, pens, my wallet and scraps of paper. I picked up my jacket from the loveseat and with clumsy fingers searched its pockets, and my worst fears were realized.

The cloning flash drive was gone. So was everything that belonged to Kay Lu. The bathroom was clean, the dresser was empty and her exotic dresses, on hangers near the door, had all checked out.

I picked up my personal effects and the scrap paper I had written Kay Lu's phone numbers on and jammed them into my pants. I searched the room carefully in the hopes Kay Lu might have dropped the flash drive or at least left some clue as to where Maxine's dad was.

She hadn't.

I weaved down the hallway and used the stairs to descend to the lobby where I spied the short, green-jacketed, Lenny. I tried to get his attention, but he was talking to a vendor who had brought back a stack of green uniforms for the desk staff.

"Excuse me," I said. "Can you help me?"

"In just a minute," he said. I watched as he rolled a little cart out and took his time hanging about 12 pairs of slacks and six green jackets. My fingers tapped nervously on the desk as he counted them and finally signed a slip for the vendor.

"See you next week," he said.

I called over to him as soon as he turned toward me. "I was wondering if you could tell me if Kay Lu has checked out yet."

"Mmmm, is she that cute little Asian girl?"

"Yes, that's her. Maybe you could check your computer."

"I don't have to do that, sir. I've been the only one here all morning. I checked her out myself thirty minutes ago, about eleven-fifteen. Mercy, she was in a hurry. She said she had to make an important meeting of some kind."

"Did she say where she was going?"

"No sir, she didn't. Must be somewhere close though."

I looked at him hopefully. "Why do you say that?"

"Because she used the desk phone to make a phone call. I was standing right here."

I waited for him to continue, but he didn't.

"And?"

"Oh, I couldn't tell you about the call. That was personal business. I'm sure if she wanted you to know, she would have left a message for you."

I reached into my wallet and slapped a twenty-dollar bill on his counter. "Maybe she did. Why don't you check?"

He took the bill and turned around to a series of boxes with room numbers stenciled on them. "Nope. Don't see any messages.

Thanks for the twenty."

I thought about this for a minute. Maybe I was doing it wrong. Should I offer him more money? I looked into my wallet and found I didn't have another twenty. I could have gone to the hotel's ATM machine, but the user fees stiff you even more than hotel clerks.

I leaned over the counter and grabbed the smiling elf by his shirt. "I expected some kind of information for the money, pal." I wondered if this is how Steadman would have done it.

Lenny didn't flinch. "I don't think what you're doing is very civilized. Let go of me or I'll call the police."

That unnerved me. I released my grip on his collar and told him I was sorry. I didn't know what else to do. My shoulders sank at the prospect of losing Kay Lu, and I turned toward the inevitable task of having to tell Maxine that I had failed.

"It was a local call."

"What?" I asked.

Lenny's smile had gone. "I said, the number she dialed, it was a local call. She called someone to tell him she had gotten something and she was on her way."

"Anything else?" I said.

"Well . . . before the call she asked if she could put a USB drive in my computer. She said she was worried she had grabbed the wrong one for her business meeting."

"Did you let her?"

"I didn't see any harm in it. I considered it a customer service. Anyway it appeared to be the right one because she got real excited and kissed me on the cheek. Then she made the call and ran out of here like someone was after her."

You didn't happen to hear the address of this business meeting?"

"No sir. I've told you all I know."

I thanked him and started to leave, but curiosity led me back to the counter. "Excuse me, Lenny. Why didn't you tell me this when I first gave you the twenty?"

He gave me an incredulous look. "Sir, you asked me to check to see if Miss Lu left you a message. I checked, and she didn't. You didn't ask me any other questions."

"Right. Okay, thanks. Sorry for the rough stuff." If I'd had time, I would have gone to the ATM and gotten Lenny another twenty.

It was a long walk from the lobby to Maxine's room. I took the stairs' trying to think of how to explain my failure to her. I rehearsed my speech a few minutes outside her door before knocking. The door suddenly swung open and Maxine faced me with a flash drive in her hand and eyes ablaze in excitement.

"Max, where have you been? Lu Fong called about 30 minutes ago. He's coming up in a few minutes. He says if I want my father back safe, I must give him the cloning formula now. I've been frantic.

"I couldn't find you, and I got to thinking. What if he has a laptop or something with him? He might check and see this copy has been erased. Thank God you're here with the real cloning formula."

I put my fingers to her lips. "Let's get out of the hallway." She backed away and I entered her room. "Where's Joel?"

"He's gone," Maxine said. "He was downstairs and saw Kay Lu leaving in a hurry. He came up and wanted the car keys to follow her."

"And you gave them to him?"

She flinched at my tone. "Well, it seemed logical to keep an eye on everybody. I thought she might lead Joel to my father. I almost went with him, but that's when Lu Fong called."

"Has Joel called?"

"Not yet," she said. "You don't think maybe he and she have run off together? Oh, how could I be so stupid?"

I grabbed her hands and squeezed. "No, Joel wouldn't do that. He's got a very level head on his shoulders. I think he wants to help you. He must know Kay Lu was using him."

"Do you think so?"

I led her to an overstuffed chair. "I'm the one you should be worrying about. I've let you down."

She tried to joke. "Oh, are you planning to elope with little Miss Fortune Cookie?"

"Maxine, she got the flash drive away from me. That's why she's run off."

Her countenance became fearful. "So we've got nothing to offer Lu Fong," her voice trailed off. "Except this erased flash drive."

There was a muted ringing in the background. It was the phone in my room. I rushed to the adjoining door, but it was locked from my side. I wondered who could have locked it. Hess? "It could be Joel calling about Kay Lu," I cried.

I ran to the hallway and fumbled for my key card in my wallet. I lunged for the phone on what I believed to be its dying ring.

"Hello." The line clicked off and on and finally there was a sound. "Hello, who is this?"

"Hello," a puzzled voice answered. "Is this Scott?"

"No, this is Max Starr. Who is this?"

"Oh, sorry. Agent Hess told me this was his room number. I must have got it wrong."

"Wait," I said. "I'm a friend of Hess's. He's staying in my room. Who are you?"

"This is Jake. I work with Scott." He was playing it careful.

"Are you calling in response to a question he phoned you about earlier?"

"Yeah, is he there?"

"No, he's -- I don't know where he's gotten off to. He should be here soon."

"Well," Jake said, "this is important. Could you find him? I'll wait."

There was something jammed behind the door of my full-length, turn-of-the-previous-century, armoire. It was a shoe and a little more. "No, I don't think so. I think he's left the hotel momentarily. Any message I can give him?" The shoe was attached to a foot.

"Nah, I'd better wait for him."

I was distracted. "Okay."

"Wait," Jake said. "Max, I think Scott mentioned your name. He said you wanted him to check up on a specific question."

"Yes—"

"Well, if you already know the question. I guess it's safe to give you the answer. The answer is yes."

I was staring at the foot. "Was it downtown?"

"Yeah, that's right, downtown. That's all I can tell you. Have Scott call me back for the rest of it. He's got my number."

I hung up the phone and paced slowly to the armoire. There was rapping on the door behind me. "Max, open up. What's going on in there?" I went to the adjoining door and unlatched it.

Maxine breezed into the room. "Who was on the phone?"

"A friend of Scott's from the FBI."

"What did he want?"

"He was calling Scott back about a special operation the FBI was conducting Friday night."

"What? Where is Scott? I knocked on the door several times in the last hour, trying to find you and nobody answered. Shouldn't Scott be laying low here?

"He is."

"What? Why are you . . . ?"

Her eyes went to the armoire. I had opened the door to see to whom the shoe belonged and its owner now was visible.

"Scott. Is he hurt?"

I held her to me. "Don't look. I think he's dead. It looks like he's been shot.

"Oh, Scott. No!" she screamed.

"I bent over the body. It lay crumpled in an awkward position at the bottom of the upright closet. His head was tilted as if asking a question. Why did someone shoot me?

His face and his hands looked waxy and his open eyes were vacant. All sign of life was gone. It was a perfunctory act for me to feel for a pulse. I could see his purple hand, a sign that his heart had stopped and the blood was settling in his extremities.

Blood stained his chest around two small holes about where his heart would be. There was blood on the carpet where he had been dragged from the center of the room. Most of the blood collected in the bottom of the armoire, where he had been thrust in death.

I stood up with blood on my hands and looked around the room for a towel. What I found instead was Steadman standing in the doorway with a blank look on his face as he stared at the former FBI agent and then at the blood on my hands.

"I heard a scream. The door was open a bit so I came in. What the . . ." In the next instant, he was all business. "Freeze!"

A large caliber gun was pointed at me, and Steadman, looking professional for the first time since I'd met him, was in a shooting stance.

I froze.

Chapter 25

Steadman walked crab-like into the room and motioned for me to step away from Hess. Maxine and I backed away together and he knelt over the body. He felt Scott's neck with one eye on us.

"He's dead. Which one of you killed him?"

"We didn't kill him," Maxine said. "We found him like this."

"He's in your room. It looks like he might have been searching it, and Starr here, stumbled onto him." Steadman rifled through the dead man's clothes and came up with a wallet. He retrieved a pen from his own shirt pocket and used it to scoop up a small caliber gun from behind Scott's body. "This gun belong to one of you?" he said.

There was a knock at the door and Steadman swung around and pointed the gun at it. "You, Red, get the door. Invite whomever it is in."

Maxine looked uncertain, but walked over to the door and opened it.

"Oh, *you are* here. I tried your door but no one answered. I remembered you saying Mr. Starr's room was next to yours."

"Come in," Steadman said. "The party's just getting started."

Maxine opened the door wider and Lu Fong took a few steps forward until he saw Steadman with the gun in one hand and Hess's wallet in the other.

"Whoa, stop right there," Steadman said. "You just come right in here and join the party."

Lu Fong looked scared. I thought he might have a stroke right in the entryway. He managed to compose himself and stepped ahead of Maxine toward me.

"What is the meaning of this?" Lu Fong said. "I told you no tricks, Maxine. Your father's life depends on it."

"This isn't my doing. Someone shot Scott." She pointed to the body, and Lu Fong quickly comprehended the situation.

"You killed him?" He was looking at Steadman, who shook his head. Lu Fong seemed more nervous asking his next question. "Are you the law?"

"Private. But I'm taking over jurisdiction here. I want you all to sit at the table by the window while I call the police."

We sat and waited as Steadman made several cell phone calls. He talked in low tones and mumbled a lot. I noticed Lu Fong carried a laptop computer with him. Maxine was right. We wouldn't have been able to bluff him with the damaged flash drive.

I wondered where Kay Lu had gone, and if Joel had managed to stay on her tail. Lenny said she had gone somewhere in Hood River. It was only a ten-minute trip to anywhere in Hood River. Why hadn't Joel called?

I picked up a discarded towel and wiped the blood from my hands. Next, I retrieved a piece of scratch paper from my coat pocket. It was the one I had jotted down phone numbers on in Kay Lu's room. I was staring at the numbers when an epiphany of sorts clubbed me over the head, as I looked beyond my own scribbling at the paper itself.

"We're all going to sit here for a little while," Steadman said. His voice was gruff and commanding. "I just called the guy from the FBI that wanted me to work for him. He's says he'll send a Bureau forensics team up from Portland. I gave him the name of the dead guy and he's an FBI agent. I'm going to be a hero and get a big reward because I've got a strong feeling his murderer is in this room."

"But my father's been kidnapped," Maxine said. "I've got to get out of here and save him. Kay Lu has stolen the flash drive, and she's going to have my father killed."

"Tut, tut, little lady. You're going to stay right here. Nobody's leaving."

Lu Fong's anxious eyes blinked at the door, probably weighing the chances for an escape. Maxine rocked in her chair and moved to get up. I grabbed her wrist and held her down. "Look, Steadman, a prime suspect has already left the hotel. Her name is Kay Lu, and she had a history with Agent Hess. We should be going after her or having the local police put out an all-points bulletin."

"That's cute," he said. "You learn that cop talk from television?" He gave me a thoughtful look. "Maybe you were sweet on this Kay Lu, yourself. Maybe you killed the FBI guy to have a clear playing field with her.

"Or maybe he was horning in on your little romance with Miss Andrews here. You'd best shut up and wait for the cops to show. The way I see it, you're the prime suspect."

Lu Fong nervously tapped the arm of his chair with a finger. "Mr. Private lawman? It would be a good idea to bring in my daughter immediately. I can tell you where she is. She must not get away. Mr. Starr is correct. It is possible she may have an involvement in this."

"Isn't he sweet?" Maxine said. "He's willing to sacrifice his own daughter to get that flash drive and the money it will bring."

Lu Fong was out of his chair and moving toward the door.

"Stop right there," Steadman said. "You're not going anywhere, and we aren't going after your daughter. It won't be difficult to pin a murder wrap on you either."

"I have nothing to do with this," Lu Fong said. "I was to meet Maxine. Since she has nothing to offer me, I have no reason to stay."

"I wouldn't say that," Steadman said. "After all, it is you the FBI is following. You might have eliminated him because he was closing in on your racket."

"That is ridiculous," Lu Fong said. "I have never seen him before."

While Steadman was being distracted by Lu Fong, I had unplugged the wire from the telephone. I heaved the telephone as hard as I could at Steadman. It struck his hand and knocked the gun from his hand into the floor. "Shit," he cried, and instinctively made a move to retrieve it.

I tackled him as he bent over to get it, grabbed his arms and pushed my knee between his shoulder blades. "Get me that telephone line."

Maxine unhooked the line from the wall, and I used it to tie his arms behind him and hog-tie his ankles. When I was done, I stood up and admired my handiwork.

"Where's Lu Fong?" Maxine said.

"He took off when I jumped Steadman. You told him Kay Lu

has the flash drive so there's no reason for him to stick around."

Steadman gasped for air. "You won't get away with this. Give yourself up."

"Get a pair of my socks from the dresser and stuff them into his big mouth," I said.

We sat in silence for a minute after we finished with the sorrowful private investigator. "Did you find anything in Lu Fong's room?" I asked.

Maxine turned excited green eyes on me. "Max, In all the confusion, I forgot to tell you. Lu Fong left his briefcase in his room. I found a list of people inside it with some notations about blood type, hair color, IQ, job specialty— that kind of stuff."

"IQ? What do you mean, IQ?"

She winced. "You know, Intelligence Quotient. How smart a person is."

"Oh."

"His briefcase was refrigerated. I mean it had ice packs in it, along with petri dishes and vials of blood. Max, there were bits of skin in little round covered petri dishes."

"What?"

"And a list of names in the briefcase corresponded with some of the names mentioned recently in the newspaper headlines. One was that friend of my father's. Remember, the newspaper said several prominent leaders had been kidnapped recently. They were all abducted, drugged and turned loose within twenty-four hours."

"Oh, you mean like that computer guy?"

"He was the latest. He was kidnapped and let go this week. The newspaper said there is a two hundred-fifty thousand dollar reward that's been posted by the government for information leading to the arrest of these kidnappers."

I felt energized and anxious, but mostly confused. I'd spent most of my thinking time trying to stay alive, and now I was missing something obvious.

"That's a lot of money. Why would the government offer a reward for such a ludicrous crime?"

"That's what I think I've figured out, Max. These kidnapped victims have something in common. Each is a specialist in their field. There was a computer engineer, a Nobel Prize physics professor, a top Pentagon military strategist, and Edward Brown, who is a member of the Fed, is an economic specialist."

"I think I remember seeing something about the Financial guy."

"The newspapers said he missed a scheduled meeting of the Fed last week because he was ill. But Daddy and Edward are old friends, and Edward told Daddy he had been abducted while jogging near his house."

"Why didn't you mention this earlier?" I said.

"Father told me about it Friday night, in strict confidence."

"So what's your theory?"

"I think Lu Fong is behind these kidnappings. "I think it's part of the package he's delivering to the Chinese Government."

"What package?"

"We think Lu Fong has developed a method of cloning humans, right?" Maxine said.

I nodded.

"Well, what if he's also supplying the tissue and blood samples of these people to be cloned. You know, our country's top scientists, like Ned Wright said."

"That might explain why Wright was at the hotel last night," I said. "But it all seems a little far-fetched. They don't even know if this technology will work."

She brushed a strand of hair from her cheek. "Maybe they do. What if they've already cloned a human? Or more than one."

I reflected on what Joel had said about the effectiveness of Lu Fong's formula. "That might explain why Lu Fong is so desperate to get your flash drive. He has the ingredients, but he doesn't have the recipe, and the Chinese are hungry. But if they've cloned something before, even if only animals, surely there would be notes or papers detailing how it was done."

"I don't know," she said. "But my intuition tells me that Lu Fong is behind these abductions and those samples of skin and blood in his briefcase are from some of those people who were recently abducted."

"How many samples did Lu Fong have?" I asked.

"I counted eleven, but Lu Fong doesn't have them anymore."

"Where are they?"

She leaned forward and whispered into my ear. "In his briefcase, under my bed. We don't want Steadman to know."

I brought her lips to mine. "You're great. So, Lu Fong doesn't have the samples or the cloning formula. I'll bet he's ready to explode."

"He might not know it yet," she said. "He didn't say anything about them when he was here."

I walked into Maxine's room and dialed the operator. A few minutes later I was talking with the salt and pepper-haired waiter from the night before. "Could you come up to my room right now? We need you."

I hung up the phone and not being able to find a pencil, picked up Maxine's purse and carried it back into my room. "Have you got a pencil in here?"

"I have an eyebrow pencil."

I accepted the substitute and went back to the scrap of paper I'd brought from Kay Lu's room. I had noticed an indentation on the paper I'd written phone numbers on earlier, when Steadman had the drop on us. I rubbed the pencil sideways across the paper and several impressed numbers and letters appeared. I kept rubbing and revealed the inscription.

"Three-thirty-three Industrial Way. Maxine, I think I know where your father is."

"What? How?"

"Kay Lu must have written it down on the pad in her room when she called Wong at their hideout." I showed her the address on the paper. "Of course it's a bit hard to read because I've written phone numbers all over it, but you can just make it out."

A few minutes later, the hotel waiter joined us. Now his mustache was gone.

"It's your friend," Maxine said. "Mr. Hollywood."

"You almost gave me away last night," he said, smiling at Maxine. "What the hell? Why have you got this guy trussed up like a hog? Max, have you gone mad?"

"This is Steadman. He's the private investigator who influenced Max to get into the business," Maxine said.

"Hold on, Jim. We've got a bigger problem." I pointed toward the armoire.

Hollywood's fierceness evaporated. "Who is this?"

"It's Scott Hess. The FBI agent we were talking about a few days ago in your office."

"Oh, man. When you called me for help yesterday, I had no idea what I was getting into."

"It gets worse. I can't tell you now, but you must trust me. Kay Lu and Lu Fong both split, and Kay Lu has the flash drive the FBI is after. There's no reason for them to keep Maxine's father alive any longer. We've got to rescue him."

"You've got to stay put. I'll take care of this, just as soon as I untie this guy."

I put my hand on Hollywood's shoulder and looked him in the eye. "Jim, please don't do that. If Steadman gets loose, he'll mess things up."

"Well I've got to call the local authorities. Hood River is not in my jurisdiction."

"Fine. But Steadman already called Ned Wright. The FBI is sending a forensics team from Portland."

"Crap. What a mess."

Maxine walked up to him and caressed his cheek. "Please, Mr. Hollywood, my father could be killed. I think you should take over."

Hollywood did something I've never seen him do. He blushed. "Well, I'll see what I can do."

"You'd better get some kind of help up here fast," I said. "Wright's agents are on their way."

"I'll need a statement from you two," he said.

"Love to," I said. "Later. Send help to three-thirty-three Industrial Avenue in Hood River. That's where we're going. Don't spare the manpower." I grabbed Maxine by the hand and we ran from the room.

"Damn you, Max. Come back here! Where's the damn phone?"

Chapter 26

We ran from the hotel lobby and into the parking lot like fugitives with nowhere to go.

"We don't have a car," Maxine said. "Joel took my rental."

"Think anyone would leave keys in their car?"

"We can look."

A moving object caught my eye. A dark car flitted between trees as it motored up the long driveway toward the hotel.

"Don't bother. I have an idea. Wait down there at the edge of the driveway for me."

"Where are you going?"

I ran back into the hotel lobby. Some of the laundered hotel uniforms were still on the rack at the end of the counter, and Lenny was on the phone. I walked calmly by him to the rack and boldly retrieved a green blazer from a hanger and replaced it with my jacket.

The blazer was a snug fit and every step was an adventure. Lenny pecked at the computer keys as I walked right past him. I started breathing again when I got outside and stopped short as a black Jaguar cruised slowly toward me.

I walked around the sleek machine to greet the driver. "Valet parking, sir?"

A thin-faced balding man with an unkempt mustache rolled the window down. "I was wondering where I should park. Will you get my bags too?"

"Surely sir, but only to the door. The deskman will signal for a footman to carry your bags up." He popped the trunk and I retrieved two small bags. The passenger door opened, and a petite young blonde stuck a shapely leg toward the ground. "Could you help me?" she said. "I'm a little stiff from the ride."

I took her hand and pulled gently. She wore a short silk gold skirt, sheer nylons and glitzy golden shoes. I bowed slightly after she was out and felt Maxine's eyes on me.

I picked up their bags again, toted them to the entryway, and placed them on a cart. "Lenny will check you in at the counter."

The bimbo waltzed past me, and the bald guy slipped me a tip. I opened my hand and saw a shiny new quarter. I handed him the cleaning stub for the jacket I was wearing. "Just present this to the valet when you want your car."

The Jag's motor was off. The tightwad was saving gasoline. I slid onto the seat and switched on the ignition, letting the engine roar a few times before starting a slow lap around the parking lot and meeting Maxine at the driveway's entrance.

"I can't believe you stole his car, but I have to admire your style." She helped me off with the borrowed blazer and discarded it in the slight back seat

I missed the gear before letting out the clutch and was rewarded with a shrill metallic outburst. "I've never driven a Jaguar before. The gearing system is a little stiff."

We coasted more than cruised down a winding road toward Hood River, while I tried to find the gears. A stop sign at the end the bottom of the hill gave me an opportunity to switch my attention from the stick-shift to the brakes, just as a large truck screamed down the highway a few feet in front of us.

I blushed and Maxine laughed. She seemed radiant for all the wear and tear she'd suffered over the past couple of days.

"How do you keep it all together?" I asked, wiping the sweat from my forehead.

"Keep what together?"

"Your father's been kidnapped, your old boyfriend's been killed, and I lost your one chance to get your dad released. Yet, you seem calm and almost carefree."

The Jag lurched on a corner I had taken too fast, and Maxine swayed with the momentum and waited for us to straighten out.

"I can assure you, I'm not carefree. I'm focused. To answer your question: I give myself positive affirmations and meditate twice a day. It keeps me relaxed and ready for anything."

I downshifted and we came to a stop at a light in downtown Hood River.

"It seems to work," I said, absently.

Maxine caught me daydreaming as the light changed. "What's on your mind?" she said.

"I was just wondering. Did you tell Steadman your surname last night when you were dancing?"

"No. The subject never came up. I'm not even sure he knows my first name. Why?"

"He called you Miss Andrews back in my room. How does he know your last name?"

"I don't know, but this light won't stay green much longer," she said.

A horn blared at us from behind, and the transmission complained as I shifted into first gear. A few minutes later I spotted a gas station, and turned in.

I typed the address Kay Lu had left behind into my phones navigation app, and a sweet feminine voice calculated the route and gave directions.

A few minutes later we were cruising up the warehouse district along the Columbia River. The address turned out to be an old two-story building with brown, weathered siding. We parked discreetly, away from the entry, at the end of the building. I counted four cars, one of them was Maxine's, and two vans parked near the double-door opening to the warehouse. We cautiously made our way to a dirt-caked window and propped two wooden boxes under the casement.

I put a finger to my mouth. "Shh."

We climbed onto the boxes and put our faces to the glass. The thick film hindered scrutiny. I rubbed my bare arm in circles against the glass, smearing the dirt into the corners of the pane and the underside of my arm.

Our eyes focused on three figures standing around a table. It was the only bit of furniture inside the empty warehouse. I heard shrill shouts coming from Wei Ming, the purported ambassador from China. It was his job to guarantee successful delivery of the cloning formula and also of the human specimens, which Lu Fong unwittingly left in a briefcase under Maxine's bed.

Wei Ming, in the same brown suit he wore at the restaurant, was apparently voicing his displeasure of Lu Fong's failure in the deal. His arms swept the air as he screamed at a subdued Lu Fong, sitting sideways at the table.

Kay Lu stood across from her father with a hand cupped under her chin, supported by an arm under her elbow. She offered no help to her father.

"Those are Kay Lu's goons over by the freezer," Maxine said. "I don't see father or Joel." I looked to where she indicated and saw Wong and two others standing at the door of a huge stainless steel box.

I looked nervously over my shoulder. "I don't guess Hollywood will be here with the cavalry anytime soon."

"He might call the local authorities," Maxine said.

"It doesn't make any difference. We have to act now."

"What's wrong?"

"How many people do you see in there?"

"Six and I think I see some of Lu Fong's men by the door. It's hard to tell through these windows."

I climbed off my box and looked down the lot toward two commercial vans. "I hope someone left their keys in their car. I'd hate to ruin that pretty black Jaguar."

Maxine jumped off her box. "What are you talking about?"

"You said yourself you didn't see your dad or Joel."

She looked blankly at me. "Where do you think they are?" Her eyes flickered and opened like an aperture on a camera lens. "Oh, no. You mean—they can't be in that old freezer."

I walked toward one of the vans. "There's no other place they could be in that barren warehouse. Did you notice the frost forming on the window of the freezer door?"

"*Oh my God, no.*" Maxine wailed. "What are we going to do?"

"Have you got a gun?"

"No."

"Neither do I. Maybe we can find a key in one of these vans or cars. If so, I'm going to drive right through the front door." I looked over my shoulder at her. "The element of surprise is all we have."

She was on my heels as we ran to the first van. "What if we can't find a key? Do you know how to hot-wire a car?"

"No."

"Why don't we use the Jaguar? You've got the keys for it."

"Maxine, *It's a Jaguar* and a loaner at that. Besides, we need a battering ram not a golf club." The first van was unlocked, so I searched for a key in the ignition, the overhead sun visors, and in the console and came up empty. Maxine fingered through the glove box and came to the same conclusion.

We went to the next van and uncovered a paradox of sorts. I could see the keys on the console as we peered in the window, but the doors were locked. "Some idiot locked himself out," Maxine said.

"Maxine, your self-affirmations are slipping," I suggested.

We tried the sliding door and the back doors, to no avail. Maxine was winding up for a foot thrust at the driver's window when I caught her heel. "You'll cut yourself."

"I don't care."

I held up an oblong rock, slightly larger than a softball, and heaved it at the window behind the driver seat. It bounced off and grazed my shoulder.

Maxine looked at the tiny chip in the glass and stepped backward for another foot thrust. "My way's better."

"Give me one more shot at it," I said.

I picked up the rock and went into a baseball windup five feet from the glass. This time the window shattered into a thousand pieces and a grapefruit-sized hole opened. I carefully poked my arm into the hole and unlatched the lock.

Maxine jumped into the driver's seat and fastened her seat belt. "I'm driving."

I hopped in the passenger side. I wouldn't have dared try to stop her. She started the engine, put the heap in reverse and spun dirt and gravel as she accelerated. She cranked the steering wheel, shifted into drive and the wheels spun again as she created a large fishhook pattern in the parking lot. She backed up for a running start and floored it toward the warehouse's wooden double-doors.

"Gun it straight through the doors," I shouted over the engine noise, as I fumbled with my seatbelt.

She hit the horn, giving a last second warning to the men standing behind the threshold, before the van collided with the structure. An overhead beam split open the top portion of the van's roof on impact, curdling the windshield onto the dashboard. Splintered lumber surged through the open windshield like jagged, wobbly arrows.

Relentless, Maxine held her grip on the steering wheel as the windshield bounced up and down on the dash. The van lost some of its force, but sped across the open space to the table fast enough to send Lu Fong scurrying from his chair. Kay Lu turned her head at the racket, screeched and leaped sideways as the van crashed into the table.

The Chinese apparently don't teach evasive tactics to their ambassadors, because Wei Ming merely stood gaping as the Ford sent him back to his homeland. The front fender struck the edge of the freezer box and my body recoiled, held tight by the safety harness.

Everything progressed in slow motion for a minute. I saw Wong and his two astonished associates, staring open-jawed at the wreck. I pushed the door open and was yanked back by my seat belt when I tried to jump out. Wong recovered from his stupor before I could free myself.

He apparently remembered me because he helped me out, headfirst, onto the concrete floor. I fought off the urge to lose consciousness. I didn't want to be rude, but this was no time to meditate and I was sure Wong wanted me in a permanent trance.

All three of the thugs came at me. I had anticipated at least one of them would go after Maxine. For them to ignore her would be a mistake.

As they grabbed me, I envisioned Maxine rescuing me as she had done before. I hoped she would go for Wong, whom I was sure she could take, and leave the other two for me. I figured I could keep them busy until she finished with Wong and then she could take care of them too.

As usual, I miscalculated.

Two of the ruffians grabbed my arms and pulled me upright. Wong was coming in for the kill. Where was Maxine?

Wong rubbed the back of his neck. "I remember you from Kwan Yin Temple." He was larger than I remembered. About the size of Alaska. "You give me great headache. Make me look bad to mistress. I vow to avenge myself."

"Maxine?" I called.

The lumbering beast brought his concrete fist down on the top of my head. My teeth rattled -- I think a few of them shattered -- and my jaws vibrated like a level eight earthquake. I collapsed and spotted Maxine, between Wong's legs, from my vantage point on the floor.

Her face, held taut by her safety harness, hung precariously inches above the steering wheel. She and the windshield, which sat in her lap, were splattered with blood. A sinking feeling overwhelmed me. It felt like my stomach had been turned inside out.

"Maxine, No!"

Wong bore down on me, eclipsing the horrendous sight. He grasped me by the neck and shook me like a rag doll. I heard the laughter of his two comrades egging him on. I opened my eyes, trying to fight off the slow numbing bout with incomprehension and thought of Maxine and her affirmations. I will not let him beat me. I will not let him beat me.

In disgust, Wong threw me to the floor. "You are not a warrior. You are a little princess. Ha." His buddies laughed at his little joke.

I had one shot while he was distracted, and I knew I had to make it count. From my kneeling position, I hit him in the stomach with an uppercut. Okay, it might have been a bit lower, but it definitely was an uppercut.

A Taifeng gushed from Wong's lungs and the great wind whooshed from his lips as he exhaled in pain. The giant dropped to the floor and stared into my eyes.

Disbelief was everywhere. I rocked back and hit him in the jaw. His pupils dilated and disappeared into two tiny pinpricks in a sad sea of yellowish white. My hand ached at the severity of the blow against the marble-like surface, but I had no time to whine.

One of Wong's comrades grabbed my shoulder and shouted something incomprehensible. He was shorter than I was, but sleek and muscular. I swung at him from my knees and missed. He stepped up and kicked me in the face with his boot. His tall, skinny friend stepped in and kicked me in the ribs and scurried away. I rolled away in pain and managed to get into a squat before the next barrage came.

The first guy, the one who laughed loudest at Wong's little princess joke, came at me, making Ninja gestures with his hands. Okay, I know Ninja's are Japanese, but it's the only term that popped into my head at the time. This friggin' Ninja is coming after me.

I advanced to a crouching position and we circled the floor. The Ninja, his careful friend, and me.

I jumped behind a square, yellow, concrete pillar in the middle of the empty depository. The two villains laughed at my absurd attempt to hide.

"K'anchien, ying yang," the Ninja said. The other chuckled.

I guessed he called me a little princess or a big chicken. I laughed too, wrenching a red cylinder from the back of the pillar.

I poked my head from behind the post. "Moo Goo Gai Pan."

I guess I startled them judging by their looks of puzzlement. Before they had a chance to regain their composure, I stepped out and swung the fire extinguisher by the end of its rubber hose. It clobbered the Ninja's face, and he fell to the ground holding onto his bloodied, broken nose.

The skinny guy watched his partner go down and gasped. I popped him in the nose with a straight-on balled-up fist before he could run away. I tossed the fire extinguisher to the floor and chuckled at the two bloodied hens squawking on the floor.

"Well done, Max. But I'm afraid this is the end for you."

I turned around and a very large gun was pointed at my face. At the end of the gun was Kay Lu. Her eyes were dark and intense and thin shadows veiled her face.

"You nearly killed my contact with your truck, and you stole my father's cloning samples. That really hurt, Max, because I was going to steal them from him. But I still have Maxine's flash drive with the cloning formula. I will get another chance. You won't."

Her finger twitched. I closed my eyes and a thunderous explosion filled my ears.

Chapter 27

Hollywood showed up 15 minutes after Kay Lu's deadly shot. She didn't get away and neither did Lu Fong or any of his men. Hood River police caught them as they were trying to drive out of the parking lot.

Hollywood walked between three ambulances at the front door and stepped over a pile of discarded lumber. The freezer door was open and Joel and George Andrews, wrapped in blankets, sat on unsteady folding chairs near a smashed table and the wry-faced van.

"Are you two all right?" Hollywood asked.

"A little cold, but we'll be okay," Joel said. "It's a good thing the freezer had been off. It took a while to get cold after they turned it on."

Hollywood knelt to their level. "What happened?"

"Has anyone seen my daughter?" Andrews said, still shivering. "Nobody will tell me anything. Where is she?"

"I don't know," Hollywood said. "I just got here myself."

A uniformed Hood River cop walked up to Hollywood and whispered something into his ear. He nodded vaguely and they talked in whispers. The cop nodded and walked out the doorway.

"It would help if you could tell me how you got here," Hollywood said.

"Lu Fong kidnapped me Friday night at the Hilton when I was leaving," Andrews said. "A bunch of hooligans with hoods over their faces shanghaied me into that heap over there and brought me here. I gathered they were holding me for some kind of ransom. I've been here for two days.

"That Asian woman showed up about an hour ago and everybody got excited about something she had on one of those memory sticks you plug into a computer. Shortly thereafter they caught this young man snooping around outside and tied him up."

"I was trying to call Max on my cell," Joel said. The big guy, Wong, caught me and hauled me in here. When Lu Fong got here they tossed us in the freezer and turned it on. It was getting pretty cold so we huddled together to keep warm and prayed."

Hollywood scratched behind his ear. "Did the police let you out?"

Joel was shivering. "Heck no. We would have been half frozen by the time they got here. We heard this muffled crash and shouting. There was a loud gunshot from right outside, and then someone opened the freezer door.

"I want to know, is my Maxine is okay?" Andrews said. "If you don't have someone find her right now, I'll make sure you're walking a beat by sundown."

Hollywood tried to smile. "A Hood River officer told me she's being treated by paramedics. She was driving the van when it smashed through the front of the building."

Andrews looked at the caved-in windshield and sheered roof and saddened. "Nobody could survive that."

"Don't you believe it." A familiar redhead stepped from behind the van. She wore a small bandage on the side of her face, but otherwise seemed okay. "How many times do I have to tell you father? I can take care of myself."

The old man sobbed, and she ran over to comfort him. "I was so worried about you, Daddy. I would never have forgiven myself if you'd been hurt because of me."

Joel smiled at the sight of father and daughter reunited as Hollywood waited patiently for the embrace to end. "Maxine, can you tell me what happened?"

"What do you want to know?"

Hollywood looked at the carnage the van had caused and shook his head. "I don't know where to begin. What happened after you guys crashed in?"

"Beats me," Maxine said. "I was knocked unconscious by the windshield. I guess Max had taken care of just about everything by the time I'd come to. I had just opened the freezer door to let Dad and Joel out when I saw Wong out cold and two of his playmates wriggling on the floor.

Her eyebrows furrowed, and she looked at the floor. "And I

saw Kay Lu pointing a gun at poor Max. I tried to stop her. She was pulling at the trigger when I hit her forearm with a karate chop."

Hollywood's eyes turned steely. "What happened to Max? Is he okay?"

"No," Maxine said. "Kay Lu shot him. I beat her up pretty bad, but she'd already done her damage. I feel so bad. I let him down." She raised her arm to her eyes. "And after all he did to help me and my father."

Hollywood looked as if he was going to cry. Joel was trying not to laugh and failing miserably, but the cop didn't notice.

"Maxine lowered her arm and smiled. "Jim, he's sitting next to the pillar with the paramedic."

Hollywood followed her gesture to me, some distance behind him. "Max, what the hell? I thought you were dead."

"I'm fine, just a little busy being patched up. I got my first gunshot wound."

"Are you okay?"

The kneeling paramedic backed away to show off the magnificent flesh wound in my side. "It still counts," I said. "If Maxine hadn't stepped in, you'd be pulling a bullet out of my brains."

"It would have saved the taxpayers a lot of money."

I looked toward the gruff voice and saw John Steadman standing next to Ned Wright, who apparently wasted no time returning to Hood River after Steadman's call.

"Well, look who finally joined the fun," I joked. "Too tied up to get away?"

Steadman had a renewed energy in his face and he practically skipped over to meet us. "I figure the FBI will put you away for about ten years," he said. "Same goes for your girlfriend."

My head started throbbing. "What are you talking about? We caught the crime ring everybody was after. We should get a medal."

"You'll be charged with obstructing justice, murder of an FBI agent, and kidnapping, if I have anything to say about it," Wright said.

Steadman looked at the back of his hand. "You know, I might just be wrong about this."

"I would hope so," Maxine said.

Steadman smirked. "Yes, I think you two could draw up to twenty-five years of jail time each."

"Come with me," Wright said to Steadman. "I want to get your account of what happened to Agent Hess."

The two of them turned and walked out of the warehouse. I thought they were a little too pleased with themselves. "Jim, are you in charge of this investigation?" I asked.

Hollywood grinned. "More in charge than Wright is at the moment. I'm working closely with Hood River police, and they're deferring to me for the time being."

"Do you suppose you could get all the players together back at the hotel? Kay Lu, her father, Steadman, yourself? I suppose the Chinese guy in the brown suit is dead."

"No, he's okay. I saw police questioning him when I came in."

"Really? He was directly in the path of the van. I could have sworn I saw him go flying."

Hollywood shook his head. "Nobody's dead. That's what I heard. Now, why do you want to go back to the hotel?"

"Well, Maxine left a critical piece of evidence back there I think we should retrieve immediately, and I think I know who killed Agent Hess."

"You do? Who is it, Max?"

"It's just speculation. I've got bits and pieces figured out, but proving murder is another thing. Still, with a little more luck and some cooperation from the suspects, we might be able to come up with some proof."

"I can arrange it, but I don't think we're going to get anything out of this crowd. That Lu Fong looks like he knows when to shut up."

"Still, I think it might be worth your time."

Hollywood looked around the warehouse and frowned. "Yeah, this is no place for an interrogation. Okay, we'll go back to the hotel. But I doubt they'll talk. They'll probably all lawyer up."

Let them," I said. "Portland is at least an hour away, assuming they could get a lawyer to drop everything and drive up here."

Chapter 28

Maxine's case turned out to be easier to solve than the sordid business awaiting me at the front desk of the hotel.

"That's the guy—he's the one who stole my car. Stop him. Arrest him. Why aren't you doing something?"

Mr. Fulbright had figured out I borrowed his Jaguar. What's the guy expecting for a quarter tip? I could imagine his surprise, and Lenny's, when he couldn't find a valet and tried to hand Lenny the laundry ticket I'd given him.

Hollywood swore and rushed me past the balding frantic hotel guest and down a long hall.

We wound up in a small conference room Hollywood had arranged for us to use for the impromptu meeting I had suggested with Thugs and Villains, Inc. Once inside he regained his cool demeanor and spoke to the small group.

"We're here because Mr. Starr and Miss Andrews have a few questions they want to ask you. I've told them that you've all been Mirandized, and you are under no obligation to speak with them."

I looked around the room at the glum faces. Kay Lu sat in a chair across from her father, and Wei Ming, who suffered only minor bruises and abrasions from Maxine's errant driving, appeared lifeless and disinterested.

Kay Lu preened herself with a makeup mirror in hand. "Is this going to take long? I haven't done anything, and I demand to see my lawyer."

"You've had your phone call," Hollywood said. "The hotel has been instructed to direct any legal calls to this room."

Joel and George Andrews sat across from them in a blue velvet settee. Maxine, Steadman, and Hollywood stood against the wall a few feet away.

"Let's get started," I said.

"You have no authority to question us," Lu Fong said. "I have done nothing. I demand to be released."

"You're not going anywhere," Maxine said. "We're here to find out who murdered my friend, Scott, and I'm going to find out. Somebody has to. His boss isn't too broken up about it."

Ned Wright wasn't even in the room. As far as we knew he was still back at the warehouse arguing with Hood River police over jurisdiction.

Steadman pulled a bent cigar out of his jacket and started chewing on it. "Just so you know. When the local authorities are done with their little investigation, the FBI will be taking over, and agent Wright told me you and the doll, here, are his main suspects."

He backed against the wall at this last declaration. I stepped to a table and poured a glass of water from a pitcher provided by the hotel staff. Nervousness seemed to pervade the room, and most of it was mine. I wiped my brow with my hand and started.

"Is everybody here?"

"Everybody except the guest you told me you invited earlier today," Hollywood said. "He hasn't arrived at the hotel yet. My men will direct him to this room if he shows up."

If anyone was curious they weren't letting on. Maxine winked in my direction. "He should be here," I said. "He's been involved in this case almost since the beginning."

I nodded at some of the grim faces in the room and wondered if a few of my indiscretions might not land me in jail beside them.

"Yesterday," my voice cracked. "I believe a series of events began, which led to the unfortunate death of Scott Hess and the theft of Maxine's computer flash drive with a cloning formula. It began when Kay Lu zeroed in on Joel at lunch yesterday."

Joel shifted uncomfortably in the settee, and I smiled encouragingly. "She decided he was the weak link. He would tell her what she needed to know."

"You mean who had the cloning formula?" Maxine said.

"Yes. Joel wasn't any match for Kay Lu's exotic charm."

Joel's face reddened. "Damn it, Max. I'm not stupid. I was just playing along."

I ignored his icy stare. "She played up to him and told him her father was responsible for Maxine's kidnapping. Joel, always the romantic, believed her. Or maybe he just played along, like he said. She told him she was in a jam and asked for his help."

Kay Lu fidgeted with her long fingernails, ignoring me.

"I watched them during dinner while I was disguised as a waiter," Hollywood said. "She was all over him. The poor kid never had a chance."

"Something interesting happened after dinner," I said. "During the dance in the banquet room last night Kay Lu ribbed me awful hard about how Steadman and Maxine seemed to be getting along on the dance floor. First Steadman tried to pick a fight by getting me to defend Maxine's honor, then Kay Lu started teasing me and egging me on to do something about Steadman."

"So?" Hollywood said.

"Granted, neither of them like me, but it seemed odd how they were tuned into the same wavelength. Later, after Maxine had disposed of Steadman, I talked with him at our table. He said Ned Wright had asked him to keep an eye on Lu Fong. Why would the FBI hire a private investigator to do freelance work when they could easily call up another agent?"

"That does seem odd," Hollywood said.

"It might make a good cover for Steadman to snoop around," I said.

"You think Steadman is involved in this cloning thing?"

"No, I don't."

Hollywood scratched his head. "Where is all of this getting us, Max? You seem to create more questions than answers."

"I'm getting to it. When Joel was dancing with Kay Lu, I noticed Steadman watching them intently. At first, I thought having struck out with Maxine, he was going to try something with Kay Lu. But his mannerisms reminded me more of someone who was jealous, not lecherous.

Steadman chewed his unlit cigar. "What are you talking about? I never saw the broad before last night."

I looked at Hollywood. "I didn't think they had ever met either. But this is a complex puzzle, and Steadman's involvement is only a part of it. Another piece has to do with Joel's late date with Kay Lu in his room after the party. He had a few drinks with her and fell asleep."

"I probably just had too much to drink," Joel said.

Kay Lu was trying to ignore me.

"We know better, don't we, Kay Lu."

"I don't know what you're talking about, and you don't either."

I stepped forward and leaned over her as she fidgeted with her nails. "You drugged him the same way you drugged me this morning."

I paused for effect, but she wouldn't rise to my challenge.

"Joel's nap was induced by some ancient herbal concoction you carry around in your purse for such matters. I'll bet the drug you slipped Joel was some kind of truth serum. At least it got him talking. I'm guessing he told you that I had the cloning flash drive, and he could have told you that the flash drive Maxine was carrying had been erased."

She looked up at me and covered a yawn with her hand. "You're boring me."

I kept pushing. "I had to ask myself how you zeroed in on me so quickly. Why didn't you go after Maxine? She's the one whom everyone thought had the flash drive. But Joel told you differently. So the first thing this morning you came to my room to steal it."

"My lawyer will surely deny that," Kay Lu said.

Maxine had been making little clicking noises with her tongue from somewhere behind me. "I'd love to wipe that smirk off her face, Max. Why don't I just . . ."

Maxine stepped swiftly toward Kay Lu, but Hollywood was quick on the uptake and intercepted her before she could launch a blow. He evaded Maxine's attempted to hook his elbow and toss him aside.

"That's enough," he huffed, and wrestled her arms behind her and tugged her backward.

Kay Lu seemed amused. "Why don't you let her go, Mr. Cop? It might be fun to see her sprawled out on the floor."

"We'll see who's lying on the floor when it's all over," Maxine said.

I waited to see if there was going to be a second round, but Maxine succumbed to Hollywood's modest arm-lock and Kay Lu returned to acting bored.

"Where was I?"

"You said my daughter had come to your room this morning,"

Lu Fong said. He was sitting up straight on his chair, hands clasped and leaning toward me. "You said she came to steal the flash drive."

"Yes. Kay Lu came to my door, but I had company so she tried to set up a meeting later. But while my door was open, you saw Agent Hess in my room. And that, I believe, was his death sentence. Hess had been making inquiries for me about a secret operation the FBI ran Friday night. I was trying to find out if the FBI set up the attempt to kidnap Maxine."

Kay Lu offered a meek laugh. "Ha, that's a good one."

"I'm sure Hess's questions didn't go unnoticed in the Bureau. So when you went back to your partner and told him about seeing Hess in my room, you sealed his fate."

"I don't know what you're talking about," she said.

Lu Fong was almost out of his chair now. "Who is this partner, Kay Lu? You are supposed to be loyal to me."

We both ignored the old man. Kay Lu was rebelling, and I was on a roll.

"Like I said, Hess's queries almost certainly sent ripples through the Bureau offices. One of your partner's cronies probably called and alerted him. When you drugged me and searched me for the flash drive, you found my room key and you gave it to your confederate. He realized that Scott might be in my room, and he took the key, let himself in and caught Hess off guard."

Joel let out a low whistle and shook his head.

"Kay Lu, why did you not tell me about this?" Lu Fong's face twisted in anger, the veins in his neck pulsating.

Kay Lu settled back into her chair and began kneading her long painted fingernails into the velvety sidearm. Her eyes glowed with a sinister darkness.

Maxine shook free from Hollywood's grip. "Then, if it wasn't Kay Lu who killed Scott, it had to be someone inside the FBI."

"Yes, Maxine. On my suggestion, Hess called a friend and asked him to check and see if the Bureau had run a covert operation the night of your attempted kidnapping at the Hilton Hotel. I'm sure that puzzled Hess. He likely wanted to know what I was thinking.

"But he never got the call that may have saved his life. I got that call later. I was talking to his friend in the Bureau at the same time I was looking at his lifeless body. If he had received the call earlier, he wouldn't have trusted his killer, would he Thomas?"

Everyone stared at me blankly. Only one set of eyes scrutinized me.

"Thomas?" someone said. "Who is Thomas?"

"Thomas was Hess's supervisor. The man who was off on a field assignment and couldn't meet with us, so he sent Ned Wright in his place."

"What?" Hollywood said.

"Haven't you noticed that even though we never see the mysterious Mr. Thomas, his name keeps coming up? Wright is reporting to him. Hess is in trouble with him. Then, this morning Wright leaves an ongoing investigation just when things are getting hot." Why? And why isn't he here now to find out who killed his agent?"

"I don't understand what you are getting at," Maxine said.

I winked at her. "The only reason Wright would have left is because he was told to by his boss, who, I might mention, has been here all along."

"But who?"

"That's what I asked myself. Some of you know I have been bluffing my way through this whole case. I'm not a real private investigator, yet by my sheer determination not to fail, I've clawed and fought and done my best not to let anyone know I was a fake.

"It's occurred to me, I'm not the only fraudulent P.I. involved in this case. Someone else has been pulling a big bluff of his own. Isn't that so Steadman? Or should I say Agent Thomas?"

"What?" Steadman said. "You're crazy. You broke into my office, remember?"

"I was in Steadman's office, not yours. You, not Steadman, came to my house. I should kick myself for not remembering the picture in Steadman's office of him shaking hands with the mayor. The thick guy, with a big nose, brown hair and a self-assured smile, is close in size and stature to Agent Thomas but didn't match the steamroller Steadman on my front porch with a red crewcut.

"You were partners with Kay Lu, and it was your job to ransack my house. I surprised you when I opened the door because I was supposed to be in a farmhouse in Camas.

"You didn't know what to say. You couldn't identify yourself as an FBI agent because I caught you breaking and entering. Being a quick thinker, you remembered the complaint from Steadman you came across when you were investigating me.

"So you pretended to be Steadman harboring a grudge. As Steadman, you could knock me unconscious and ransack my place. And assuming his identity would allow you to take a more active role in the investigation. You could have just hauled me back to Kay Lu, but you thought you were being clever."

"You've got quite an imagination," Steadman said.

I turned to Hollywood. "Thomas was working with Kay Lu. I don't know how they got together. Maybe he hooked up with her during the investigation into Lu Fong's restaurant in Portland.

"When I was looking through Kay Lu's address book in her room this morning, I found the initials 'TK' and a Portland phone number. Later, I realized the Chinese go by last name first. 'TK' in reverse could stand for Ken Thomas. I'm willing to bet if I call that number I'll get his FBI office.

"Another thing that bothered me is that Steadman called Maxine Miss Andrews this morning in my room when he held a gun on us. How did you know her last name, Thomas?"

"I'm not Thomas. She told me her name when we danced last night."

"No I didn't," Maxine said. "You were too busy groping me."

I chuckled at Maxine's indignity. "The FBI knew about Maxine's relationship with Hess somehow and as the senior agent Thomas was in a good position to know these things. I figure Kay Lu was looking for an opportunity to get out from under her father's control, and she persuaded Thomas that twenty million dollars could be better spent than a government pension. She can be very persuasive when it comes to men.

"Thomas is the one who blew the investigation, not Agent Hess. Thomas didn't want to put Kay Lu in jail, and Hess was in a position to ruin their new partnership, so I'm betting Thomas and Kay Lu set him up. They drugged Hess, and the Lu operation blew town. Kay Lu probably told her dad the FBI was onto them, and Thomas used Hess as the scapegoat for the blown investigation."

"A lot of words," Steadman said.

"Maybe not. I talked to the real John Steadman on the phone

this morning. I told him who I was and how you were using his name. Of course, he thought I was doing it again. He told me he had checked with the state of Oregon and found out that I wasn't licensed.

"He also said he reported me to the state after talking with the employment counselor across the hall. He put things together quickly. I think he's actually pretty good at his job.

"Then he told me about how someone from the FBI had been referred to him from the state licensing office. Apparently the same state clerk had talked to both men. He said the agent he talked with grilled him over the phone for twenty minutes.

"I asked him which agent called, and he said it was an Agent Thomas. You see that's the part that fooled me. When you told me you were Steadman, and you knew everything that happened in Steadman's office, I had no reason not to believe you.

"But the real Steadman is on his way to Hood River, and I'll bet he has identification. So if you want, we can sit here and wait for him."

The FBI agent deftly slipped behind Maxine, looped his arm around her neck and pointed his gun at her head. Hollywood started to go after him, but stopped at the sight of the gun.

Lu Fong took an impotent swing in the air with his ancient cane. "Is this true, Kay Lu? What were you thinking, forming a partnership with this man?"

"I don't know, father. Right now, I'm wondering the same thing."

Chapter 29

Hollywood stepped toward Thomas, who waved the gun in a menacing tone. "What do you think you're doing?" he said. "You'll never get away. It's an hour's drive to Portland, and I'll have a statewide bulletin out on you before you get out of Hood River."

Thomas spoke through clenched teeth. "I don't think so. Kay Lu's father is the big fish in this thing. I just saw an opportunity and hitched a ride. Lu Fong was the one who set it all up: the kidnappings, the cloning formula, and the big score with the Chinese government. He's the one you want; I'm just the one with the gun taking advantage of an opportunity."

"Be silent, fool." Lu Fong's feeble manner was gone. He stood inches taller with menacing eyes and a curled lip. In one long stride he was within striking distance of Thomas.

"Look out!" Maxine cried.

An antique cane transformed into a thin metallic blade as Lu Fong discarded the wooden facade. The blade careened down on Thomas as we all stared in stunned awe.

Maxine tried to get out of the way, but Thomas managed to use her as a shield. The saber tore Thomas's jacket sleeve and drew blood from Maxine's arm. Thomas fired off a wild round at his attacker, striking the old man in the shoulder. Lu Fong brushed at the wound as if it was an annoying insect and sneered.

"You're crazy!" Thomas screamed, dragging Maxine toward the exit door.

"I have not worked this hard to let you take it all away," Lu Fong said. "And you will not turn my daughter against me. No matter where you go, I will find you and kill you."

I had to stop the crazy old lunatic from killing Maxine. I jumped him from behind, grabbed at the saber and tried to wrestle it from his grip. He twisted and turned and scowled at me. His rage transformed into superhuman strength. He discarded me on the floor like a speck of lint and turned toward Thomas, who now was aiming his .38 special straight at Lu Fong's head.

Instinctively, I wanted to grab at the pain in my side from my own gunshot wound. Instead I went for Lu Fong's feet as Thomas squeezed off another shot. Lu Fong tripped and fell forward. I didn't know if I was in time to save him.

He moaned and rolled over on his back. His eyes caught mine and he glared. "You have ruined everything." The monster was gone; the meek subdued old man was back.

"Father," Kay Lu said. She ran to him on the floor and stroked his forehead. "It's all right Father. I won't let him hurt you."

Maxine struggled, but Thomas's chokehold stopped her. "Is he dead?" Thomas asked.

Kay Lu looked at her father's face, turned and smiled sweetly at Thomas. "He is fine. I want you to leave him alone. Do you hear me?"

"Hey, he started it," he drawled.

I climbed to my feet and felt my wound to see if it had begun bleeding again. "So. Lu Fong is behind the kidnappings of those tech people and scientists. Maxine was right."

Thomas didn't flinch. "Yeah, you two are pretty clever for amateurs."

"What are two you talking about?" Hollywood asked.

"It's been in the headlines for the past three weeks," I said. "Don't tell me you missed it."

"I only read the comics," Hollywood quipped. "News is too depressing, especially in my line of work." He paused and I watched him turn it over in his head. "But that's all been happening in California and back east."

"It started with this bunch and spun out of control when Thomas joined up and murdered Hess," I said.

Thomas offered an unctuous smile. "You had it figured," he said. "Hess asked me if I knew about a covert operation to kidnap Maxine when I stumbled upon him in your room. After you told him to call his friend in the Bureau, he started putting it together. But I got the drop on him. I shot him with my silencer and tucked him into your closet with the idea of tagging you for his murder.

"And I would have too, if you hadn't jumped me and tied me up. I had already planted the gun in your room, and you were all set for the frame. Now I'll have to come up with another plan."

"Are you going to kill all of us?" I asked.

"I won't have to. You're not going to be able to stop me."

Kay Lu got up from the sofa and walked over to Thomas. "What now, darling? You said you were going to get me out of this. Now you are in it as badly as I."

"Shut up," he said. "Take that stuff of yours and mix it up with some water. Our guests are getting thirsty. Then get Maxine's hotel key and go up to her room. I think you'll find your father's cloning samples in a briefcase. Look under her bed. Then, meet me in the lobby."

I figured Thomas must have heard Maxine whispering its location when he was all trussed up. Kay Lu took the hotel key from Maxine's purse. "But what about the flash drive?"

"Good point," he said. "Who has the flash drive?"

"That policeman took it from me," Kay Lu said.

"He gave it to me," Maxine said. "It's in my purse, in the inside zipper."

Kay Lu fumbled with a zipper and retrieved a black flash drive. "I've got it."

She stopped and studied it carefully. "Wait a minute. This flash drive is the wrong color. The one I had earlier was red."

"I thought you were color blind," Maxine said. "Why else would you wear those awful gold and lime-green dresses?"

"Check the cop." Thomas said.

Kay Lu put her fingers into Hollywood's shirt pocket and fished out a red flash drive. "I've got it. What now?"

Thomas took the flash drive from Kay Lu. "Mix some stuff up for them. It will keep 'em busy dreaming for a few hours."

Kay Lu went to a sink and opened cupboard doors. She found some paper cups and began filling them with water from the pitcher.

Wei Ming apparently recovered from his indifference, because he stood up from his slumped position in his chair. "You must take me with you," he said. "I will arrange for the money."

"The cops already have the twenty million you brought," Thomas said. "This stuff's going on the open market."

"No," Wei Ming said. "I will be able to arrange for more money when we get away. Twenty million dollars is nothing for my government. I can get you fifty million if you take me with you."

Thomas loosened his grip on Maxine and looked over his shoulder to Kay Lu. "What do you think, Kay?"

Kay Lu secreted a yellow filmy liquid from an eyedropper. "I don't see a downside. We're out nothing if he doesn't deliver. But what about my father?"

"It's up to you," Thomas said.

"Let's leave him here with the police. I don't want him chasing after us too."

A few minutes earlier she was practically sobbing when she thought her father was shot, and now she was cold again. I wondered what had happened in that family.

Lu Fong, his dangerous cane confiscated, steadied himself on the top of a chair. "Kay Lu, you must not leave me behind. I'm your father."

"Sit down and shut up," Thomas said, waving the gun. Lu Fong stumbled into the chair and mumbled something under his breath.

Thomas turned and smiled at me. "Looks like you get to keep the old man, unless he wakes up first."

"One thing I don't understand," I said. "Why is this flash drive so important? Didn't Lu Fong have other copies of the formula?"

"My father is a very cautious man." Kay Lu said, stepping carefully across the floor with a tray of paper cups filled with the yellowish-tinted water "He had his scientists working in several groups unknown to each other. A different team worked on different parts of the formula. He had labs in Hong Kong, Seattle and Portland. When Maxine began snooping around, he worried someone was onto him so he collected the data for all of the experiments and scanned it on his computer."

"He destroyed all of the paperwork?" I said.

"Yes," Kay Lu said.

"So, when Maxine sabotaged his computer and the backup flash drives, she destroyed everything?"

Kay Lu nodded. "He is an old fool. He had left the cloning flash drive in his computer instead of putting it back in his safe.

We thought he lost everything until Kenny called me and told me about Maxine's e-mails to Agent Hess. Hess had told her to collect information so we hoped she had taken the formula with her."

"Were they monitoring the email of Maxine or Hess?" I asked.

"Both." Kay Lu set the paper cups on a table in front of me. "Kenny monitored Agent Hess as a matter of standard practice, I think, and my father didn't trust Maxine. When she emailed Agent Hess it was a complete surprise to us. I told Kenny about my father's suspicions of Maxine so he helped me set up a method to intercept her emails."

"Geez. So when I was suspicious about Hess's intentions and called his boss . . ."

Kay Lu displayed a wicked smile. "Yes, we already knew Maxine was in town, and that she probably had the cloning formula."

"That's why you kidnapped her."

"Of course," Kay Lu said. "Kenny called Maxine on her cell phone. He had managed to intercept her call to Agent Hess earlier and realized she had the formula. Technology is such a wonderful thing in the hands of the FBI."

"Yeah, I called Maxine and set up the meeting with her," Thomas said, smirking. "Kay Lu's father was still running the show at that point, so I did surveillance across the street.

"I heard two gunshots and saw two of Lu Fong's men rush out of the Kwan Yin Temple and drive off in a car. I followed, figuring they had the cloning formula."

"Yes, but your men lost them in traffic," Kay Lu said. "You bungled it, but I didn't. I hung around the temple and saw Max enter the building. I watched from a distance, and I saw father's men come back. I saw Max and Maxine sneak out the back door, and I watched as father's men drove into the path of the oncoming van.

"But you didn't see me, did you, Mr. Starr. I followed you home, and my men were waiting for you when you left the next morning."

Her timing was awful. I did remember the headlights behind me, following me for a while that night.

But I had picked that moment to rush Thomas, who looked over at me as I moved toward him, and he tightened his grip on

Maxine.

He pulled her back toward the door and pointed the gun at my face. "Stop."

I backed away. "No problem. Have you got any other questions, Maxine?"

"None, except, has this guy ever heard of mouthwash? His breath smells like a lizard factory."

The door flew open and banged into Thomas, and he lost his grip on Maxine while struggling to keep his balance. She raised her foot and stomped her heel across the top of his foot. He hopped on the other foot and fell to the floor with the gun still in his grasp. Maxine grabbed his wrist, twisted it behind him, and wrestled the gun from his fingers.

The rest of us could only stare at the figure that opened the door.

"Is this a bad time?" It was the real John Steadman. "Someone wanted me to come in here and talk to the cops." He looked at the FBI agent prone on the floor with Maxine's foot pushed into his back. "Looks like fun. Can I play?"

"Good timing, Steadman," I said.

Kay Lu stared in disbelief at the sedated Thomas, groaning pitifully on the floor. "I guess that's it." She held something at her side and waltzed toward Thomas. "Are you okay, honey?"

Maxine held the gun now and let Thomas sit up. Kay Lu bent over him and stroked his crew cut with her fingernails. Her voice was sugary sweet. "Poor thing. Here, have some water." She tilted his head backward and poured the cup of water down his throat. The confused man gagged as the drink went down his esophagus. "What was that? You drugged me."

Her sweetness turned to venom. "Damn right. Happy dreams stupid."

Chapter 30

I trudged up the steps with Maxine in tow, and we stopped to gaze again at the script emblazoned on the window of the massive concrete building.

Maxine read the emblem aloud, pausing between words for emphasis. "Federal... Bureau... of... Investigation. It sounds more intimidating from this viewpoint."

And so, we began our second journey into the depths of the halls that led to further questioning into our roles in the Vampire Cloning Affair, as newspapers now called the case.

In our first interview, interrogators implied Maxine was a spy for the Chinese government. We were questioned in different rooms and the cross-examiners went back and forth between us, comparing our stories. The interviews lasted a dreadful 10 hours straight with no time out for meals. At the end of the day my interrogator pounded his fist on the table and bounced out of the room.

When Maxine and I compared notes over a late dinner afterward we determined that our stories were harmonious. Her testimony had evoked similar frustrations from her accusers.

It had been three days since that first meeting when we were summoned again. This time we lawyered up. But instead of being led to interrogation rooms, we were all ushered into an office area. As we waited to be admitted to an inner office, I noticed a man in painter's clothes scratching the remnants of Ken Thomas's name from the door we had been directed toward.

I smiled to myself and wondered who would take his place, now that he was sitting in the Justice Center jail in downtown Portland, awaiting federal charges.

In a moment I got my answer. A man wearing oval-shaped glasses greeted us and our lawyers like we were long-lost friends.

It was Thomas's vicious flunky, Ned Wright.

"Max, come in, come in," he said. He greeted Maxine in the same fashion and urged us to sit down. We sat on the edges of our chairs.

"I hope you will understand I was just following orders from my superior, Agent Thomas," Wright said. "I had no idea in what he was involved. Believe me, I spent twenty-four hours in an interrogation and took two lie detector tests before I convinced my superiors I was just a pawn in the whole thing.

"Seems like you landed on your feet," I said.

"Oh this is just temporary. I'm the one most familiar with his caseload. I probably won't be promoted. At least not right away. This kind of stuff leaves a scar that takes time to heal. So what do you say? Shall we put all this adversity behind us?"

Our lawyers warned us to be cautious with our statements. For the record, Maxine's lawyer, Christina Barnes, was prettier and tougher than mine. Of course, mine was a 20-something freckle-faced kid; hers was an aggressive take-no-prisoners blonde.

"Really," Wright said. "No more fighting, I promise. I just want to clarify a few things about your statements, and we'll wrap this thing up."

I leered over my shoulder, unable to ignore the two humorless agents in dark suits standing outside Wright's new office. He noticed my distraction and lowered his voice. "They're waiting for me; I have a press conference in a few minutes."

"If you think you're going to haul my client off to jail, you'd better think again," Christina said. "Any information you obtained from these two in the first interview will be inadmissible by the time I'm through with you."

"Yeah," my lawyer said. "Inadmissible."

Wright looked at his watch. "Well in that case, maybe I'd better skip my questioning for now." He stood up from his desk and smoothed his suit with his hands. "Let's go."

"Where?" Christina demanded.

"Yeah, where?" my lawyer said.

Wright smiled at the blonde. "I promised to make Max and Maxine available for a few more questions. Of course you can always advise them not to speak."

We were ushered out of Wright's office and escorted down a

long, gloomy hallway by the serious FBI agents. At the end of the hallway we turned to the right, opened a door, and stepped out of the darkness and into harsh sunlight. I could see a jail bus parked on the curb and a large group of people milling around in front of it.

So this was to be our fate, I thought. I felt bad for Maxine, who shielded her eyes from the sun. She looked weary, and I knew how she felt. I felt ill too, as the realization of doing jail time smacked me in the gut.

But the prisoners waiting to get on the bus weren't wearing orange. Most of them wore ties and business suits. A few of them were armed and one of them shoved an instrument into my face.

"Are you Max Starr?" he shouted. "Tell us how you caught the Vampire Cloners."

As my eyes adjusted to the sunlight, I could see the prisoners were actually media types.

"You'll get a chance to ask your questions in a minute," Wright said. "First, I have a statement I would like to read on behalf of the Federal Bureau of Investigation."

Wright cleared his throat. "The FBI, with the assistance of private investigators Maxwell Starr and Maxine Andrews, arrested four persons as leaders of the so-called Vampire kidnapping attacks on the West Coast and in other parts of the country.

"The names of these suspects are being withheld pending a grand jury indictment expected later this afternoon. The goal of this organization in kidnapping various scientific leaders appeared to be to obtain blood and skin samples with the objective of cloning their kidnapped victims.

"We believe the suspects would then have sought to sell their DNA cells to other world powers in attempts to further their defense systems and develop technology equal to the United States some twenty or thirty years down the line."

Voices from the media rose in frenzy, and Wright raised his hands to quiet them. Television cameras angled for key positions as he continued.

"I'm not saying cloning technology has gotten to the point where scientists can clone humans. Most scientists agree that even the successful cloning of an animal is very difficult. But this group of speculators obviously thought they struck upon the right formula for cloning humans. In this case, we will never know how successful they might have been because the only copy of the formula was on a computer flash drive that was somehow destroyed."

Maxine winked at me in her mischievous way and smirked. She had given the FBI her copy of the magnetically erased flash drive, and at her insistence we had tossed the only good copy of the formula into my fireplace before our initial questioning by the FBI. We celebrated the action with a bottle of champagne and a romantic evening.

She was as good as her word. The introduction of human cloning wasn't going to happen on her watch. Hollywood knew about the deception, but he wasn't talking, and Lu Fong and Kay Lu wouldn't even acknowledge there was a cloning formula as they prepared for their day in court.

"What role did Maxwell Starr and Maxine Andrews play in this investigation?" a reporter asked.

Wright pushed his egg-shaped eyeglasses further up his nose, showing irritability at the reporter's question.

"Mr. Starr met with our agency early on and advised us of a kidnapping attempt of Miss Andrews. During a subsequent investigation on their part, this scheme was uncovered. The FBI worked with the Multnomah County Sheriff's Office, the Hood River Police Department and Mr. Starr and Miss Andrews to trap the suspects in a warehouse in Hood River."

"I understand an officer of the FBI was slain while working on this undercover operation," another reporter said. "How did this happen?"

Wright wiped sweat from his forehead. "Mr. Hess was slain in the course of duty, allegedly by his supervisor, Ken Thomas, whom we believe was in league with members of this alleged cloning scheme. Mr. Thomas is in the Justice Center awaiting a grand jury indictment."

With this news a thousand questions were launched toward Wright. This story had so many angles the FBI would be on the defensive for a year.

He put his hands up again and held them up for minutes before the throng retreated. "I'm not going to answer any more questions now. I would, however, like to introduce Mr. Starr and Miss

Andrews and thank them for their role in this investigation." Wright winked at us. "They are newly licensed private investigators with the state of Oregon, and I believe they will have many more exciting cases in the years to come. I would also like to announce they will be issued the offered award of two-hundred and fifty thousand dollars for their role in catching the kidnappers of prominent scientists and technology experts."

Wright, having diffused the FBI scandal by offering us up as fresh news fodder, smiled and stepped back to where we stood, open-mouthed. Away from the microphone he made a startling announcement to us.

"Maxine, I've cleared you with Interpol and all other governmental agencies. You won't be hassled again. Go ahead and answer their questions. Just don't tell them anything official about the case."

The reporters heard this last statement and moaned.

"What are you going to do with the reward money, Max?" asked a reporter wearing a blue blazer.

I leaned over and whispered something to Maxine. She nodded. "I guess we're going to give half of it to John Steadman. He's the P.I. who helped get me going on the case, and I feel obligated to give him half of any earnings. He also helped capture one of the suspects."

After what seemed like a hundred stupid questions, an anchor from the six o'clock television news finally asked me one I wanted to answer. The tall woman shook her short-cropped yellow hair toward me and thrust her microphone in my face. "What are you two going to do next, now that this is all over?"

I looked at Maxine, her bright red hair twinkling in the sunlight, her impish smile now fading beneath the barrage of questions.

"Well, we've both been through a lot. We've been shot, kidnapped, stabbed, drugged, and beaten up. I thought we might wrap up a couple of legal matters, take a week off and book a flight to Maui. I've never been there, and I noticed one of the travel agencies is offering a special for honeymooners."

At first, my comment didn't register with Maxine. She had that 'Oh, a vacation would be nice' look. Before the reporter could respond, however, she wrinkled her face at me.

"Honeymooner's special? We aren't honeymooners, Max."

"Well, I hoped we might qualify before the plane takes off."

Her puzzlement quickly turned to an amused grin. "Oh, you did, did you?"

ABOUT THE AUTHOR

Don Weston lives in Portland, Oregon, most likely known as of late as the location for TV shows Portlandia, Grimm and Leverage. He is a member of Willamette Writers and Oregon Writer's Colony. He has coordinated volunteers for the annual Willamette Writers Conference with approximately 1000 attendees, and worked on the OWC conference committee staging author workshops.

He writes thrillers and mysteries "but somehow humor manages to sneak into my writing voice," he says. He also writes a blog on writing and getting publishing called *I Love A Mystery*.

Made in the USA
Las Vegas, NV
23 January 2024

84821016R00134